Love Finds You™

IN

Camelot

TENNESSEE

Love Finds You™

IN
Camelot
TENNESSEE

FIC
HANNA
2011

BY JANICE HANNA

summerside
PRESS™

Summerside Press™
Minneapolis 55438
www.summersidepress.com

Love Finds You in Camelot, Tennessee
© 2011 by Janice Hanna

ISBN 978-1-935416-65-4

Scripture references are from The Holy Bible, New International
Version®, NIV®. Copyright © 1973, 1978, 1984 by International Bible
Society. Used by permission of Zondervan.

The town depicted in this book is a real place, but all characters are
fictional. Any resemblances to actual people or events are purely
coincidental.

Cover Design by Koechel Peterson & Associates | www.kpadesign.com

Interior Design by Müllerhaus Publishing Group | www.mullerhaus.net

Cover image: iStock

Photos of Camelot provided by Janice Hanna.

*Summerside Press™ is an inspirational publisher offering fresh,
irresistible books to uplift the heart and engage the mind.*

Printed in USA.

Dedication

....

To the only wise King,
the One who sits enthroned upon my heart.
You've taught me that sometimes we have to
go backward in order to go forward.
Thank You for sending me back to Camelot.

Acknowledgments

....

To my choir and drama directors from Milligan
College, 1977. Your willingness to place me in the fall
production of Camelot as a lady-in-waiting changed
my life and gave me the foundation for this story.

To my daughters and grandchildren. You are the true ladies-in-
waiting and knights in this fairy tale that my life has become.

To my mom. Thanks for humoring me when I insisted upon
driving through Camelot on our way out of Tennessee.
That beautiful scenery is forever etched in my mind.

To my critique partners. Thanks for holding my hand and
walking me through this one. Tough stuff, writing about Camelot.

To my agent, Chip MacGregor. Thanks for the role you
continue to play in my writing life. In so many ways, you
are a true knight, championing my "writing cause."

To my copyeditor, Connie Troyer. Thank you for adding
your sparkle and shine to this fanciful story.

To the wonderful team at Summerside—how can I thank
you? You've given me opportunity after opportunity
to weave these fanciful tales. I'm so grateful.

To the only true "King" in my life. It's been
worth it all, just to sit at Your feet.

So we fix our eyes not on what is seen, but on what is unseen.
For what is seen is temporary, but what is unseen is eternal.

2 CORINTHIANS 4:18 NIV

Preface

....

My tie to Camelot goes back to the fall of 1977 in East Tennessee, where I played the role of a lady-in-waiting in Milligan College's production of the Lerner and Loewe musical. The story is rich with personal symbolism and always reminds me of that precious season of my life. And though I'm a Texas girl at heart, there's something about East Tennessee that leaves me breathless. It calls out to those who've wandered away in much the same way a loving father welcomes home his wayward child—particularly in the fall when the leaves are turning.

The elusive kingdom of Camelot has always been shrouded in mystery. Perhaps that's why we love it so much. Within its boundaries, we're swept up in a world of knights and ladies, chivalry and dreams, romance and sacrifice. And in the tale of Camelot, we find a symbolic portrait of a very real King, One willing to give His very life for those He loves, even those who break His heart. What an honor to dedicate this story to Him.

Camelot, Tennessee

Tennessee boasts not one but *three* Camelots, all in the Knoxville area. I knew from my research that they were all very tiny, so I chose what appeared to be the largest of the three. Then I crafted my story idea, using my college memories of the Knoxville area.

In the fall of 2009, while on a road trip with the seniors' ministry from my mother's church, I was given the opportunity to make a trip to Tennessee. I detoured off of Interstate 40 so I could see this elusive place called Camelot up close. What I found was more of an area than a town. Still, I couldn't help but be enraptured.

Camelot is nestled near the spot where the Oak Ridge Highway meets the Pellissippi Parkway. A gorgeous bluff with towering pines kept me mesmerized as I meandered up and down streets with names like Excalibur Circle, Lancelot Lane, and Merlin Circle. My imagination was stirred. I could see my characters interacting in this breathtaking place. Their dreams of grandeur would parallel those of the real—or was he imagined?—King Arthur. Like the town of lore, the Camelot I stumbled upon was little more than a dream rising up from the fog. Oh, but what a lovely dream!

Janice Hanna

Don't let it be forgot
That once there was a spot,
For one brief, shining moment
That was known as Camelot.

FROM THE MUSICAL *CAMELOT*
BY ALAN JAY LERNER AND FREDERIC LOEWE

Chapter One

....

Acting should be bigger than life.
Scripts should be bigger than life.
It should all be bigger than life.

BETTE DAVIS

An early morning haze hung over the sleepy town of Camelot, Tennessee. Amy Hart squinted to get a better view of the road as she maneuvered her Jeep Liberty around a tricky bend. On a clear day, the journey into town would prove challenging. But on a morning like this—with the heavy April skies pressing in around her—the curvy road seemed to slip away into a foggy mist. How many times had she imagined she could drive off into the dreamy haze and find herself in a world of knights, ladies, castles, and kings?

Once she rounded the turn, Amy reached over and flipped on the radio then settled back against the seat as a familiar worship song came on. Perfect. Pretty soon the skies would clear and so would her mood—just as soon as she arrived at work and shared her latest idea with Steve. Only then would the tightness in her chest dissipate. She lost herself in thought as she pondered her best friend's reaction to her latest plan. Likely he would think she'd lost her mind. Just like the last time. And the time before that. Oh well. She would prove him wrong—this time.

Amy made her way down Excalibur Drive and turned off onto

Lancelot Lane, taking a shortcut to City Hall. Another turn to the right landed her on Camelot Court. She sighed as she caught a glimpse of the abandoned car lot to her right. As usual, nothing much stirred there. Or at the bank. Or at Gwen's Grooming, Camelot's only pet-friendly store. No, at this time of morning, not much fluttered but the birds. Well, the birds and Lucy Cramden, who always walked her ferret, Fiona, at the crack of dawn. Strange sight, a ferret on a bright pink leash. Just part of the quirkiness that made Camelot… Camelot.

As Amy turned into the parking lot at City Hall, the sun peeked through the fog for one magical moment, taking her breath away. She took it as a sign. A confirmation, of sorts. Surely the Lord Himself had performed this wondrous act to boost her courage. She whispered a prayer of thanksgiving and her spirits lifted immediately.

After pulling into her usual parking space, Amy turned off the car. Instead of heading for her office, she lingered in the car for a few moments, watching the colors of the sky morph from dizzying gray to pinkish blue. She used the extra time to get a handle on her thoughts. Last night's town hall meeting had left her reeling, but this morning she'd awakened with the perfect plan, one she hoped others in town would go along with. In fact, it was such an amazingly simple idea, she had to wonder why no one had thought of it before.

She glanced out over the bluff, the panoramic view mesmerizing her as always. For as long as she could remember, Amy had always loved the dewy mornings in East Tennessee, and the changing of the seasons only made her love them more. The vibrant colors had proven spectacular last fall when the leaves turned. As a child, she'd believed her father's tale that an artist's paintbrush swept in across the bluff while she slept, leaving behind strokes of amber, hazy orange, and brilliant gold. Of course, she'd believed all her father's tall tales as a kid, including the one about meeting King Arthur face-to-face and pulling Excalibur out of the rocky ledge near Beaver Creek. But who could blame her? Dad's stories carried her away to a place deep in her imagination, and sometimes a girl just needed to travel.

"You've won my heart with those stories, Dad," she whispered. A smile tugged at the corners of her lips. She allowed herself one last glimpse over the bluff before thinking about entering the real world. It offered the promise that things could be different in her sleepy little town. Yes, now that spring was finally upon them— winter's frost finally gone—the leaves danced in brilliant shades of green. The trees that housed them stood sturdy and strong, so close together that she could scarcely see where the branches of one ended and the next picked up.

Kind of like the people of Camelot.

"It's better than any work of art." Amy closed her eyes to imprint the photo of the bluff on her imagination. "Only God could paint a picture like this."

A tap on her window nearly sent her out of her skin. She let out a yelp then looked over to discover her best friend, who also happened to be the town's newly elected mayor, grinning on the other side of the glass. Rolling down the window, she scolded him. "Steve, you scared me to death!"

"Sorry." His gorgeous blue eyes twinkled as he flashed a smile. "Just couldn't stand the idea of you sitting there with that goofy grin on your face. Daydreaming again?"

"N–no." She shook her head. "Not really."

He gave her a pensive look. "You're up to something. I can always tell by the expression on your face."

"W–who...me? Never!" Amy did her best to hide the smile as she rolled the window back up and climbed out of the car. Drawing in a deep breath, she tried to figure out how to begin. As they made the walk toward the front of tiny City Hall, she decided to start with the obvious. "I don't mind telling you, that meeting last night really had me worked up. I hardly slept a wink."

Steve sighed, and his boyish smile disappeared. "No point in worrying about it, though. God's got this under control, Amy."

"I know." She waited while he opened the front door with a gentlemanly flair, allowing her to enter. "But I love this town. And the idea that it might…" She wouldn't say the words that flitted through her mind. She didn't dare.

"God has a plan. I know it."

"Right." She turned to him, ready to share her idea. "Just remember you said that, okay?"

"O–okay." He cocked his head and gave her a what-are-you-up-to-now look as they trekked down the hall, side by side.

Amy knew that look well. She'd seen it hundreds of times over the years, going all the way back to the seventh grade when she'd decided they should turn all the desks in the classroom upside down during recess. And that time in high school when she'd laid out a plan for stealing the opposing team's mascot for a day. And last month, when she'd suggested the city-council members host a citywide bake sale to raise funds.

Her current idea might be amazing, but Amy realized it would be a hard sell to the others on the city council. She needed to win Steve's support first.

"Okay." She paused at the door in front of her tiny office. "As you know, our city needs money to stay afloat. Lots of money."

"Right." His brow wrinkled.

"We've tossed around a lot of ideas, but none like the one I've just come up with."

"I'm bracing myself."

She rolled her eyes. "Problem is, we've been coming at this from a logical left-brained angle. I think we need a right-brained approach for once."

"I have a feeling you're about to be more specific. Not sure why that worries me." Steve crossed his arms as if preparing for a showdown of wills.

"Before I tell you, I just want to reiterate that I love this little town," she said. "I was born here, after all. And even though I left for college, I've seen it through hundreds of ups and downs. More downs than ups."

"Right. Me too." He nodded.

"I feel like the morale of our citizens is on a decline with everyone so worked up about our lack of revenue, and that breaks my heart. A place called Camelot should be idyllic, shrouded with a lovely sort of mystery."

Steve snorted. "The only mystery around here is whether or not Old Man Brenner will have the good sense to put his dentures in before coming into town. And whether Woody Donaldson will remember that Officer O'Reilly threatened to take away his driver's license if he goes plowing through the plate-glass window of the Sack 'n Save again in that old Mustang of his."

Amy slugged Steve in the arm. "Be serious."

"I am." He chuckled but paused when she reached to take his hand. Steve glanced down at it for a second then directed his attention to her eyes.

Good. I have him now. Maybe he'll focus so I can get this out.

"I've always thought of Camelot as a lovely romantic painting, a place people would want to step inside to escape the harsh realities of life. But lately it feels like the colors are fading. I'm starting to wonder if we'll even continue to exist if someone doesn't step up to the plate and do something, or if we'll just…" Her voice drifted off. "Fade away like the legend," she managed to whisper. Amy felt the sting of tears but willed herself not to cry. Not in front of Steve, at any rate.

"You know me. I'm a realist," he said. "That's not to say I don't have faith, but someone has to be practical. If we can't keep our budget out of the red for more than a couple months, Camelot really *won't* exist. That's the cold, hard reality."

"Exactly. But I think I've come up with a way to convince people this is the perfect place for romance. A place where people young and old can fall head over heels in love and be swept away by the possibilities of what could be."

"Um, okay. Have you been watching the Lifetime Channel again?"

"No." She groaned. "Please hear me out. According to legend, Camelot is a place for happily-ever-afters."

"Unless you happen to be King Arthur," he said. "In which case, it's a place where a handsome younger man sweeps in and steals your woman while your back is turned. And then you end up at war with his country and with several of your best men dead because you made the mistake of putting your trust in someone who really couldn't be trusted." Steve crossed his arms and gave her a funny look. "But never mind all of that. You were saying?"

She sighed. "I'm just saying, Camelot should be a place where people can come to have their faith renewed. A place where they can dream again, hope again."

"Ah." A smile tipped up the edges of his mouth. "Now you're talking. Go on."

Amy didn't let his playfulness deter her. Not this time. No, this time she had the perfect answer. "Camelot." She nodded as she spoke the word. "The answer is as simple as the name of our town. Camelot."

"O–okay." He still looked confused.

As she opened the door to her tiny office, the CITY PLANNER sign fell off and clattered to the floor. She picked it up and stuck it back on the door then turned her attentions once again to Steve, ready to do business.

"We've never taken advantage of the one thing that should be as obvious as the noses on our faces."

"And that would be…?"

"*Camelot*. The musical." She drew in a deep breath then let the idea fly. "I think we should perform the musical *Camelot* and charge money for the tickets. Can you imagine it? People would come from all over the country to see folks from Camelot put on the musical *Camelot*."

"Wait." He shook his head. "You're talking about a *musical*? Like, song and dance numbers and an orchestra and the whole bit?"

"You've got it!" She nodded then clasped her hands together. "It's the answer we've been looking for, Steve. I can see it all now— the sets, the costumes, the musical numbers, the jousting scene.…"

"Jousting scene?" His eyes widened. "You can't be serious."

"I am." She grinned, her excitement growing more with each word. "And it's going to be awesome! Think of the money it'll bring in."

"But how? And where?"

She could hardly contain her excitement as the words ushered forth. "We'll build an outdoor theater behind the Civic Center, near the bluff. And we won't have to go very far to find an audience. People are always heading over to Pigeon Forge to see the shows, and that's just an hour and a half away. Getting tourists to stop by Camelot on their way should be a piece of cake. We'll just have to advertise. We'll start with a website and a great PR campaign." She dove into a lengthy discussion about all the ways they could market this production to ensure success.

"Amy." Steve stared at her like she'd just landed in a spaceship. "Don't get me wrong. I like a fun idea just as much as the next guy. And the people in this town are all talented in their own ways. But… musical theater? Are you serious? I can't imagine we would be capable of pulling off something like that. And who would direct?"

"Woody Donaldson." She nodded, feeling more secure by the moment. "We'll ask him to be our team leader. He used to teach drama at the Junior College in Knoxville, you know."

"A lifetime ago!" Steve countered. "The man is nearly eighty years old. And his hearing is almost gone."

"The city can buy him a new hearing aid," she said. "We'll write it off. Besides, I'm sure he would love to help out. Getting others to participate won't be a problem, Steve. Think of all the people who sing in the choir at church. And what about Prissy Parker?"

"Prissy Parker?" Steve groaned. "The homecoming queen? Are you serious?"

Amy's enthusiasm grew with every word. "I have it on good authority that she has the best voice in town."

"Who told you that?" Steve asked, the creases between his brows deepening.

"Her mother."

"Naturally."

"You're not giving this a fair shake," Amy argued. "I'm telling you, this production will be the perfect solution. I wouldn't have taken on the job of city planner if I didn't care about this town, Steve. You know that."

At this point, she felt the sting of tears. Steve, of all people, knew her love for their community. Why else would she have come back here after years away in Knoxville? Camelot was in her blood.

She took a seat behind her desk, wondering what he would say next. Unfortunately, Amy never had a chance to find out. In that moment, the sign fell off her door once more, this time breaking into two pieces as it landed on the floor. Steve picked it up and laid it on her desk with a sigh.

"Just promise me you'll pray about it." She reached for a stack of papers on her desk then gazed up into Steve's worried eyes.

"Mm-hmm." He nodded. "I'll pray, all right. But just answer one question first."

Amy tried to sound confident as she responded with, "Sure." Looked like she had him right where she wanted him.

"Camelot took place during medieval times, right?"

"Yeah." She shrugged.

"Is this going to be one of those shows where the guys have to wear tights?"

She felt the color drain from her cheeks as she stammered her response. "Well, I…um, I guess so."

"Mm-hmm. That's all I needed to hear." Steve gave her a pensive look then stepped out into the hallway and closed the door behind him.

Amy leaned back in her chair, more determined than ever. Never mind Steve's silly questions. Tights or no tights…the show must go on!

* * * * *

Steve Garrison took a few determined steps down the narrow hallway, his thoughts tumbling a thousand different directions in his head. "She's got to be kidding!" He spoke the words to no one but himself.

Then he began to have a chat with the walls about how this would never work. Never in a million years.

His secretary looked at him with some degree of curiosity as he approached her workspace outside his office. "Everything okay, boss?" The soft wrinkles around Eula Mae Peterson's gray-blue eyes deepened in concern.

"Mm-hmm. Unless you count the new city planner's crazy idea to save the town by making men put on tights and dance around in the park like a bunch of ballerinas in tutus."

Did I really just say that out loud?

"Oh, wow." Eula Mae looked at him, her eyes wide. "Now *that* I would pay money to see."

Alrighty, then. Maybe Amy was on to something after all.

Chapter Two

....

Acting is also working with people who invite you into their dreams and trust you with their innermost being.

<small>CATHERINE DENEUVE</small>

The following Monday evening, Amy approached the Civic Center with a sense of excitement. Steve had balked at her idea, but she felt confident the city council members would see the good in it, once they caught a glimpse of the income it could generate for their little town. Desperately needed income, no less.

The sunset over the bluff distracted her temporarily as she pulled into the parking lot. She settled on a spot and then glanced over as Pete Jones eased his van into the spot next to her. Amy prepared herself—psychologically and otherwise—for seeing him. Or, rather, for smelling him. Pete couldn't help it that his job as Camelot's only pest controller created such a pungent odor. Not that he appeared to notice. No, the genteel fellow seemed oblivious to the pinched noses of his fellow townspeople.

She watched as he climbed out of his old Chevy van—a 1980s number with a large plastic cockroach on top—and approached her car. Amy opened the door of her SUV and climbed out, holding her breath in a non-obvious way.

"Evening, Amy." A genuine smile followed his words. "Can't wait to hear what you've got to share tonight. Should be exciting, as always."

"Thanks." As always, her eyes began to water and Amy took a

teensy-tiny step backward. She diverted her attention to the tagline on the side of his van, which he'd hand-painted—Pete's Pest Control: Contract Killer Onboard." Ironic, since the fellow didn't have a mean bone in his body.

The squeal of tires alerted her to the fact that someone else was arriving. A rusty red Mustang convertible came tearing into the parking lot, barely missing her Jeep as it whipped into the next-closest spot.

"Slow down, Woody!" Amy called out. She shook her head, wondering how the seventy-nine-year-old managed to keep his license.

Seconds later Woody emerged from his car, first adjusting his glasses then fidgeting with his hearing aid. As always, he moved slowly and remained in a somewhat hunched-over position. Age spots shone through his thinning wisps of white hair, as he leaned forward to yank the hearing aid from his ear. He whacked it against his palm and muttered something indistinguishable.

"Thought you were in a hurry to get to a funeral or something, Woody," Pete said, giving him a pat on the back.

"Eh?" Woody looked Pete's way, the wrinkles around his eyes growing deeper as he fiddled with the hearing aid in his hand.

Amy raised her voice a notch. "Pete wants to know why you're driving so fast."

Another grunt escaped as Woody attempted to stand upright. "No power steering on that car, and the brake pads are worn, so I have a doozy of a time keepin' up with her. Besides, this old body of mine won't move fast anymore. Figure the car's the only chance I have left to really live it up." He pressed the tiny device into his ear, made a face, then pulled it out and shoved it into his pocket. "And speaking of living it up..." He narrowed his gaze as he looked at Amy. "You're up to something. I can feel it. What's this meeting all about?"

"Oh, you'll see." She shrugged and tried to act nonchalant.

"Hope it's not another one of your goofy ideas," he said. "Like that time you talked me into dressing up like Uncle Sam for that ridiculous Fourth of July pageant." He gave her a pensive look.

Thankfully, their conversation was interrupted by another vehicle pulling into the parking lot. Lucy Cramden approached in her powder-puff pink Crown Victoria, circa 1993. Her Mary Kay bumper sticker had faded over time, but the amount of makeup she wore had not. Lucy always provided a colorful distraction.

A couple of minutes later, the middle-aged diva climbed out of the car and eased the strap of a large purse over her shoulder. Her hot-pink T-shirt boasted the words *Shut Up and Kiss Me, You Fool* in shimmering sequins. Lucy flashed a smile almost as bright and offered a "Hi, y'all."

"Hi yourself, Lucy." Pete's focus had clearly shifted from pest control and the topic of tonight's meeting. His gaze remained fixed on the inviting words blazoned across Lucy's ample chest. "G–good to see you." His focus abruptly shifted to her face, with his cheeks now crimson.

A high-pitched squeal from the oversize purse alerted Amy to the fact that Lucy must have brought along her pet ferret. Uh-oh. Not again. Not after the fit Eula Mae had pitched at the last meeting. Lucy clutched her bag tightly under her arm and sauntered over to Pete, who wrinkled his nose.

He rubbed his nose with the back of his hand. "What is that unusual aroma?"

"Maybe it's my perfume," Lucy said. "I'm wearing something new."

Eau de Fiona, no doubt.

The sound of crunching gravel caused Amy to look up. She smiled as her father's blue Ford F150 pulled into the parking lot. Even after all these years, Dad still enjoyed serving on the city council. It had filled a void in his life after Amy's mother passed.

He pulled into a spot on the opposite side of the parking lot then sprang from his car and headed toward the group.

Lucy pivoted on her heel, the words on her shirt now directly in his line of vision. His eyes widened as he read the inviting message—and then his face turned redder than Woody's car. "Charlie, it's so good to see you," she crooned.

"I, um, well, it's good to see you too, Lucy." He now focused on the others. "And all the rest of you too." He drew near the group, gave Amy a hug, then wrinkled his nose. "What is that…" He didn't get the word "smell" out before glancing Lucy's way. "Hmm. Risky move on your part, Lucy, after last month's fiasco with Eula Mae. She's allergic to Fiona, you know."

Lucy rolled her eyes. "Allergic, my eye. That story is a ruse."

"Oh? What do you mean?" Amy asked.

"She's not allergic. Eula Mae has been jealous of me ever since I told her that the pastor's wife was a better choice for the song 'O Holy Night' last Christmas. We're not speaking." She shrugged. "Besides, Fiona is in my purse, safely hidden from view. I had it made just for her." She held up the cotton-candy pink bag; the ferret's nose peeked out of one end.

"Unless that bag comes with a built-in deodorizer, I don't think your plan will work." Amy's father rubbed his nose.

Pete shook his head. "Eula Mae's gonna flip. So's Steve."

"Speaking of which…" Amy's dad gestured to the door of the building, where Steve stood with his mom's best friend, Caroline, at his side.

"What's the holdup out here?" Steve called out. "Are we meeting outside tonight?"

"Nah." Amy took several steps in his direction. As she passed by him, he rested his hand on her shoulder and gave her a playful wink. Her heart fluttered as he gazed into her eyes. *Hmm.* She'd been noticing that a lot lately—the same feeling she'd gotten in junior high whenever he donned that football uniform. Not that she'd ever come out and told him that her heart fluttered in his presence, of course. How did a girl go about telling her best friend that she suddenly wanted...well, more?

"You ready to share your idea with the masses?" he whispered, his breath warm against her ear. Tingles ran all the way down her spine.

"What idea is that?" Caroline's voice rang out. "The one where all the men of Camelot dance around in tights?" She laughed and slapped her leg. "I heard all about it from Eula Mae. Can't wait to see how *this* one goes over." She disappeared into the building, laughing all the way.

"What's Caroline talking about?" Pete looked at Amy, his eyes widening. "Men in tights? I hope that's some sort of a joke."

"No kidding," Grady Knowles, owner of the hardware store, said as he joined them at the door. "I'll be ding-dang-donged if anyone thinks fer a minute I'd be seen in girly tights." He raked his hands through thinning gray hair. "Ain't gonna happen."

Amy groaned. "I'll be sharing my idea in a few minutes," she said. "But don't be so quick to judge, okay? What I'll be proposing could turn out to be the best thing that ever happened to Camelot."

"Oh, I'm sure it will be lovely, whatever it is." Lucy slipped through the door and into the hallway next to Amy. "We could stand a little shaking around here. This town has drifted off to sleep." She headed off in the direction of the meeting room, shushing Fiona, who'd started that high-pitched squeal again.

"Sounds like you've come up with another one of your hair-brained ideas, Amy."

Amy turned as she heard the voice of her one-time best friend, Gwen Meadows. The beautiful blond took a couple of steps in Steve's direction. She batted her overly mascaraed eyelashes at him. "Honestly, I don't know how you put up with her, Steve." She paused and punctuated her next words. "As her *friend*, I mean."

Amy caught her meaning. Gwen wanted everyone to know she'd set her sights on Steve. *Hmm.* Strange, the sensations that passed over Amy. Though she held no official claim on Steve—other than best friend, of course—she still couldn't imagine him dating Gwen. In a parallel universe, perhaps, but not here. Not now.

"We'd better get inside." Steve put his hand on Amy's back and guided her down the narrow hallway toward the meeting room.

A couple of seconds after they greeted the others, Eula Mae entered with a tray of cookies in hand. She turned toward the group with her nose wrinkling. Sniffing the air, she voiced the inevitable question. "*What* is that stench?"

"Oh, I, um…" Amy shrugged, unable—or would that be *unwilling*?—to divulge the information.

"I distinctly smell…" Eula Mae's gaze circled the room, finally coming to land on Lucy Cramden's purse. "Ferret." She marched Lucy's way. "I can't believe you've done this again. I've told you a half dozen times at least that I'm allergic to Fiona. Why you persist in…" At once, her eyes began to water. Eula Mae sneezed. And sneezed again.

"How could you be allergic?" Lucy pulled her bag a bit closer. "That's just silly. People aren't allergic to ferrets. Why, they're the sweetest, cleanest—"

A voice at the door distracted them. Pastor Crane, who also owned the Knox County Funeral Home, swept in. His forehead glistened with tiny beads of sweat. "Evening, everyone."

Eula Mae turned toward him and handed him the tray of cookies. "Evening, Pastor. Help yourself."

He clutched the tray, his eyes growing large as he took in the variety of cookies. "Don't mind if I do. Natalie's Chicken Surprise casserole left something to be desired."

"How's she doing, anyway?" Amy asked.

"Oh, a little better, now that she's nearing the end of the second trimester," he said. "Still can't believe the baby's due in July. Hottest time of the year." He snatched a cookie, bit into it, then sauntered across the room and sat next to Amy's father, while still holding the tray.

"I can't wait to greet that new baby," Caroline said with a broad smile. "We need to have a shower for Natalie and that sweet baby boy."

"She would love it," Pastor Crane said. "She's in that nesting stage already." He began to talk at length about his wife's latest attempt to scrub down every square inch of their parsonage, chuckling all the while.

At five minutes after seven, Steve interrupted the pastor's story to call the meeting to order. Amy glanced across the room, taking in the various city council members. Of the 172 people who lived in Camelot, more than a dozen resided on the city council—mostly business people, of course. Well, all but her dad and Caroline, who had both recently retired.

Amy smiled as Blossom Dale, an over-the-top stylist from Such a Tease! salon, entered the room, her hair styled high and firmly cemented in place with spray. And glitter. Interesting look for a forty-something.

Next came Annabelle Baker, a chubby but bubbly clerk from the local Sack 'n Save grocery store. The fun-loving twenty-something was followed by Chuck Manly, the town's only butcher. Amy had it on good authority that Annabelle and Chuck were sweet on each other, but neither appeared to be ready to admit it, at least not publicly.

Hmm. Seemed to be an epidemic of that in Camelot. For how many months had Amy secretly longed to tell Steve that her heart went into overdrive each time she saw him? And yet, she could not. Something stopped her every time. Fear, perhaps? The potential loss of their friendship?

She watched as the man who captivated her thoughts rose to greet the council members. Though she'd tried not to notice his handsomeness tonight, she could not avoid it. That gorgeous dark hair. Those amazing blue eyes. His five-o'clock shadow, beautifully placed over a perfectly sculpted jawline. Dimples that teased her every time he smiled. That great blue button-up shirt over his broad-shouldered physique. Perfectly fitted jeans.

Man. She'd never get through the evening if she didn't focus on the reason for tonight's meeting. Thankfully, Steve opened the meeting in prayer. Something about a handsome man lifting up his voice in prayer did her in every time. It might not be the way folks did it in other places, but here in Camelot, every meeting started with an invitation for the Lord to join them. He finished and then introduced Amy, who rose and approached the front of the room. She whispered a quick "Lord help me!" before facing her fellow townspeople to lay out her plan.

Chapter Three

·····················

Acting is a question of absorbing other people's personalities
and adding some of your own experience.

PAUL NEWMAN

Amy had no sooner opened her mouth to share her plan than a grunt
at the door shifted the attention of all in attendance. She groaned
inwardly as her gaze fell on her father's best friend, Sarge Brenner.

"Woulda been here sooner, but my rheumatiz's been givin' me
fits." Sarge rubbed his hip joints and eased his way into a chair. "Feel
like I've been run over by an army tank."

This, of course, led to a story about his days serving in Vietnam.
On and on he went, talking about how he'd hidden out for weeks in
a swamp, finally contracting a strange and exotic illness, before a
young American private happened by and came to his rescue.

Amy didn't want to hurt Sarge's feelings but knew she had to
keep everyone focused. After getting their attention, she laid out
her plan in three simple sentences. "Folks, I think it's high time we
brought in some money so that the town of Camelot can get back on
its feet. We need to take advantage of our name, do something we've
never done before."

"We've tried for years to draw people in by using the Camelot
name as a hook," Pete said. "Nothing has worked. You saw what
happened to Lance's Used Car Lot. Didn't last three months before
Lance closed up shop and moved to Knoxville."

"He's right," Lucy interjected. "None of our Camelot-themed businesses have succeeded. Remember that trailer park on the outskirts of town called King Arthur's Court? It was condemned by the county years ago."

"And the hotel," Woody said, giving Amy a pensive look. "Your dad drew up plans for an over-the-top castle-themed hotel but never came up with the funding."

"Hey, now," her father interjected as he swallowed another cookie from the tray in front of Pastor Crane. "That hotel was a great idea."

"I always thought it was a lovely plan," Caroline added.

"Yes, I remember." Amy shook her head, remembering her father's grand scheme for Excalibur Inn. "But this is different, I promise."

Gwen smirked. "The only Camelot-themed business that's ever really worked is my dog-grooming business. Guinevere's Grooming is doing well, thank you very much." She looked down her nose at Lucy, who shrugged.

"Yes. Still, what I'm proposing is altogether different," Amy explained. "I'm not talking about naming a business after anything in the legend of King Arthur. I think it's time we link arms and perform the musical *Camelot*."

"*Camelot*, did you say?" Her father grinned. "Marvelous idea!"

"Oh, I love musicals," Caroline added. "Always have."

Annabelle clasped her hands together. "What a great idea!"

"I think I'd like to audition," Lucy said. "I did a little acting back in high school."

"I'd make a mighty fine King Or-a-thur," Grady Knowles drawled. "My wife—God rest her soul—always called me the king o' the castle." He snorted then took a sip from his coffee cup. "Get it? King o' the castle?"

A nervous chuckle went up from the crowd. Surely everyone

knew that the slow-drawlin' owner of their local hardware store could never fill the role of the famed king. Not that Amy could really peg any of Camelot's men for the King Arthur role. *Hmm.*

"Where did this idea come from, anyway?" Gwen asked. "Seems a little far-fetched."

"Dad and I took a little trip to Pigeon Forge last month to see some of the shows," Amy explained. "They were wonderful, but once I saw how many people they brought in, the idea took hold. After praying about it, I realized that *we* could bring in folks too."

Her father piped up. "Lotta great country singers in Pigeon Forge. And we went to Dolly's place too. Even rode the roller coaster."

"Yes, we did." Amy nodded. "The town is a mecca for tourists. I think Camelot can be too, if we play our cards right."

"I can't imagine we would ever be as popular as Pigeon Forge," Lucy said. "I just love it there. There's a wonderful outlet mall on the highway leading to Gatlinburg. Why, that's where I got this shirt." She turned once again to face Amy's father, whose gaze darted to the trees outside the window.

"Oh, speaking of malls, did you see my new outfit?" Annabelle stood and showed off her snug jeans and frilly blouse. "I bought it in Knoxville last week when I went to my Jenny Craig meeting."

"Jenny Craig?" Caroline piped up. "I knew it! You've lost weight, haven't you, Annabelle?"

"You noticed?" Annabelle released a giggle as she tossed her dark-brown curls. "Well, as a matter of fact, I have. Two and a half pounds. Only fifty-seven and a half more to go before I reach my goal."

Amy groaned inwardly. How had they transitioned from musicals to weight loss? She cleared her throat. "Attention, everyone." When they finally stilled, she tried again. "Here's my point. People pay good money to see those shows. Everyone loves to be entertained."

"I know I do." Blossom nodded. "I can't wait till Tuesday nights to watch *American Idol* on TV. I just love it. It's so entertaining, especially when they have all those big-name stars come on to encourage the kids. I'd pay money to see that. In person, I mean. I can watch it on TV for free, of course. Well, not really free, I guess. I do have to pay for the cable service." She giggled.

"*American Idol*?" Pete asked. "Whatever happened to the great television shows of the past? *Dragnet*? *Mission Impossible*? Now *those* were entertaining." He and Annabelle began to debate at length and ended up in an argument.

"If we're talking true entertainment, there's nothing like a great book." Amy's father rose, cleared his throat, and began to share a story from King Arthur's legend, his favorite story of all. The story started with the part where Arthur met Guinevere for the first time and ended with their eventual marriage by candlelight.

"Yes, that's a great story," Amy said. "Very entertaining. My point is, if we're strategic, we can compete with all those great shows over in Pigeon Forge. We just have to capitalize on our name. Oh, and we'll need to build a theater of some sort. I suggest we put it behind the Civic Center, which we can use for our rehearsals. And I'm not talking about building anything elaborate. Maybe an amphitheater type of setup, carved into the terrain with the Civic Center directly behind it. The area is on a hill, so it will work perfectly. And the view is out of this world." She paused to get a feel for the crowd. No one responded. "I know I'm asking for a lot here, but if we build it, they will come."

"*Field of Dreams*," Pastor Crane interjected as he reached for another cookie. "James Earl Jones gave the performance of a lifetime, don't you think?"

"I love his speaking voice," Eula Mae threw in.

"And wasn't Kevin Costner the cat's meow?" Gwen sighed. "I've always thought he was sinfully handsome in that role."

You've always thought every man was handsome. Amy forced a smile. "I'm just saying that we'll build a theater where we can do shows all weekend long. A show on Friday night, two shows on Saturday, and a Sunday matinee after church."

"I cain't work on Sun–deez," Grady drawled. "Against my ree–ligion."

Pastor Crane snorted. "You don't even go to church, Grady. What's the difference?"

"Church is against my ree–ligion too. Too much bickerin' goes on in them-there churches."

"Hey, speaking of religion, did you see that new cable channel with the great gospel sing-alongs?" Eula Mae asked. "I just love those old songs. They take me back to my childhood days." She began to hum "When the Roll Is Called up Yonder."

"What about that old hymn we sang last Sunday?" Pastor Crane added. "'Trust and Obey.' I thought I did a pretty good job of working it into my sermon."

Annabelle sighed. "I don't mind saying, your message on temptation really convicted me that I need to stick to my diet."

"Speaking of temptation, I'm reminded of a story from the war, during '69," Sarge said. "It was me and my guys, over in Vietnam." Off he went, into another lengthy story.

Amy did her best not to sigh as the minutes ticked by on the clock. As always, she'd lost control of the meeting. Nothing new there, only this time she'd had an agenda. A real one. She cleared her throat, hoping Sarge would take the hint. He did not. His story continued until Eula Mae—God bless her—steered the ship back on course.

"I do like the idea of the play," the elderly woman said, as she circled the room to refill coffee cups. "And I see the potential for making money, if it's handled right."

"I just have one question," Gwen said. "Who's gonna direct this shindig?"

Amy's gaze shifted to Woody Donaldson. She cleared her throat. At this point, the others looked his way as well.

Woody seemed perplexed by the attention. "Eh?"

"Turn up your hearing aid, Woody," Eula Mae raised her voice. "They want you to direct this play."

"Correct display?" He looked confused. "Don't have a clue what that means."

"No." Amy exaggerated her next words. "Direct. The. Play. We want you to direct the play." She sat next to him. "You're really the only one with any know-how, Woody."

"Well, shoot," he drawled. "I was countin' on playin' Merlin."

Steve drew near and slapped him on the back. "Make you a deal. If you agree to direct, you can play any role you like."

"Really?" Woody's eyes lit up. "Well, I'll pray about that. Might just take you up on it."

"I'm no actress," Amy added, growing more excited by the minute, "but I'd love to help you direct."

"If you think you could work with her, Woody." Pete laughed. "She'll keep you on your toes with all those ideas of hers."

"Hey, now." Amy quirked a brow.

"Ideas are good things. It's the 'idea people' we need to be listening to. They spur us on to do great things." Pastor Crane lit into a story about how his father had come up with the idea to open the funeral home back in the '70s, which led Pete to a discussion about what life was like during the decade that birthed disco, which led Annabelle to share that she hadn't even been born in the '70s, which somehow led Amy's father to telling a story about how the passage of time had no bearing in the legendary land of Camelot. Thankfully, he'd led them right back to the matter at hand.

"So…" Amy clapped her hands together. "I can tell you're all excited about the idea. I know I am. We'll have several shows per weekend, as I said. And I was thinking we could serve a meal at each show. Something medieval."

"Something evil, you say?" Woody looked perplexed. "I don't know that I'd go so far as to say food is evil. Filled with preservatives, sure. But at my age, I need all the preservatives I can get!" He slapped himself on the knee and laughed.

"She didn't say food is evil, Woody." Caroline spoke with a raised voice. "She said we're going to serve a Renaissance-themed meal to the patrons."

"Speaking of great food, did any of you taste that delicious chicken-and-rice casserole I made for last Sunday's potluck at the church?" Lucy batted her eyes in Amy's father's direction. "It was de-*lish*."

"Very tasty," Pete chimed in. "Almost as good as the pie you baked the month before. Blueberry, right?"

"We're having a sale on our frozen banana-cream pies at Sack 'n Save," Annabelle threw in. "You all need to come in and check it out. They're only on special till Tuesday." She frowned. "Not that I can eat pie. This diet is killing me."

"So, about this medieval meal…," Amy interrupted. "We'll feed the audience members a great dinner while they're watching the show. Very authentic, of course."

"Well, I think this whole idea is just ridiculous," Sarge spouted. "Almost as nutty as the decision to put Wi-Fi in at the Flying J gas station last month. Who in the world needs to check their e-mail at a gas station? That was the goofiest idea Amy ever came up with."

"It's called progress, Sarge," Steve said. "We try new things so we can keep up with technology."

"Well, back in my day, folks wrote letters. Why, I remember that when I was stationed in Texas back in '65, my sweetheart sent me three letters a week, sometimes four."

Off he went on another tangent about life in the military. This, for some reason, led to a story from Blossom about hairstyles, which led Eula Mae to a story about orthopedic shoes. At this point, a strange, high-pitched sound filled the room. Lucy Cramden's purse began to stir, and seconds later Fiona emerged and headed straight for the cookie tray in front of Pastor Crane. As the ferret jumped on top of it, every lady in the room let out a scream and cookies flew through the air along with the tray, which landed on the floor with a clatter.

At this point, everyone went wild, chasing after the ornery ferret. Well, all but Gwen, who waggled a thinly plucked brow in Amy's direction as if to say, "See? I told you so. You'll never be able to pull off a show with this motley crew."

Maybe she was right. Maybe this was just another dumb idea.

Yes, just another in a long line of dumb ideas by Amy Lyn Hart.

* * * * *

Steve looked on as Pete dove under the folding chair to snatch Fiona, hollering something about extermination techniques. Blossom jumped up on her chair, squealing nonstop, while Annabelle picked up cookies from the floor and stuffed them into her pockets. Eula Mae said something about grabbing a broom to clean up the mess, and Amy's dad began a story about how King Arthur would have dealt with all of this.

And Amy...poor Amy. She sat in her chair, a defeated look settling across that beautiful face. She brushed a loose blond hair behind her ear and sighed.

Steve hated to see her unhappy. And when the tears welled up in her eyes, he could only think to do one thing. Rising to his feet, he called out above the mayhem. "I say we go ahead and take a vote. All in favor of putting on the musical, stand up. All opposed, sit down."

Okay, so maybe not everyone had heard him. Or maybe they all just liked the idea of putting on a play. For, with the exception of Woody Donaldson, who continued to mess with his hearing aid from a seated position, everyone remained on his or her feet, chasing after—or escaping from—Fiona.

Steve glanced at Amy, who rose from her chair in response to his request. The edges of her lips curved in a tearful smile, and it melted his heart. Suddenly he realized he'd do whatever it took to keep that smile on her face, even if it meant building an outdoor theater...or wearing tights.

Well, maybe not that last one. Still, he'd do just about anything to win this fair maiden's heart. First, however, he'd have to garner the courage to tell her how he really felt. Staring at the chaotic scene transpiring in front of him, Steve concluded the obvious: sharing his heart would have to wait till another day.

Chapter Four

....

I know very little about acting.
I'm just an incredibly gifted faker.

ROBERT DOWNEY JR.

On the first Saturday in May, Amy met with Woody in the tiny fellowship hall of Grace Church. The townspeople would arrive in the sanctuary in a half hour, but before the auditions could begin she had to talk through some issues with the show's director. Well, director-slash-actor. Woody had shown up in his Merlin costume, ready to get into character. Hopefully his acting skills would prove to be as good as his directing skills. Not that Amy actually had any idea about his directing skills; she only knew what she'd heard through the years from others.

She settled down at the table, flipping open her copy of the script to the page marked CHARACTERS. "Look at these roles we have to fill." She pointed to the audition form. "Arthur, Lancelot, Guinevere, Merlin."

"Don't need to fill that one." Woody raised a makeshift wand. "Merlin's right here, ready to perform a little magic."

"I wish you could. I'd have you wave that wand and make this whole idea disappear."

"I know, I know." He chuckled. "Another goofy idea by Amy Lyn Hart."

"Ugh." She groaned. "If people keep saying that, we're going to have to embroider it on a pillow or something." Amy continued looking at the script, fear settling over her like a dark cloud. *Oh well. Back to the matter at hand.* "We'll also need knights, ladies-in-waiting, jugglers, milkmaids, a cobbler…"

"Cobbler?" Woody licked his lips. "I've always loved cobbler. Cherry is my favorite."

Amy forged ahead, making a mental note to address the issue of raising funds to provide Woody with a new hearing aid at the next city council meeting. "And we'll also need animals—horses and dogs. And then we have to think about costumes and set design. We'll need a castle, a moat, a field for the springtime scene, and a backdrop for the jousting scene." She dropped her head onto the table and groaned. "What was I thinking? This is nuts. We'll never be able to pull this off."

"Deep breath, girlie." Woody chuckled. "You won't make a very good codirector if you're losing your cool before the auditions even begin."

"True." She lifted her head and attempted to collect her thoughts, giving herself an internal pep talk. *You can do this, Amy, with God's help. He hasn't nixed the idea yet, so He must be for it.*

She hoped.

Woody opened his script and looked inside. "It's not as complicated as you think. Just three major roles in this show—Arthur, Guinevere, and Lancelot. The rest will be easy to fill."

"Thanks for the encouragement. I was just starting to think I must be crazy for coming up with this idea."

"Eh?" He gave her a curious look then tapped on his hearing aid. "You calling me crazy?"

"No, Woody, of course not. I couldn't do this without you. The only crazy person here is me. Agreed?"

"Agreed. No argument there."

A knock on the door caught her attention. She turned and smiled as Steve peeked his head inside. "Crowd control is becoming an issue in the foyer. The pastor's wife is feeding everyone cookies and punch, but they're getting restless."

Amy felt her pulse quicken. "Already? Should we open the doors to the sanctuary and let them in? They could wait for us in there."

"Yeah, if you think that will work." His eyes widened just before he came bolting into the room, several people pushing in behind him.

"I wondered where you two were hiding." Lucy Cramden turned to show off her low-cut medieval gown in a shimmering shade of blue. "Don't you love my dress? Perfect for Guinevere. Woody, what do you think?"

"Did she say I *stink*?" Woody crossed his arms over his chest.

"Oh, of course not." Lucy drew near and ran her fingers through Woody's wisps of hair. "I would never say anything ugly about our show's fabulous director."

"Now she's calling me ugly?" Woody closed the script and leaned back in his chair.

Lucy tried to explain, but he couldn't seem to hear her over the voices of the others, which were now rising to a chaotic chorus.

Natalie Crane swept in with a tray of cookies in hand. "Have one, Amy," she said. "You're going to need your strength."

Amy almost declined…until she saw those peanut butter–chocolate chip cookies she loved so much. "Mmm. Thanks." She grabbed two. Hey, a girl needed all the strength she could get.

Blossom made her way to Amy's side, beaming ear to ear. "I fixed my hair just like Vanessa Redgrave wore it when she played Guinevere in the movie version." She patted her beautifully coiffed updo. "What do you think?"

"Well, I—" Amy never got a chance to respond, though she had to admit, Blossom's auburn locks looked pretty amazing in that style. And from what she could gather, there was enough hair spray holding things together to keep it looking good for months to come.

"I think there's more to the part of the leading lady than just her hair, for heaven's sake." Gwen pushed past Blossom and clutched her hands to her chest. "The real Guinevere wasn't middle-aged, ya know. She was young and beautiful."

Amy swallowed a bite of her cookie, preparing to take Gwen down. How dare she say such a thing?

Blossom's happy-go-lucky expression faded. "Oh, well, I—"

Prissy Parker, the town's homecoming queen, pressed her way through the crowd; her shimmering crown caught the light from the fluorescent bulb above. It, however, was nothing compared to the glittering ball gown she wore. "I say we go with someone *really* young for Guinevere. Beauty before age." She giggled then clamped a hand over her mouth. Removing it, she whispered, "Did I really just say that out loud?"

Amy sighed, already troubled by the direction this conversation seemed to be heading. She shoveled the rest of the first cookie into her mouth to keep from responding. Apparently Steve had the same idea. He took a couple of cookies from the tray and swallowed them in rapid succession.

"Actually," Amy's dad interrupted as he forced his way through the crowd, "Vanessa Redgrave was thirty years old when she played the part of Guinevere. And Richard Harris was no spring chicken when he played Arthur. I rather think we'll be better off casting older, more experienced folks in the roles." He narrowed his gaze in Amy's direction. "Don't you agree, honey?"

"Oh, well, I..." Thank goodness for the peanut butter in the cookie. It seemed to have glued her tongue to the roof of her mouth.

"I think we'll figure it all out after we've listened to everyone audition," Steve said. He flashed a desperate look Amy's way then drew near, lowering his voice as he spoke to her. "Are we ready to start? If so, I'll usher these folks into the sanctuary. Putting them up on the stage will give us a chance to see if they can handle the heat."

"Handle the heat. Hmph." Prissy's mother grunted from behind Amy. "Just wait till you hear my girl sing. Then you'll know she can handle the heat. And you'll rethink that age thing, too. You'll want a young, pretty Guinevere, I guarantee you."

Steve cleared his throat and addressed the crowd. "Let's get this show on the road, folks."

"Get it? Show on the road!" Grady laughed as he entered the room. "That was a good 'un, Steve! Maybe we really will take this show on the road someday. Maybe we'll go all the way to Broadway!"

Amy glanced at the clock on the wall and shrugged. So much for having time to reflect and pray before kicking this thing off. She grabbed her script and the audition forms, which she quickly passed out to all in attendance. Then, after nibbling on the second cookie, she headed into the sanctuary, where Steve gathered the crowd into the first ten or twelve rows. Amy brushed the cookie crumbs from her hands and did a quick head count. Thirty-two people. Thirty-two! And Steve had been worried that no one would be interested. She smiled, relieved at the show of support from the community.

Until the questions began.

"How do I fill out this paper, Amy?" Blossom asked, looking more than a little confused. "It's all Greek to me."

"Just mark down any acting or singing experience you might have had in the past," Amy said. "And add your contact information. Hand the forms to us when you're done. We'll pull them in random order and call you up to the stage to audition."

"But I haven't had any experience." Blossom bit her lip. "Well, except for that time I played the role of Mary Magdalene in the Easter play, but I only had one line." She giggled. "And I forgot it."

"My Prissy has starred in several school productions," Ellie Parker said. She brushed her daughter's bangs out of her face. "And she played Mary, the mother of Jesus, in the church Christmas pageant. We might need two forms to list all her credits." She reached into her bag and came out with a photo. "Oh, and we brought a professional headshot, of course. Wouldn't go anywhere without it."

Amy did her best not to roll her eyes. She gave those who were auditioning a few minutes to fill out the form and then glanced at her watch. "Okay, if I can get someone to move the pulpit off the stage, we'll get started. Woody and I are going to sit in the front row so we can take notes, and Eula Mae is available to run sound or accompany you on the piano. Steve has agreed to take on the role of production director, meaning he's the one you go to with any big questions related to funding the project. He'll also help us out by overseeing the various departments involved, like set design, theater construction, and so on. Does anyone have any questions before we begin?"

Annabelle's hand shot up in the air. "Can we stay in here while the others audition, so we know what we're up against?"

"I'm not sure that's the best idea," Amy said. "Might be unfair to those who go first."

Steve drew near, whispering in her ear, "Still, it would be nice to give folks an audience. That way we'd know if they could handle the pressure of being in front of people."

"True." She turned to the crowd. "Okay, it's fine if you stay. But keep your comments to yourself. Understand? Absolutely no interruptions will be tolerated."

"Good luck with that," Steve whispered. He followed his words with a wink, which almost made her forget they were in a room filled with people. In that second, she saw only him. Felt only the familiar lurch of her heart as she pondered her ever-growing feelings for him.

"Wow." Gwen rolled her eyes. "Amy's really letting this director thing go to her head. Give a girl a little bit of power, and she wants to rule the world."

"I heard that," Amy said. "And just for the record, I'm not trying to be bossy. I'm attempting to keep things orderly."

Steve snickered then walked to the stage and, with Grady's help, moved the pulpit off to the side. Amy took a seat in the front pew of the church, fewer than eight feet from the stage, and Woody sat beside her, fidgeting with his hearing aid. She thumbed through the audition forms, pulling one out.

"Prissy Parker," she called out.

Seconds later, the teen bounded onto the stage, giving a flirtatious curtsy. Her beautiful smile offered a glimmer of hope.

"Which part would you like to read for?" Amy asked.

"Mama says I'm supposed to try out for Guinevere." Prissy brushed back her hair and fluttered her eyelashes.

"Is that the only part you'll take?" Amy asked as she scribbled some notes.

The teen giggled. "Mama says it's the only role I'm suited for. Anything less would be, well, you know…less."

"That's right," her mother called out.

So much for no interruptions from the crowd.

"I see." Amy swallowed hard. "Well, Eula Mae will give you a copy of the audition script." She rose and turned to face the crowd. "Those reading for Guinevere will turn to page twenty-seven and read the monologue they find there."

Prissy accepted the offered script then read the appropriate lines. Not bad, though she did sound a little young for the part. Still, she had clearly prepared herself for the audition, memorizing several of the lines.

As soon as she finished, Ellie Parker cheered. "That's my girl!"

Woody cleared his throat and then looked Prissy's way. "Are you prepared to sing for us?"

"Of course. I brought a vocal track for *The Simple Joys of Maidenhood.*" Prissy passed off the CD to Eula Mae, who put it in the player and pressed the PLAY button. Seconds later, the teen dove into the song. In the wrong key.

"Oh, sorry." She giggled. "Must just be nerves." She tried again, this time coming in on the right note. Unfortunately, it happened to be the only right note in the song.

Someone in the audience snorted, and before long, folks were doubled over in laughter. Steve turned and gave them a warning look.

"That's enough, folks. We need to treat others the way we want to be treated."

They settled down in short order—all but Prissy's mother, who rose, fuming. "This is clearly a case of sabotage. Someone must've done something to the CD." She glared at Eula Mae. "I'm completely sure the song was in a different key when we—I mean, *she*—practiced it at home." She gestured for Prissy to come down from the stage, and the two left together in a huff.

Amy drew in a deep breath and counted to ten before pulling out the next audition form. *Thank goodness. Someone reasonable.*

"Blossom, it's your turn."

The sweet-hearted beautician took her place on the stage, looking a little nervous. As she began to read Guinevere's lines, she stumbled and bumbled, finally giving up altogether. "Guess I'm not supposed to be an actress," she said at last. "Maybe I should offer to do the hair and makeup? What do you think?"

Amy nodded. "That would be nice. We'll definitely need someone to fill that role, and I can think of no one better suited than you. But I think you could play a lady-in-waiting too, Blossom. You wouldn't have any lines, and the costume would be beautiful."

"Perfect!"

Next came Annabelle, looking a little green. She, too, wanted to try out for Guinevere. "I'm so nervous," she whispered as she untied her Sack 'n Save apron and tossed it to the side of the stage. "But I've been practicing."

After a little prompting from Amy, she did a fine job with the lines. More than fine, actually. And her rendition of the show's theme song sounded pretty good. Not particularly strong, but her beautiful pitch surprised Amy. The bubbly clerk didn't exactly fit the part from a physical standpoint, and her nerves might be a bit of an issue. Still, she received high marks from Amy, who felt a wave of relief wash over her. Thank goodness someone in Camelot could act and sing.

Amy squinted, giving Annabelle another glance. If they didn't come up with anyone else, she could play the part of Guinevere. Maybe. Amy scribbled a few more notes onto the page then raised her head, ready to move on.

Grady Knowles entered the stage next. "Whul, here I am," he drawled. "Ready ta read them-there lines from that play you've been talkin' 'bout. Wanta try out for that-there King Or-a-thur part, cuz he's the King o' the castle."

Wonderful.

Eula Mae handed him a script, and he tried to conquer the British accent. *Butchering it* might be a more apt description. Still, he seemed rather proud of himself at the end, and all the more as he attempted to sing. Well, not really sing, exactly, but lip sync. Turned out he was pretty good at mouthing the words to Richard Harris's version of "I Wonder What the King Is Doing Tonight." The whole thing would've made a great Internet video.

The audience cheered at the end, and Grady gave a deep bow. "Thank you," he said, offering an over-the-top Elvis impression. "Thank you very much."

Amy glanced at Woody, who shook his head and put Grady's audition sheet at the bottom of the pile. "Might make a good knight-in-shining-armor," Woody whispered. "With some work. And a really great costume."

Amy nodded then pulled out another form. "Sarge?" She rose and faced the audience. "I didn't realize you were auditioning."

"Yep." He took a few hobbling steps toward the stage. "Soon as I heard about the jousting scene, I hurried right over."

"Jousting?" Amy couldn't believe her good fortune. "You know how to joust?"

"One of the advantages to spending years in the military," he said. "I can joust with the best of 'em. Give me a sword and I'll show you I've got the goods."

Woody tossed his fake sword Sarge's way and the older fellow began to swing it this way and that in an impressive show. Not bad, considering his arthritic condition. He wielded the sword in several directions, nearly losing it once or twice in the process. But the joyous expression on his face captivated Amy. She'd never seen him more in his element. Yes, things were certainly looking up.

"Can you ride a horse?" she asked when he finished.

"Can I! Haven't you seen my mare?" Sarge asked. "She's a fine specimen."

Woody looked puzzled. "Your hair is a fine specimen?"

"His *mare*, Woody," Amy said. "His mare."

"Perfect." Woody adjusted his hearing aid then turned to Sarge with a grin. "Would she like to audition too? We need horses in this production."

"Well, sure." Sarge beamed. "I'd love to see old Katie Sue play a role. Maybe B-52 would like to participate too."

"B-52?" Amy gave him an inquisitive look.

"Must be another horse," Woody whispered. "We can use more than one for the jousting scene."

Pete took the stage next, still wearing his pest control uniform and smelling of pesticide. He looked more confident than most. "I've been working on my lines." He held up several pieces of paper. "I found the script on the Internet."

"Awesome." Amy nodded. She appreciated an actor who took an audition seriously. "Which part?"

"Lancelot." His cheeks flushed. "I know I'm a little older than the guy who played the role in the movie, but it's the part I feel most comfortable with."

"Fine," Amy said as she nodded. "No problem."

Pete began to quote from the scene where the handsome Frenchman sang his own praises. The whole thing was a little over-the-top. Still, he did a decent job. Not bad at all, in fact. And the crowd apparently found him humorous. They cheered when he finished the soliloquy.

"Do you sing?" Amy asked, feeling more hopeful by the moment.

"Hmm." Pete stared at his feet. "In the shower. That's about it."

"Lancelot has a couple of really great songs," she explained, "so he has to be a strong singer. One of the strongest in the show, in fact."

"That might be a problem." He wrinkled his nose.

"Well, let's try it and see." She rose and walked to the stage. "Eula

Mae, can you play the opening lines from 'If Ever I Would Leave You'? Pete, I'll sing a few of the opening notes to help you out. Just follow my lead."

"O–okay." He managed the words but did not look convinced. In fact, he looked downright terrified.

Eula Mae's gaze narrowed as she looked at Pete. "Sure hope you're up for it."

His cheeks reddened. "I'll give it my best shot."

"You can do it, Pete!" Grady hollered.

Pete offered a weak thumbs-up but still looked unnerved.

Amy sang the first few words of the song to offer a demonstration. As the familiar romantic lyrics rang out, she found herself glancing at Steve. The lyrics seemed to fit their budding relationship. From the moment they'd met as kids, she'd been drawn to him in such a strong way.

"If ever I would leave you," she sang out, her heart motivated by the lyrics, "it wouldn't be in summer. Seeing you in summer, I never could go…"

Her gaze shifted again to Steve. She couldn't leave him…or this town, even though she'd tried. No, she couldn't leave him in springtime. Or in summer, when afternoon sun shimmered through the trees on the bluff, bringing the whole place to life. Or in autumn, when the leaves turned from orange, to red, then brown, finally releasing their hold on the trees. Or in winter, when pristine layers of snow covered everything in sight, creating a magical wonderland. And judging from the pounding in her heart right now, she could never leave him even if the town of Camelot drifted away into the hazy mist, like the fabled town of lore.

After a couple of lines, she stopped, embarrassed. A roar went up from the crowd. Well, from her father and Sarge, anyway. Lucy Cramden didn't look terribly happy, and neither did Gwen.

Steve, on the other hand…well, he offered a comforting smile and then approached the edge of the stage, where he led the audience in a round of applause.

"How is it possible that I didn't know you could sing like that?" he asked.

"Oh, I, well…" She felt her cheeks grow warm as she struggled to find the right words.

"He's right, Amy," Pete said. "You sound great. But I'm going to be gut-honest with you here. I'm not sure *I* can sing like that. Ever. In my wildest dreams. So playing the role of Lancelot is completely out of the question for me."

"Just try." She gestured for the music to begin again. As Eula Mae played, Pete attempted to eke out the notes but couldn't. He tried a second time with no luck.

"Steve, come and help him." Amy turned to her best friend, desperation creeping in.

After a few words of complaint, Steve entered the stage looking a little weak in the knees. Still, when the music began again, his voice rang out in perfect pitch. The words resonated across the sanctuary with such beauty that Eula Mae stopped playing and stared at him.

"Well, for Pete's sake," she said.

"Yes?" A look of confusion registered on Pete's face.

"Oh, I wasn't speaking literally," Eula Mae said. "I just meant I'm surprised Steve can sing like that. I've heard him belt out a worship song or two, and he's great with a hymn—but never a Broadway ballad. It's remarkable."

Amy narrowed her gaze, sizing Steve up. Yes, indeed. *Remarkable* would be an understatement. Her thoughts wandered to the lyrics, and she found herself forcing back a smile.

Somewhere in the middle of her pondering, they lost Pete. He slinked off the stage. Only the clanging of the door at the back of the sanctuary alerted her to the fact that he'd disappeared.

Not that it mattered. Eula Mae started playing once more and Steve managed the first few words of "If Ever I Would Leave You." Amy followed suit, adding her lines to his. And by the time they reached the chorus, the audience members—well, most of the audience members, anyway—were on their feet, cheering.

* * * * *

"Bravo!"

Steve felt his cheeks warm in embarrassment as Eula Mae shouted her praises from the piano.

"I knew it! I knew you two would blend like tea and honey."

"W–what?" Steve shook his head, hoping he could pull himself back to the present. Looking into Amy's twinkling eyes, he found it more than a little difficult. The two of them stood in silence for a moment, but his heart was nearly thumping out of his chest. He tried to make sense out of what had just happened but couldn't.

Only one thing was crystal clear. They'd sung their first duet. Well, the first since that play in the seventh grade where he'd been forced to dress up like John Smith and sing to the fair Pocahontas. He smiled, remembering how out of place Amy looked in that Indian costume with her long blond hair…and yet how beautiful. Almost as beautiful as she looked today. Back then, a strange tightness in his chest, coupled with an inability to breathe correctly, had almost made him bow out of the performance at the last minute. That same feeling returned now, making him wonder if he might be ill. Strange. He hadn't noticed till just this moment. Did he have a fever? And what was up with the constricted feeling in his throat? Maybe he was coming down with something.

The cheers startled him back to reality. Steve tugged at his collar as he felt a warm sensation creep up his neck and into his cheeks. Now what? Apparently they'd lost Pete. And it appeared they'd lost control of the audition too.

Amy gave him a wild-eyed look. "I—I think we need to take a break." She shot across the stage but looked back at him for a moment with her cheeks pink as Lucy Cramden's lipstick. Glancing out at the audience, Amy hollered, "Take five, everyone. Then we'll pick up where we left off."

"Pick up where we left off, eh?" Eula Mae's eyebrows wiggled playfully. "I'd daresay, that will be exciting."

Steve did his best to hide the smile that threatened to erupt as a peaceful feeling settled over him like the early morning fog over the bluff. What he wanted to do was run after Amy and reiterate the words to the song in person with just the two of them listening. He wanted to tell her just what he'd been thinking and feeling over the past few months. How thrilled he'd been when she came back home from Knoxville. How he looked forward to seeing her every day at work. How, in spite of her crazy ideas, he cherished every word she'd ever spoken.

Still, every time he thought about opening up and sharing his thoughts, fear gripped him. Would he ever get past this crazy shyness? *C'mon, Steve. Are you a man or a mouse?*

He looked at the audience and shrugged. Until he caught a glimpse of Fiona, leaping from Lucy Cramden's hands directly into Blossom's over-the-top hairdo. The unsuspecting beautician let out a scream as her auburn tresses came unwound. She leaped from her seat and ran squealing toward the back of the auditorium.

From there, the ferret leaped onto the floor and began to travel up the aisle. Just as she reached the stage, Woody reached down and caught her in his right hand. He held up the little mongrel and shouted, "I've caught you, you vixen! You shall torment the kingdom no more! Tonight Merlin will boil you up in a pot of stew and feed you to the king's enemies!"

This, of course, caused Lucy Cramden to go into a panic. She raced toward Woody, grabbed Fiona, and began shouting a few lines that weren't exactly in the script. At this point, Pete reappeared and bounded down the aisle to calm Lucy. Not that she noticed. No, she took to chasing Woody, who ran—if one could call it running—from one side of the sanctuary to the other.

Steve watched it all, laughter bubbling up in his midsection. What a strange turn of events. Oh, what a wonderful, chaotic mess. Yep. Just another day in Camelot.

Chapter Five

....

Acting is happy agony.

Sir Alec Guinness

Amy paced the small bathroom, trying to make sense of what had just happened on the church's stage. Forget the fact that she'd sung in front of people. That wasn't such a big deal. Okay, well, maybe it was, considering the fact that she'd never done it before. Not as an adult, anyway. But singing with Steve? Hearing their voices blend in miraculous harmony? Memorizing the magical look in his eyes as he'd sung? She'd never experienced such a perfect moment in all of her twenty-nine years. Oh, but how she wanted to experience it again—and again. Not necessarily in front of an audience, of course, but gazing into his eyes? Hearing words of love sung directly to her? A girl could get used to that, for sure.

Amy could hardly stop trembling as she reflected on it all and had to wonder why. Actually, she did know why. Clearly, her feelings for him went far beyond what she'd ever allowed herself to think before. As he'd sung those words, that he would never leave her, in front of the crowd, she realized the truth.

I'm crazy about him…but I can't tell him.

Only, now she couldn't *not* tell him. Right?

But how? And when? Her mind reeled as she considered the possibilities. Maybe after the auditions she could bring it up. No—

he had a meeting. Maybe tomorrow morning when they met for breakfast to finalize the cast list. Sure, that would be just the right time. Except that everyone else at the local diner might overhear and the rumor mill would get started. That would never do. Could two city employees date? Hmm. She'd never thought about that before. Would they be breaking some kind of rule? Did he even want to date her?

Amy's emotions plummeted. Maybe he didn't feel the same way. Maybe he would find this all laughable. Or worse—pitiable.

"Amy, you okay in there?" Eula Mae's shaky voice rang out, startling Amy back to reality. "It's been more than five minutes."

"Oh?" She ducked into a stall as the elderly woman entered the bathroom.

"Yes, I was getting worried. You're not gonna chicken out on us, are you?"

"Chicken out?" Amy spoke from behind the closed door. "I don't have a clue what you mean."

"Mm-hmm. Anyway, half the town is still out there, waiting to audition, including your father. And Lucy Cramden. She's fit to be tied that this is taking so long. So is Gwen."

"Of course she is."

"Chuck Manly just called the church office," Eula Mae continued. "He's not feeling well but wants you to hold a spot for him, if you can."

"Ah." Amy made a point to flush the toilet and then walked out of the stall. As she did, Caroline entered the bathroom. Amy washed her hands, glancing in the mirror at her reflection. "Ugh. Why didn't someone tell me my hair was such a mess?"

"Your hair is perfect." Caroline drew near and the two of them stood side by side, staring into the mirror. "He thinks you're beautiful, you know."

"W–who?" Amy turned to face her. "Chuck Manly?"

"Don't be ridiculous. You know who." Caroline grinned and slipped her arm around Amy's waist, giving her a little squeeze. "Steve has always been nuts about you. Do you know how many times his mother and I talked about it over the years? She's always known it."

"Really?"

"Yes. And when she married Bob and moved away to Memphis, she made me promise I'd keep praying for the two of you. So I have a vested interest in your relationship as the future groom's mother's best friend."

"Wow. Now we're in wedding planning mode. That's quite a jump." Eula Mae turned toward the door. "Not that we have time to be planning a wedding today. C'mon, girlie. We've got a show to cast. Let's get to it." The bathroom door closed behind her and Caroline, but Amy couldn't seem to move. Or breathe. So, others had noticed... even prayed that she and Steve would one day marry. Crazy.

She drew in a few deep breaths as she made her way back to the sanctuary. The minute she saw Steve, a butterfly farm sprang to life in her stomach. For a minute, she thought she might be ill. Drawing in a deep breath, Amy turned her focus to those left sitting in the auditorium. *Hmm.* Probably ten or twelve more people still to audition, including her father and Lucy. And Gwen, who looked about as sour as a lemon drop.

Her father drew near, a concerned look in his eyes. "You okay, honey? You don't seem to be yourself."

"Yes, I'm fine." Amy offered a weak smile and patted his arm. Steve gave her a curious look. She quickly took her seat and motioned for Woody to do the same. Unfortunately—or fortunately, depending on how she looked at it—Steve took the seat on her left. Amy reached into the stack of audition forms, ready to get this show back on the road.

Is there some reason my palms are sweating?

She brushed them against her jeans and kept going, putting on her most professional voice, anxious to get this next one over with. "Gwen, it's your turn."

Gwen touched up her lipstick and then approached the stage, brushing her long blond hair behind her shoulders. Without using a script, she started quoting Guinevere's lines, beautifully memorized...but poorly acted. Over-the-top in every conceivable way. And as she sang the words to "The Simple Joys of Maidenhood," the notes were right—mostly, anyway—but the overall presentation was not. Something about her performance simply didn't ring true. As she ended, Gwen flashed Amy a look of "See? I told you I'm the best" and then marched off the stage, flipping her hair once more.

Instead of focusing on her feelings, Amy decided to keep things moving. "Pastor Crane," she called out, reaching for the next audition form. "It's your turn."

He came forward with his expectant wife, Natalie, in tow. "Natalie's here to help me out," he said. "We came up with a new twist on one of the scenes in the show."

"Sure. Of course."

Amy settled back in her seat as the couple proceeded to act out the scene where Guinevere was burned at the stake. Interesting. Pastor Crane did a fine job of playing the henchman. Definitely a role he could handle in the production. But Natalie looked a bit odd in her role, being six months pregnant and all.

When they finished, Natalie looked at Amy with a grin. "I hope you realize I just did this for him. I can't really participate in the show right now." She rubbed her tummy and smiled. "I have my own little production going on."

"Of course." Amy chuckled. "But we'll miss you, Natalie. You have the best singing voice in town."

"Why, thank you." The woman's cheeks flushed pink. "That's the sweetest thing anyone's said all day. But I might have to argue the point. You have a mighty fine voice, yourself."

"Sure does," Eula Mae chimed in.

"Thanks." Embarrassment washed over Amy. She turned her attention to the audition process. Next up were Jimmy and Timmy Billingsley, local twin boys, who auditioned to be knights in shining armor. They weren't bad, though Jimmy's acne would likely challenge Blossom as a makeup artist. Amy might have to call in someone more heavy-handed with the cosmetics, say, Lucy Cramden. Still, the teens were willing...and able. Amy couldn't argue with that. And they seemed capable of pulling off the part.

"Would you boys like to read for Lancelot?" Woody peered over his glasses at them.

Timmy's eyes widened. "Can't carry a note in a bucket, sir."

"Me neither," Jimmy echoed, before shrugging.

"Fine." Woody waved them off the stage. "No idea what we're gonna do about that Lancelot role."

"Me either," Amy whispered in response. "But we'll figure it out." She reached for the stack of audition forms and came up with her father's. "Dad?" She turned and gave him an encouraging smile. "Your turn."

"Praise the Lord and pass the sword!" He reached into his belt and pulled out his own version of Excalibur. Amy had seen the sword before. Dozens of times, in fact. He used it every time he told one of his Camelot tales. Only, now he apparently planned to use it on stage.

"What role would you like to try out for, Charlie?" Woody asked.

"Is there any doubt?" He entered the stage, moving so quickly that he almost tripped. "Arthur, of course. It's a lifelong dream of mine to play the great king." His face radiated pure joy at this proclamation.

"Ah." Amy swallowed hard, trying to imagine how she might handle this. She knew from previous experience that her father couldn't sing to save his life. Still, his storytelling skills were great.

Help me out here, Lord. Please!

Eula Mae began to bang out the intro for "I Wonder What the King Is Doing Tonight," and Amy's father squared his shoulders as he began to sing. As Amy suspected, his vocal abilities were anything but good. Still, he gave it the old college try…in several keys… none of them the key that Eula Mae happened to be playing in. She finally halted the music and turned to him with a grunt.

"Aw, look," he said, looking deflated, "I know I can't sing. But maybe we can dub my voice."

"Dub your voice?" Amy shook her head.

"Well, sure. That's what happened in the movie version. Franco Nero played Lancelot, but he wasn't a singer—so they dubbed his voice."

Confusion registered in Woody's eyes. "We're not going to snub you because of your voice, Charlie," he said. "But we do have to take it into consideration. Arthur has to sing. No way around that."

"He didn't say *snub*, Woody," Amy explained. "He said…aw, never mind."

"Well, how about this, then." Amy's father began a rousing rendition of "Knights of the Round Table" from *Monty Python and the Holy Grail*, making quite a show of things. Woody chuckled and then began to clap along. So did Steve, for that matter. Before long, they were all quoting lines from the movie, one after the other.

Amy drew in a breath and waited until they finished, wondering if she'd ever be able to take control of the audition again.

"Dad, that was…great. But still…"

"Not convinced?" The edges of his lips curled down. "I understand."

She wasn't sure he did, but she also wasn't sure what she could do about it. Honestly, if things didn't turn around soon, she'd just as soon walk out of here and forget this whole thing. Why, oh why, had she come up with the idea to do a musical in the first place? What was she thinking? Oh yes. She was thinking that, perhaps, she could save her town from ruin.

She gave her father another glance, and an idea registered. Perhaps he could play King Pellinore, Arthur's friend. Yes, he would be perfect for that part. And there was no singing required. Perfect! Hopefully the idea would settle well with him.

At this point—with no introduction—Lucy Cramden entered the stage, still dressed in her medieval gown and now carrying Fiona. Her eyelashes nearly took to flight, fluttering up a storm. "It's my turn! Oh, I can hardly wait."

"O–oh?" Amy fought to keep her gaze off the low-cut dress. She distracted herself by scrambling for Lucy's audition form.

"If you're casting Charlie as Arthur, let me try out for Guinevere." A girlish giggle erupted. "Anything I can do to share the stage with such a *talented* actor." She shifted her attention once more to Amy's father.

Amy sighed. "Turn to page twenty-seven of the audition script and read Guinevere's monologue."

"Face us, please," Woody said. "I need to hear you."

If he managed to keep his gaze on Lucy's lips, Amy would have to give him a gold star. Thankfully, he turned his attention to the audition form, glancing up only on occasion.

Lucy did as Amy suggested but stumbled over the words. She

tried again but botched it once more. Her giggles became contagious, and before long several others in the audience were laughing. Hopefully *with* her, not *at* her. Fortunately, her singing audition went better. Turned out her pitch was pretty good.

"Maybe I could be one of the fair maidens," Lucy said at last. Eyeing Amy's father, she added, "But only if you pair me up with just the right knight for the lusty-month-of-May scene."

Amy's dad shifted his gaze to the floor, muttered something about the weather, then shot out the door at the back of the sanctuary. Who could blame him? If Amy had her way, she'd run out the back door too. In the meantime, she'd just pretend she'd dreamed all this.

Her eyes misted over, and she swiped them with the back of her hand, determined to keep going.

"There's no crying in theater, kid," Steve whispered from the seat to her left.

"I thought that was baseball," she whispered in response.

"That too." He flashed that boyish smile and then winked. Her heartbeat skipped a beat.

Stay focused. Stay focused.

"Why are we talking about baseball?" Woody turned to them, the wrinkles in his brow deepening. "Someone hit a home run? Is that why your dad took off so fast?"

"Um, no." She sighed. "I think he had an emergency of some sort."

Steve buried a laugh that ended up sounding more like a snort.

"Are you done with me?" Lucy asked. "Because if you are, Fiona wants to audition." She lifted the ferret, showing off a frilly pink outfit. "She dressed for the occasion."

"What part, exactly, is she auditioning for?" Amy asked.

"I felt sure Guinevere would need a pet." Lucy cradled Fiona near her cheek. "And who better to play the part?"

"I'll think about that." Amy offered what she hoped would look like an encouraging smile, and Lucy nodded. Then she took off toward the back of the auditorium, muttering something about finding Amy's father.

With Lucy gone, Amy and Steve turned their attentions to the only auditioner left in the room, Steve's older brother, Darrell.

"What's it gonna be, Darrell?" Steve asked.

"Shoot, I don't care." Darrell pulled off his baseball cap and shrugged. He stuffed the cap in his back pocket and ambled toward the stage, the heels of his cowboy boots clicking against the floor. "Whatever you think, as long as I don't have to sing. I couldn't sing my way out of a paper bag."

"Hmm." Amy flipped through the script, trying to come up with the right part. "Oh, I know. Why don't we have you read for Mordred, Arthur's wicked son?"

"That sweet boy doesn't have a wicked bone in his body," Caroline said, slipping into the seat behind Amy.

"We'll see if he can pull off the part of the evil son," Amy said. "If so, then we'll know his acting skills are really good."

Darrell sighed. "I always have to be the bad guy." He chuckled as he looked Steve's way. "It's been that way since we were kids. He was the good brother, I was the bad one."

"Hey, now," Steve said. "It's not my fault I've always been a mama's boy. I'm the youngest, after all."

"I have it on good authority that you were both mama's boys," Caroline said. She chuckled as she leaned back in her seat. "Still are, in fact."

"Yeah." Darrell chuckled. "I spent a half hour on the phone with her last night. She misses us. In fact, she misses the whole town. Wishes she and Bob could be here to try out for the play."

"Acting runs in the family," Caroline said.

"Hmph. We'll see about that." Darrell took the script that Eula Mae offered him, still looking a little uncomfortable.

"Turn to page forty-two," Amy instructed. "And give us your most evil voice as you deliver the lines, okay?"

"Will do." He laughed. "I'll just be thinking about that time Steve got me in trouble with Mom back in the eleventh grade when I borrowed her car without asking. That should help me get into character."

"I remember that day," Steve said. "You drove into Knoxville to see a girl you'd met at church camp. Nearly gave Mom a heart attack."

Darrell—likely frustrated by all of this attention—lit into Mordred's lines, delivering them perfectly. Every evil inflection. Every wicked nuance. By the end of his speech, Woody, Amy, and Steve were on their feet, cheering.

"Finally!" Amy clutched her script to her chest, overcome with relief. "Someone with acting abilities."

"My brother can act too," Darrell said as he pointed at Steve. "You wouldn't believe the great acting he did every time he got caught doing something wrong as a kid. Very convincing. Mom bought it every time."

"Very funny." Steve gave his brother a stern look.

From the seat behind Amy, Caroline chuckled. "Boys will be boys."

Amy looked at Steve, an idea percolating. "Steve, why don't you read Arthur's lines on the next page? Just for fun, of course—to give Darrell someone to read against. That way we'll know if he can handle the back-and-forth movement from line to line. There's a really intense scene between Arthur and Mordred, and I'd love to see him tackle it."

"Oh, I really don't act." Steve shook his head. "Seriously. He was just kidding. Right, bro?"

Darrell shrugged. "How do you know unless you try?"

"Yeah, how do you know unless you try?" Amy pressed her script into Steve's hand. "Besides, you're just doing this to help out your brother. Give him someone to play against."

Steve rose and sighed then made his way to the stage to join his brother, mumbling something about how it didn't make sense that Darrell would read the part of his son, even if they were just messing around.

"Pick up with the line at the top of page forty-three," Amy said. "Let's see how this goes." She leaned back against the chair, praying that this little scheme of hers would work. And praying that Woody and Steve would go along with it, if it did.

Darrell delivered the opening line, and Amy held her breath as Steve countered with his. Not bad. His next line was even stronger, though the British accent could use a bit of work. By the time Steve got to his fourth or fifth line, he had it.

Amy closed her eyes and listened to the exchange between the brothers, believing, truly believing, that they were Arthur and Mordred. And for the first time all day, she believed something else too. They could pull this off. The town of Camelot really *could* put on a musical, and folks would pay to come see it. Before long, the town's residents could breathe freely again.

Leaning back in her chair, she released a sigh. A loud snore from the seat next to her startled Amy back to attention. She giggled as she glanced Woody's way. Poor guy. Looked like he'd slept right through Steve's audition. He must be exhausted from the day's proceedings.

Well, never mind all that. He would surely be tickled that they'd found their Arthur. Perhaps the land of Camelot would be saved after all.

She prayed so, anyway.

Chapter Six

....

I have only one rule in acting—
trust the director and give him heart and soul.

AVA GARDNER

The following morning, Amy drove to the Camelot Diner to meet Steve for breakfast. Though exhausted, she also felt more encouraged than the day before. She prayed he would concur with her decisions related to the cast list, one in particular. Would he go along with the idea of playing King Arthur? Hopefully she could convince him to do so. Steve knew how important this was to the town—and to her.

She entered the diner and was surprised to find Steve seated in a booth across from Gwen. A ripple of jealousy ran through Amy, but she pushed it aside. As she drew near the booth, Gwen looked up. Her expression hardened.

"Oh, hey, Amy."

"Hey." Amy looked back and forth between Steve and Gwen, trying to decide where to sit.

"Here, sit by me." Steve moved over on the bench, making room for her. She slid into place, noticing at once the frown on Gwen's face.

"We were just talking about the auditions yesterday." Gwen laughed. "Honestly, have you ever seen so many talentless people in one room? The whole thing was a joke. Too funny, really...in a *not*-so-funny sort of way." She rolled her eyes then took a sip from her cup of coffee.

"What?" Amy found herself stunned at Gwen's bluntness. "Actually, I thought a few of our townspeople did a great job. Some better than others."

"Surely you don't actually think we can pull off a professional show, Amy. One people would pay money to see?" Gwen leaned forward with her elbows on the table. "It's ludicrous. You need to stop this before people get hurt and it destroys the reputation of our town."

"What?"

"Yes." Gwen gave her a pensive look. "People are going to get their hopes up and then dashed when this thing doesn't work out. It's not fair—to them or to the people who are going to pay money to see the show."

"But that's always how it is in theater," Amy said. "Things are rough at first, but the show must go on. Everything works out in the end."

"How would you know?" Gwen leaned back against the booth, crossing her arms. "Exactly how many shows have you been in, again? Since junior high, I mean."

"Well…"

"Exactly. Look, Amy, this was a clever idea, and we all know how you love to come up with clever ideas. But this one's just a little too much. You need to let it go."

Steve shook his head. "Gwen, I disagree. I think it's one of the most brilliant ideas Amy's ever come up with. And most everyone agrees. As for ruining the reputation of the town, I don't think it's possible. Camelot is such a small place that most folks haven't even heard of it."

He emptied his coffee cup and leaned back against the seat, his shoulder rubbing against Amy's. She tried not to let his closeness distract her from the conversation at hand, but, man! Being this close to him was getting harder every day. She tried to focus on Gwen, who continued to talk.

"That's just it," Gwen argued. "We want to be known as a respectable town. I don't want to become the laughingstock of East Tennessee."

"That's not going to happen," Amy said. "I won't let it."

"We'll come up with the perfect cast list," Steve added. "Just watch and see. God will work it all out. Have a little faith."

"Hmph." Gwen rolled her eyes. "Well, at least we know who's going to play Guinevere." She rose and gave him a knowing look.

"We—we do?" Amy looked back and forth between them. "Who?"

"Isn't it obvious?" Gwen laughed. "I've already got the name. And my audition went great. You might as well give me the part. Everyone expects it. You should have heard Blossom and Annabelle talking about it. Lucy too. They're all expecting to see me in the role. Some things are just a given."

"But…" Amy let her words drift. There was no point in stating her opinion. She and Steve could talk about it later. But if he'd promised Gwen the role because of her name, he could think again. Everything in this show was going to be fair and square. Parts weren't for sale, not now, not ever.

Gwen gave Steve a little wink. "You tell her, Stevie. Talk some sense into her."

"Yes, Stevie," Amy echoed. "Tell me all about it."

"Well, I…" He sighed and gave Amy a wide-eyed glance. "That's what we're here to discuss. The cast list, I mean. So, I guess Amy and I had better get to it."

"Yes." Gwen nodded. "Better get to it, then." She blew him a kiss. "Thanks for the breakfast date. I had fun."

Breakfast date. Ugh. The very idea made Amy feel queasy. She watched as Gwen left the diner, the bell at the door jingling as she shoved her way past an incoming customer. Amy turned to Steve, her temper near the boiling point.

"You promised her the role of Guinevere? Why? Don't you think you should have run that by Woody first? Or me? I hardly think it's fair to—"

"Whoa, there." He shook his head and lowered his voice. "I never promised her a thing. Ever. I don't know where she got that idea. Just conjured it up in that overactive imagination of hers, I think."

As he spoke the words "overactive imagination," Amy flinched. Was he sending her some sort of signal? Did he realize she was currently imagining how she might pull every lovely blond hair out of Gwen's head?

"You two were pretty cozy," Amy said. "So I just figured…"

"You figured wrong. And just so you know, I came to the diner a little early to read my Bible, have a cup of coffee, and get a little perspective. I had no idea Gwen would be here."

A wave of relief washed over Amy. She didn't even try to hide the smile as she responded. "Gotcha."

"My mom called yesterday to say that she's worried about Caroline."

Amy's heart twisted within her at this news. Caroline had been a mother figure to Steve and Darrell for several years, ever since their mother had remarried and moved to Memphis. "What's going on with Caroline?"

"Not sure. From what my mother said, she hasn't been herself lately. Not that you can really tell over the phone, but something might be up."

"If anyone would know, your mom would," Amy said. "They've been best friends forever." As she spoke the words "best friends forever," her heart lurched. She and Steve had been best friends forever, hadn't they? And they knew each other equally as well.

"Mom asked if I'd keep an eye on Caroline to make sure she's okay, so I stopped by her place this morning to check on her. I have to admit, she's been acting a little odd. Secretive."

"In what way?"

Steve shook his head. "It's like she's got something to hide. I'll stop by her house when she's on the phone, and she'll end the call right away."

"Hmm." Amy paused. "What are you thinking?"

"Honestly? I've been worried about her health. She went through a spell last year with that lupus flare, and she's not been the same since. I think she's keeping something from us."

"Weird. You think she's struggling with something and doesn't want you guys to know?"

"I don't have a clue. I just know that she's been gone from the house more than usual. Sometimes I'll come for a visit and her car will be gone."

"Maybe she's gone off to Knoxville on a shopping spree. You know she loves to shop. Remember how she and your mom would head off to the mall in Knoxville and not tell anyone?"

"Right." He shrugged. "But I don't see her wearing any new clothes. So I have to think there's something going on. And my gut tells me it's not good. I've been half-tempted to ask Mom to call her rheumatologist."

"I'll be praying for her then," Amy said. She pursed her lips, not saying any more. If Caroline was really headed back into another lupus flare, then she had a tough road ahead of her. Amy swallowed hard, thinking of her own mother—and how deeply that loss still affected her, even now. Oh, how she wished for one more minute of conversation, one more mother-daughter talk.

Amy's thoughts were interrupted by a familiar voice. "What would you two like to order?"

She looked up at Prissy. "Oh, um...yes." Amy glanced at the menu. "I'll have the Camelot Special."

"How do you want your eggs?" Prissy's voice had a bit of an edge to it as she refilled Steve's coffee cup.

"Over easy," Amy responded. *Just the opposite of your attitude today.* "No, make that scrambled. I'll try something different today."

"Adam and Eve on a raft," Prissy hollered back to the kitchen. "Wreck 'em!" The teen turned her attention to Steve and fluttered her eyelashes. "Mama said to tell you that your breakfast is on the house. Since you're the mayor and all."

"Well, thank you." Steve glanced at Ellie Parker, who stood at the register and gave a little wave.

Amy did her best not to sigh out loud.

"So, what would you like to order, Steve?" Prissy asked, her eyelashes still going to town.

"I'll have the same thing Amy's having, but add a bowl of grits. And bring extra packets of sugar, okay?" He gestured to the empty container and the stack of opened packets to his left. "I go through a lot of it."

"Sweets for the sweet. That's what my mama always says." She flashed a bright smile and walked away.

Hmm. Well, at least one of them still had the ability to make people smile. Thankfully, Steve slipped into easy conversation about something to do with the new theater, and Amy relaxed. She could read the excitement in his eyes and praised God for it. Before long, the food arrived. He took her hand and gave it a squeeze then bowed his head and prayed. Oh, how she loved listening to the sound of his voice as he chatted with God in such an easygoing manner.

The next few minutes were spent eating and talking about everything except the play. By the time Amy swallowed the last of her eggs and toast, she was ready to get to business. She reached into her purse and came out with the page she'd stayed up half the night creating.

"What have you got there?" Steve tried to sneak a peek, but she pulled the paper back, not ready to show him just yet.

"Hear me out, okay?"

"Okay." He shoveled a spoonful of grits into his mouth then gave her a curious look. The same look she saw every time he doubted her sanity. "Whatever you say, Amy. You're the director."

She drew in a deep breath. "Woody and I talked on the phone till the wee hours last night. We filled most of the roles."

He gave her a look of admiration. "Good. I knew you could do it."

"I'm still waiting to hear back from Chuck Manly. He was running late yesterday because of a doctor's visit."

"Oh? Is he sick?"

"Strep throat. So I told him we'd give it a couple of days and then let him try out for Lancelot. He's the right age, right look...."

Steve's brows elevated. "Chuck Manly, the butcher, is your ideal Lancelot?"

"Well, not ideal, exactly. But I think he could do it. If he can act and sing, I mean."

"Hmm." Steve took another sip of his coffee.

"What?" Amy looked his way. "You think it's crazy?"

"Not sure. I'm trying to imagine Chuck up on stage with a meat cleaver in his hand and that bloody apron he wears all the time. Brings into question the peacefulness of the knights of the Round Table."

Amy laughed. "Trust me, it's hard to imagine any of the people of Camelot up on the big stage. But the more I think about it, the more convinced I am."

"In spite of what Gwen said?"

"Yes, in spite of Gwen." Amy sighed. Steve leaned over to read her notes. As he did, the scent of his cologne captivated her. She leaned closer, drawing in the aroma. *Mmm.*

"Um, Amy?" Steve gave her a curious look. "What, um…what are you doing?"

"Oh, sorry." She paused. "I, um…I like that cologne you're wearing."

"It's aftershave, actually." He patted his face. "I just shaved." A broad smile lit his face.

She studied his face, noting that his usual stubble had been replaced by slick skin. "Wow. That's the cleanest I've seen you since the seventh grade."

"Hey, I can't help it if my five-o'clock shadow shows up before noon," he grumbled. "It's a curse, not a blessing, trust me. But I'm getting a little tired of Eula Mae ragging me about it every day. She goes on and on about how scruffy I look. And she's not keen on my sandals, either." He sighed. "I just like to be comfortable. Is that a sin?"

"Of course not." She smiled, thinking of how awesome he looked with a little stubble on his face. How manly. For whatever reason, she reached up and ran her fingers along his now-smooth cheek, smiling as she enjoyed their nearness.

"What?" His eyes narrowed to slits. "Say what's on your mind."

I don't dare. Better get busy. She dropped her hand and redirected her gaze to the cast list. "We don't have it all figured out, but there's a good foundation. We liked Darrell in the role of Mordred. And I think Sarge could probably pull off the role of a jousting knight, thought it might take a bit of prayer for his safety, if you know what I mean."

"Of course." Steve chuckled. "This whole thing's going to take a lot of prayer, Amy."

"Um, yeah." She paused and looked at the paper, knowing that prayer was the only answer. They certainly couldn't pull this off without intervention from on high. "Pete can play Sir Lionel and Grady would be okay as Sir Dinadan. The twins did a fine job, so they can be knights, too. Oh, and Woody will be Merlin, of course. That's a given."

"And you're hoping Chuck can pull off Lancelot."

"Yes." Amy nodded. "And I think my dad would make a fine Pellinore. Now let me fill you in on the women's parts." She turned the paper over and glanced at the names she'd written down, happy for the distraction. "Prissy, Gwen, and Blossom can play ladies-in-waiting. I don't see any of them as Guinevere. I know that Natalie could have pulled it off—I've heard her sing a hundred times in church—but not six months pregnant."

"By the time we get around to our first performance, the baby will be due," Steve added. "Can you imagine how much fun that would be?" He chuckled as he pushed his plate back and took another drink of his coffee.

"No kidding." Amy laughed. "But don't worry, I have some other ideas for Guinevere. I was thinking that maybe—"

She paused as Prissy drew near the table with the coffeepot in hand. "You want some more?" she asked, her gaze fixed on Steve.

"No thanks." Amy and Steve spoke in unison.

Prissy leaned forward. "What are you two doing over here, anyway? Talking about the cast list? Can I see it?"

Amy pulled the paper off the table and held it close. "We'll be posting it on the door at City Hall at eight o'clock on Monday morning. You can see it then."

"Okay." Prissy shrugged and a hint of pain filled her eyes. "Not that it matters. I'm going to be too busy trying out for Miss Teen Tennessee to be in that stupid play, anyway. Mama said it would be a waste of my time, since it's not a professional production."

After she left, Steve sighed. "Let's get out of here, okay? We can wrap this up at the office, if you're okay with that."

"Sure. I think we're better off in private, anyway. I feel like everyone around us is listening in."

They rose and made their way to the register, where Prissy checked them out. Amy noticed the still-pained expression on the teen's face. She tried to decipher it but could not. Embarrassment perhaps? Frustration? Yes, she'd suffered both during the audition process. Well, Amy would do her best to encourage her, should she choose to participate in the play after all.

Minutes later, Amy and Steve reconvened in his office at City Hall. Thankfully, Eula Mae had not yet arrived for the day. Amy had a few things on her mind that required Steve's full attention.

"I'm glad we're alone," she said. "There's something I need to talk to you about."

"Oh?" He smiled. "I'm glad we're alone too."

Amy paused, noting the flirtatious look in his eye. Interesting.

"Okay, well, here's where things get serious." Amy worked up the courage to say the rest. "I need you to do something for me, Steve."

"Other than build a theater and change the direction of an entire town?" He grinned.

"Yes." She swallowed hard then forged ahead before her nerves got the better of her. "We've joked around about this long enough. It's time to get serious."

"Serious is nice." He wiggled his brows.

"Good." Amy grinned. "Glad you feel that way. Because I've made up my mind once and for all. I need you to play the lead in the show. You've got to be our King Arthur."

* * * * *

Steve stared at Amy, his thoughts tumbling madly as he struggled to come up with an adequate response to her request that he play the role of Arthur.

"Oh, no no no." He rose and began to pace the room. "It was one thing helping my brother audition. But you knew I was just doing that to be nice, right? I didn't really plan on trying out, myself. Not for real. I think we all just got carried away in the moment. Playacting. You know?"

"Yes, but…"

"It's enough work just being the mayor. And I've already agreed to oversee the production, to make sure we're covered financially and otherwise. I'm your production director, not your star."

"Right. I'll still need you to do that," she said. "And there will be a thousand details to iron out along the way. I figure you'll be in the thick of it. But I need you to do this for me, Steve."

"You need me to put myself on display? Total strangers will be watching. Not to mention, all my friends and neighbors."

"They're going to love you."

"And you made a random decision—even though I didn't technically audition—"

"Yes, you did," she argued. "You were great, by the way. By far the best man there."

Steve couldn't hide the smile that followed. "Thank you. But I didn't technically try out. Besides, Arthur is the one who's betrayed by Guinevere and his best friend, Lancelot. Not exactly a happy-go-lucky part, if you know what I mean."

"Steve, you've got to do it. I need you to…." She paused, and tears filled her eyes.

He took her by the hand, his eyes riveting into hers. Would the trembling in his hands give him away? "Need me to what?"

"Pull the sword out of the proverbial stone," she whispered. "Save the day. For the town…and for me."

"Ah." He chuckled and brushed a loose hair out of her face, happy to be of service. "Looking for a hero, are you?"

Amy nodded. "Yeah." Tenderness filled her eyes as she added, "And you're the best possible choice. I really mean that."

Oh, how he wanted to sweep her into his arms! To tell her that he'd gladly slay giants on her behalf. For now, though, he'd better stick to the topic at hand.

"Arthur is the lead in the show," he said. "It's a huge part. A big commitment. How in the world am I going to balance that against my workload? That's why I didn't officially audition, Amy. It's going to be impossible to oversee this production and play a role in it too." *Keep talking, though, and you'll eventually win me over. Anything to keep the light shining in those beautiful eyes of yours.*

"I don't know if it's going to work, Steve," she said. "But if you don't agree to do this, we don't have a soul who can play the part of Arthur." Amy's eyes lit up. "Oh, but I did have some thoughts about Guinevere. I know Annabelle's not physically right for the part, but maybe by the time the show gets here she will be slim and trim. She's on a diet, you know. Lost two and a half pounds already."

"With fifty-seven and a half more to go. And I don't see that changing anytime soon. Did you see the cookies she put away at the last meeting?" Steve shook his head. "I daresay she won't be any trimmer by the time we put on the show."

"Well, even if she's not, it won't matter. Whoever said that Guinevere had to look a certain way? Annabelle will do just fine."

Steve struggled to find the right words. "I'm not judging her because of her weight. It's not that. I just don't think she's right for the part." He shook his head, determination setting in. "No, if I'm going to be Arthur—and I'm not saying I am—I want the right Guinevere." His heart quickened, but he did his best not to let it deter him.

"The right Guinevere?" Her brow wrinkled. "What do you mean?"

"I don't want to waste the next season of my life romancing the wrong woman. If we're going to do this, it's got to be right in every conceivable way. We want this to be believable to the audience, and that's going to require more than good acting on my part. We've got to have chemistry."

"Chemistry. Hmm. I see." She bit her lip. "Well, it's clear you and Gwen have a lot of chemistry. And her audition wasn't really bad. Just...odd. She's convinced we're giving her the role, anyway, and I know you two are close." Amy's gaze shifted to the ground.

"Close? To Gwen Meadows?" *Good grief.* Either Amy was really bad at taking a hint, or he was lousy at giving them. Didn't she realize the only Guinevere he wanted...was Amy herself? Steve shook his head. "Gwen would think we were acting out a real-life scene, and I can't risk that. Trust me when I say that's the last thing I want."

A look of relief flooded over Amy's face as she looked into his eyes. "I'm glad." A hint of a smile followed. "Okay, well, what about Prissy Parker, then?"

A shiver ran down Steve's spine. "She's what...sixteen? And you were there. Don't tell me you didn't notice."

"Notice what?"

"She's totally flat."

"Excuse me?" Amy's eyes widened.

Steve chuckled. "Her *singing* voice," he explained. "Flat as a pancake. She can't possibly carry the role musically, despite her mother's best-laid plans."

"Ah. Well, there is that." She paused. "What about Lucy?"

"Lucy Cramden? As Guinevere? Are you kidding? She's a little old for the part, don't you think? And can you even imagine what she'd try to wear? It would be too risky. And weird." Another shiver ran down his spine.

"True." Amy held up her index finger in teacherly fashion. "But she's certainly got the flirtatious part down. And you saw her rendition of 'The Lusty Month of May.' "

"Oh, it was something to behold, all right. But, Amy, she's fifty years old if she's a day. I'm only thirty. You don't think that would be a little...?"

"Creepy?" Amy paused. "Yeah. Might not be our best bet, and we don't want to encourage her already-flirtatious behavior."

"Exactly. And she's insisting Fiona play a role too."

"I can't believe she expects us to cast a ferret as a muse. Crazy." Amy paused. "I don't know, Steve." She sighed, and all of the energy seemed to drain out of her. "With Natalie out of the picture and Gwen's audition being so over-the-top, Annabelle is really the only one who makes sense. Like I said, she's not exactly what I had in mind physically, but she can sing and her acting skills were the best. And she has some experience from her college days. Probably more than everyone else put together, in fact, which could be very helpful."

He finally worked up the courage to speak his mind. "I know one thing that would be helpful."

"What's that?"

"Well, for one thing, I think it would be helpful if I tell you how I really feel." He swallowed hard and tried to collect his scattered thoughts. No point in botching this up. Not when he'd waited so long to do it. "If I'm just honest with you, I mean. It's about time, after all."

"How you really feel?" Her eyes filled with tears. "You mean, about putting on the show in the first place?"

"No, I—"

"Oh, Steve, you think I'm an idiot, don't you? You think this play is another one of my lousy ideas. Another dumb idea by Amy Lyn Hart. It's going to be a total and complete flop. Is that it?"

"No." He took his finger and placed it over her lips. "Did any-one ever tell you that you talk too much?"

"Only every day for the last twenty-nine years." She sighed.

"Exactly."

Her mouth opened and then promptly shut. Looked like he'd stopped her from whatever she might say next. Not that he minded. With the tip of his finger, Steve traced her lips until they curled upward in a contented smile. He slipped his free arm around her waist and drew her close. His heart felt as if it had gravitated up into his throat, but somehow he managed to speak. "I've been wanting to say this for months. Don't know what took me so long."

"Say what?" she whispered, her eyes now fluttering closed.

"This." He leaned forward and placed a gentle kiss on her lips. She responded by wrapping her arms around his neck, a wonder-ful sign. As the kiss intensified, every emotion he'd kept bottled up for the past several months poured out. "You're the only Guinevere for my Arthur," he whispered when the kiss ended. This was fol-lowed by another tiny kiss on her nose.

"W–what? What are you saying?"

"I'm saying that I can't imagine entering into this venture with anyone other than the one fair lady I've had my eye on for years. You."

"But—" She grinned, but he felt her trembling in his arms. "Are you serious?"

More so than I've ever been in my life. And if I can figure out how to go about it, I'm going to tell you just how crazy I am about you.

"What if your Guinevere can't act or sing?"

"I know for a fact that you can act," he said, his heart still pound-ing out of control. "You've been acting for months like you just wanted to be my friend and nothing more. You could win an Academy Award for that performance." When Amy sighed, he paused then gave her a little kiss on the cheek and tried to quiet his heart. "I almost fell for it, by the way."

"O–oh?" She gave him an embarrassed smile.

"So don't argue with me about your acting abilities," he said. "Or your singing abilities, either. We all heard you belt out that song. You were amazing."

"I was just playing around, helping Pete. Or trying to, anyway."

"Well, you've got the best singing voice of any of the women in Camelot," he said, every word the truth. "And then there's the fact that you're beautiful. Guinevere has to be beautiful."

Amy's cheeks flushed pink. "That's sweet." She didn't say anything for a moment. "I just wonder what people will think."

"About what?"

"About the director taking one of the lead roles. It won't seem fair."

"Amy, just so you know, the decision to place you in the role of Guinevere came from Woody. We talked it through first thing this morning. He called me at six a.m. The decision has been made—from the top. He and I both agreed. There's no one else to play the role but you."

"What?" She stared at him, eyes wide. "When did he decide this?"

"The minute you sang that song. You should have heard him singing your praises to me." *And vice versa.*

"Wait a minute." She shook her head, confusion registering in her eyes. "He called me last night and said that you should play Arthur—and then he called you this morning and said that I should play Guinevere?"

"Looks that way. I just know the man is convinced you're the greatest thing since sliced bread, and I couldn't argue the point. Putting you in that role is the right thing to do…not just for me, but for the town. We've got to pick the strongest possible cast, and none of the women who tried out yesterday are even close. And that includes Annabelle. Yes, she sings relatively well, but she's got to realize she doesn't look the part. You do. Besides, you've got star quality, something none of those other ladies have."

"Star quality?" Amy chuckled. "I do? What makes you say that?"

"Because every night when I close my eyes, you're center stage. Have been for as long as I can remember." He pulled her close once again and planted several tender kisses along her hairline.

"Why didn't you tell me?" Amy whispered.

Steve sighed. "Because I'm more like the real Arthur than you know. Nervous. Shy." He paused, deep in thought. "Remember that scene at the beginning of the movie where Arthur hid out in the woods, too nervous to face Guinevere?"

"Yes."

"That's me. I don't know that bravery is one of my strong suits. It takes me longer to say what I'm feeling."

"Well, you've been pretty brave today." She kissed him on each cheek.

"Guess it's about time." He squared his shoulders. "But the need for bravery is just beginning, Amy. What we're about to do is huge—the biggest thing we've ever tried to pull off. So we're going to have to make a pact that we'll be tough, even when things get difficult. Agreed?"

"Agreed." She stuck out her hand and he shook it.

Then kissed it.

Then kissed her.

* * * * *

Amy felt light-headed as she melted once again into Steve's embrace. Was she only imagining it, or was Steve actually kissing her? Surely this whole thing was a dream. No girl could be this blessed. Especially not a girl like her, who'd made such a fool of herself in front of so many, time and time again.

The kiss ended and he looked deep into her eyes. "Just one question," he asked. "And it's an important one."

"Sure. What is it?"

"Arthur's costume. Do I—I mean, does he really have to wear tights?"

Amy laughed, caught off guard by his question. "Steve, is that really what you're most worried about? Seriously?"

"Yeah, actually." He shrugged, a panicked look in his eye. "You have no idea what this could do to a man's psyche."

"Well, in that case, we'll call them pants, not tights. But whatever you call them, you'll have to wear them. You don't want to stand out in the crowd."

"That's just the problem," he argued. "Every man in town will make fun of me."

"No, they won't," she countered. "Because they'll all be wearing them too. But don't get hung up on the costuming yet, Steve. We've got so many other things to think about first—the stage, the set, the props, the acting, the food, the tickets, the programs, the orchestra, the promotion...." Amy suddenly felt a little nauseous. She leaned against him. "What was I thinking?"

"You were thinking of Camelot," he whispered, his words tickling her ear.

"The legend, or the real place?" she asked, lowering her voice to match his.

"What's the difference?"

What was the difference, indeed? The kiss that followed was, after all, the stuff legends were made of.

Chapter Seven

....

The actor should be able to create the uni-
verse in the palm of his hand.

<small>SIR LAURENCE OLIVIER</small>

On Monday morning at eight o'clock, with her knees knocking and her pulse racing, Amy posted the cast list to the front door of City Hall. With Steve's help, she and Woody had managed to fill every role but one. Lancelot. Turned out Chuck Manly couldn't sing a note...and it couldn't be blamed on the strep throat. His acting abilities also left something to be desired. In the end, she'd assigned him a role as the town butcher, doubling as a knight in shining armor. Woody agreed to write in a couple of lines for him.

Thankfully, she had a lead for an out-of-towner who might be willing to play the Lancelot role, someone with plenty of experience. That decision she would just have to leave in the Lord's hands. At least the other roles had been filled. Now came the moment she'd been dreading...sharing the news with the townspeople.

The crowd roared as soon as Amy taped the paper to the door. People flocked around her, but she managed to scoot past them. Sprinting toward the ladies' room seemed the best solution. Perhaps she could spend some time hiding out from the crowd. Amy could only imagine what the other women would say once they saw her name next to the role of Guinevere. Likely it would be the end of her.

Would they buy the story that Steve and Woody had cooked up this plan? Hopefully—since it happened to be the truth.

A few minutes later, Eula Mae showed up in the ladies' room. "You've been in here a long time. Feeling poorly?"

"Not really." Amy groaned. "Well, not physically anyway."

"When the going gets tough, the tough hide out in the john?" Eula Mae's laugh lines deepened as she got a case of the giggles. "This is becoming a regular habit for you."

"I'm afraid they're going to lynch me when they see what Woody and Steve have decided."

"You mean the fact that you're playing Guinevere?"

"Yes." Amy sighed. "You know it wasn't my idea, right?"

"Well, I for one think it's brilliant," Eula Mae said. "After that duet you and Steve sang the other day, there was no doubt in my mind. You're perfect for each other." She giggled. "As Arthur and Guinevere, I mean." She muttered something indistinguishable under her breath as she pulled the door open and headed out into the hallway.

Amy glanced at her reflection in the mirror. She tried to imagine herself as the fair Lady Guinevere, dressed in a regal gown and singing alongside the handsome King Arthur.

Suddenly her spirits lifted. Playing Guinevere meant that she would be spending a lot of time with Steve. In a romantic role, nonetheless. Her fears dissipated and she felt her courage return as the memory of their kiss—or would that be kisses?—resurfaced. She could do anything with Steve at her side. And how ironic that the Lord had placed them in this situation, where they would have to declare their undying love for each other—as Guinevere and Arthur—in front of the masses. Man. When the Lord moved, He moved fast!

Amy spoke to her reflection in the mirror. "You can do this, girl. Just go out and face them like a man. Er, woman."

"Amy, who are you talking to?"

She looked over as Caroline stepped inside the ladies' room with Lucy following directly behind.

"Oh, well, I..."

"You're hiding, aren't you?" A hint of a smile graced Lucy's overly made-up face.

"Yeah." Amy sighed. "But I'm about to go out there. As soon as I work up the courage."

"Not sure that's the best idea just yet," Caroline said. "The ladies are, um..."

"Mad?"

"As hornets. Well, mainly Gwen. The others are just confused. Trying to absorb the news. Give them time to get used to the idea. Woody is talking to them."

"Did he tell them this was his decision? Well, his and Steve's?" Amy asked. "Because I didn't do this. I promise. Trust me, the last thing I wanted to do was put myself up in front of people as an actress and singer. I'm not." She started to add, "I'm not even a director," but stopped short.

"Oh, honey, don't worry about that," Lucy said. "No hurt feelings from me, anyway. I tried out for the part, sure, but I didn't really put any stock in getting it. Besides, I was there when you sang that song with Steve. It's so obvious that you were meant to do this. And a few other things are just as obvious too."

"O–oh?"

"Of course." Lucy's painted-on eyebrows elevated. "You think you can hide your feelings for Steve from someone as discerning as me? Think again."

"You're as obvious as a rosebush blooming in my front yard," Caroline added. "Maybe more so."

Amy sighed. "I'm done trying to hide it, anyway. We both are."

"Well, good." Caroline grinned and reached over to give Amy a hug. "Steve and Darrell have always been like family to me, so I've taken a special interest in you, Amy. Always have. I hope you know that."

"Me too," Lucy said, joining the circle. "After all…" Her cheeks turned pink. "I guess it's no secret that I have a little crush on your dad." She giggled.

Ugh. Awkward. And apparently just as awkward for Caroline, who looked as if she might be ill at this news.

Thankfully—or not so thankfully—Amy didn't have time to think about Lucy Cramden as potential mother material. The door to the restroom swung open and Gwen entered. Yikes. The twenty-something's eyes narrowed as she looked Amy's way.

"Is it true?"

"W–what?" Amy asked.

"You gave yourself the lead in the show?"

"Well, actually…" Amy stopped and shrugged. What difference would it make if she told Gwen who had decided it? She still wouldn't believe her.

"So it's true." Gwen crossed her arms and stared at Amy. "Pretty brazen, I think. But I see what you're up to. You set this thing up from the beginning, didn't you?"

That last accusation took Amy's breath away. "Of course not. And to clarify, Woody and Steve made this decision."

"Sure they did." Gwen glanced at her appearance in the mirror then looked back at Amy.

"They did. And I've agreed—reluctantly, I might add—to go along with it."

Annabelle and Blossom squeezed in behind Gwen.

"I think it's a great idea," Blossom said, her eyes sparkling with excitement. "Amy is absolutely perfect for the part."

"You're just saying that because you're tone-deaf," Gwen said. "You never stood a chance like I did."

Blossom's smile disappeared. "I, um…" Her eyes brimmed with tears.

"That was rude, Gwen." Annabelle stepped up next to her. "And just for the record, I happen to agree with Blossom. Amy *is* the better choice. We'd have to be crazy not to see it."

"You're not disappointed?" Amy took Annabelle's hand and gave it a squeeze. "Your audition was so good."

Gwen made a *hmph* sound and rechecked her reflection in the mirror.

Annabelle shrugged. "I'm a little disappointed, sure, but I never counted on playing the lead." She gestured to her midsection. "Look at me, Amy. I'm no Guinevere."

"You would have made a beautiful Guinevere," Amy said. "I have no doubt in my mind. But if you're okay with playing a lady-in-waiting…"

"Okay?" Annabelle laughed. "I'll be a nervous wreck, just like I was when I auditioned. And besides, my work schedule is terrible. Making the rehearsals is going to be tough."

"Same here." Blossom sighed. "I hope I can work it out."

"Well, to be honest, I'm not even sure I'm going to try to work it out." Gwen reached inside her purse for her lipstick and then swiped a streak across her bottom lip. "I'm trying to run a business, after all. I could see bending over backward to play one of the leads in the show, but a bit part? No thanks." She tossed the lipstick back in her purse and then turned and walked out of the bathroom, the door slamming behind her.

"Should I go after her?" Amy asked.

"Don't you dare." Caroline shook her head. "You just give her time to cool down." After a pause, she gave Amy a tender look. "You realize what she's really upset about, don't you?"

"What?"

"You and Steve. I think she realizes this seals her fate."

"Her fate?" Annabelle and Blossom spoke in unison.

"What do you mean?" Amy asked.

"I mean, she's been trying to get her claws into Steve for years," Caroline explained. "And she's not happy that you're going to be playing his love interest."

"Well, technically, Guinevere is a love interest for both Arthur and Lancelot," Lucy said with a wink. "So Amy gets to romance two men, not one."

A shiver ran down Amy's spine as she contemplated that idea. Didn't sound appealing.

"Speaking of which, there's no Lancelot listed," Annabelle said. "What's up with that?"

"We haven't cast that part yet," Amy explained. "Woody says he's got someone special in mind and not to worry. Someone from out of town with a lot of acting experience. Anyway, I'm trusting that he knows what he's talking about. For now, we'll get started with the players we do have and go from there."

A knock sounded at the door and a man's voice rang out. "Everyone okay in there?"

"Pete?" Lucy pushed the door open, and he took a tentative step inside, looking more than a little nervous. "What in the world are you doing in the ladies' room?"

"We were getting worried about you." He gestured to the hallway, where all of the men stood in a huddle. "Thought maybe someone was sick or something. Do you need us to call 911?"

"Of course not." Lucy rolled her eyes. "But thanks for checking on us." She closed the door and giggled. "Men. Can't live with 'em, certainly can't live without 'em!" At this proclamation, the ladies erupted in laughter.

Eula Mae entered once more. She looked back and forth from Amy to the others. "I had no idea we were holding a business meeting or I would've prepared appetizers. Anyone else hungry?"

"Starving," Annabelle said, rubbing her stomach. "That pizza I ate last night barely hit the spot." As the others looked her way, she shrugged. "Yeah, it's true. I'm off my diet. But who cares, really? If I can't love myself in my current fluffy condition, then I've got a deeper issue than a few pounds."

"My thoughts exactly." Eula Mae gave her a warm hug. "So, what do you say? Let's all head over to the diner for breakfast. My treat."

"Your treat?" Amy gave her a funny look.

"Yes, I'm feeling generous." Eula Mae grinned. "And a little giddy too."

"Why is that?"

"That's for me to know and you to find out," Eula Mae said with a wink. "Now, c'mon out of the ladies' room and face up to the people. They're grown-ups. They can handle it."

"And don't worry about Gwen," Lucy added. "She's got her panties in a knot, but they'll come unwound soon enough and she'll be back to her old self."

"Mean and rotten?" Blossom asked.

A ripple of laughter made its way around the room, and before long Amy felt her spirits lift. It looked like most of the ladies were on her side. Not that she really wanted anyone to take sides. Honestly, all she really wanted with Gwen was peace. And possibly a little taste of what things were like back in junior high, when they were still good friends.

Didn't look like that day was coming anytime soon. Amy sighed then reached for her purse and tagged along on Lucy's heels, ready to tackle her role as Camelot's leading lady.

* * * * *

Steve paced the hallway, wondering when Amy and the others would come out of the restroom.

"She up to her usual tricks?" Charlie asked, drawing near.

Steve looked his way. "Sir?"

"Oh, you know. She always hides in the restroom when she's nervous about something. Remember that cheerleading audition in the ninth grade? It took her mother over an hour to talk her into coming out of the ladies' room at the school. And she did it the day of the auditions too, remember? At the church."

"Now that you mention it, I do see a common theme." Steve paused. "What do you suppose they're doing in there, anyway?"

"Who knows." Charlie slapped him on the back. "Who can ever tell with women? They always go to the restroom together. Besides, you know what I always say, son: 'Women. You can't live with 'em...'"

"And you can't live without 'em." Steve chimed in for the last few words and then chuckled. For the first time in his life, he finally understood what it was like to not be able to live without a woman. The words to "If Ever I Would Leave You" flitted through his mind, bringing a smile.

The door to the ladies' room swung wide and Eula Mae stepped through. Then Lucy Cramden, wearing a lime-green T-shirt about three sizes too small. Then Annabelle, eating a kolache that she pulled from her oversize purse. Then Blossom, fussing with her hair. Then Caroline, offering him a motherly smile. Then, finally, the woman he'd been waiting for.

Amy.

She looked his way and sighed.

"Our star is ready for her close-up, Mr. DeMille." Eula Mae pushed Amy his way. Then she took Annabelle and Blossom by the arm and led them in the opposite direction. The crowd cleared and Steve found himself alone with the fair maiden. Well, the fair maiden with the look of terror on her face.

"So..." He stifled a grin. "Anything I need to know?"

"Just one thing." She reached over and gave him a kiss on the cheek. "If anyone ever accuses me of being faint of heart, defend me, okay?"

"Of course."

"Honestly, this is the bravest thing I've ever done."

"Braver than owning up to the fact that we're more than friends?" He glanced around to make sure no one was looking and then kissed the tip of her nose.

Amy paled. "It's just so terrifying to think that I'll have to stand up on a stage and sing my heart out in front of hundreds—no, thousands—of people."

"Let me understand this." Steve crossed his arms and looked into her eyes. "You're perfectly willing for *me* to stand up in front of thousands."

"Well, that's different. You've sung in church before."

"But these will be total strangers who are paying to see the show."

"Oh, Steve." She rested her head against his shoulder. "What have I done? Seriously? This is going to turn out to be the dumbest idea I ever had."

"Doubtful."

When he grinned, she slugged him. "Thanks a lot."

"Hey, now. I'm not saying it's a dumb idea. Just the opposite, in fact. And you'll do fine, Amy."

"As actor or director?"

"Both." His gaze narrowed. "Only one problem I can see."

"What's that?"

"When I kiss you, am I kissing Amy the director, Amy the actress, or Guinevere—the woman who's going to eventually break Arthur's heart?"

"Ugh." She shook her head. "Let's just say you're kissing Amy, the girl who's been nuts about you since the seventh grade."

"Seventh grade, eh?" He chuckled. "That's really saying something. I had acne and skinny legs in seventh grade."

"You still have skinny legs," she said. "But who's looking?"

"Obviously *you* are." He kissed her soundly then wrapped her in a loving embrace. As she lingered in his arms, his heart swelled with joy. Steve suddenly felt like the king of the world. And with Lady Guinevere in his arms, he felt sure he could conquer any foe.

Chapter Eight

....

All the world's a stage, and all the men
and women merely players.

WILLIAM SHAKESPEARE

Less than one week after auditions for the play, Steve rode to Knox-ville with Amy's father. He prayed they would make it to the build-ing supply store by noon to make their purchases so that they could load up the truck and be back in Camelot in time for their first rehearsal at the Civic Center. The afternoon was sure to be chaotic.

From the passenger seat in Charlie Hart's truck, Steve observed the cloudless sky. "It's supposed to storm this afternoon, so I hope we make it back without any trouble."

"We will." Charlie quirked a brow and picked up the pace.

"Praying it passes over quickly," Steve added. "With all the men coming on Saturday to start working on the new theater, we'll need clear skies."

"Yep." Charlie nodded but kept his gaze on the road. "I've already checked the weather report for Saturday. It's supposed to be clear with temperatures in the seventies. Should be perfect for a project like this."

"I don't imagine we'll get a lot done that first day," Steve said. "But I think we can get a start on the seating area first."

Charlie's words interrupted Steve's thoughts. "Did that daugh-ter of mine tell you what she's thinking?"

"As far as the layout of the new theater?" Steve nodded. "Yes. She wants to take advantage of the hill behind the Civic Center. She apparently wants to pattern the design after some theater you took her to as a kid—in Texas."

"Palo Duro Canyon." Charlie braked as he approached a stop sign. "The amphitheater was cut out of the slope of a canyon, so there was basically no construction except the stone for the stage and some wood for seating. It was a clever idea. Very creative and very little cost involved." He turned on his right signal and eased his way out onto the road.

"Right." Steve nodded, giving the idea further thought. Made perfect sense to him. "I like the idea of using stone. It's perfect for an outdoor environment. And with the Civic Center being right there, we won't have to worry about bathrooms for the patrons. We've already got those."

"Right." Charlie nodded. "I think she wants us to build on some sort of awning behind the Civic Center, though. That way we could have a covered area where people could purchase sodas and snacks."

"Good idea. Great way to bring in some extra money."

"That's my girl, filled with great ideas." Charlie laughed and slapped his hand against the steering wheel. "Well, maybe not all of them are great, but you have to admit, they're creative."

"She is definitely creative," Steve said. "I have to give her that. I just hope the people at the county office will go along with her plans. My gut says they're going to have a couple of issues with what I sent them."

"Hope not." Charlie sighed. "That poor girl's been through so much in her life already. If she has to jump one more hurdle…" He paused and shook his head. "Well, I suppose she'll jump it, but I hate to see her struggle so much. Seems like nothing comes easy for her.

Ever since her mother died..." Charlie grew silent, his gaze focused on the road.

"I understand," Steve said, "And my heart goes out to her. That's one of the reasons I usually go along with her ideas, even when they sound a little..."

"Far-fetched?"

"Yeah." Steve chuckled. "I love that she's always thinking outside of the box. Wish I could be more like that sometimes. I'm also pretty impressed that she's always interested in putting others first. Seems that way, anyway."

"Oh, she's in the habit of putting others first." Charlie sighed. "She's definitely like her mother in that respect. But we'll have to keep an eye on her, Steve. You know how she is. If we're not careful, this project is going to swallow her whole. We can't let that happen."

"Right." Steve nodded. "I plan to keep an eye on her. And since I'm acting as the production director, I can always step in and help, if she needs it."

"Thank you for that." A pause followed, and then Charlie's tone grew more serious. "I want to thank you for doing all this for my girl, Steve. It means the world to her."

"For your girl?" Steve's curiosity piqued. "What do you mean? I'm doing it for the whole town, not just Amy."

"Aw, c'mon now. I know you're not really keen on building a theater or putting on a play. You're doing this to humor her. And I think I know why. I've got eyes, you know." He gave Steve a knowing look.

"O–oh?"

"You're sweet on her." Charlie nodded. "And she's sweet on you. A person would have to be blind not to see it."

"Ah." Steve forced back the grin that threatened to erupt. "So, you've figured us out, eh?"

"Yep. I'm just glad you two finally figured it out."

"Took us awhile."

"True, but it's worth the wait. I'm a firm believer in love," Charlie said. "I married my best friend thirty years ago, and I never regretted it. Not one day."

"Well, you know how things ended for my parents," Steve said. The pause that followed left him feeling a little weighted down.

"Yeah." Charlie patted him on the arm. "I used to feel really bad about the fact that your dad didn't stick around. But your mom did a great job of handling things on her own. And she found love in her later years, so all's well that end's well, right?"

"True." Steve swallowed hard, as if he could somehow force away the negative images his father had left behind. "But I have to admit that watching the way my parents' relationship played out has definitely kept me from being able to express myself. I guess that's why it took me so long to finally let Amy know how I felt."

"Oh, you've told her, have you?" Charlie grinned. "I was wondering why she's been beaming for the past few days. Must have something to do with that."

"Yes, well…" Steve thought about his response. He hadn't exactly opened up and shared his heart with Amy, not in full. Sure, he'd told her that she had star quality. That she was center stage in his thoughts. And he'd kissed her. They were off to a good start. But getting to the crux of things—telling her that he'd fallen so hard he couldn't think straight when she was around—well, he hadn't done that yet. Hopefully soon.

"Don't feel bad about the fact that you're a little gun-shy," Charlie said. "That's nothing new in Camelot. The real king Arthur found it hard to express his feelings too. He hid out in the woods before marrying Guinevere, you know."

"Yes, I was just telling Amy that story." Steve paused, reflecting on Charlie's words. "It's funny, listening to you talk about Arthur like he was real. You don't really think he existed, do you?"

"Of course I do. And just for the record, I think he needed to be a little more assertive with the woman he loved. That's why he lost her to Lancelot, you know. Lack of assertiveness. A man needs to be ready to lay down his life for the woman he loves. But first he's got to let her know that she's adored."

"The woman he loves?" Steve smiled as he contemplated the possibilities of that statement. "I do wonder sometimes what it would be like to marry a girl like Amy. Only problem is, we're so different. Can you even imagine how chaotic it would be?"

"Nothing wrong with a little chaos." Charlie grinned. "And just so you know, God made people different on purpose. The greater the contrast, the more brilliant the painting. I'd say there's a lot of contrast between you and Amy. She sees it too. I'm sure of it. But I'm pretty sure she likes what she sees."

"I know I do." Steve did his best not to grin. Still, he did like what he saw when he looked at Amy—and all the more as time went on.

Charlie navigated a bend in the road, nearly veering off into a ravine as he paused to point to the east. "Speaking of liking what you see..." He went off into a story about the contrast of colors in Tennessee's landscape and how great it was to live in Tennessee. "Either your heart connects with the beauty of the state or it doesn't," Charlie said. "But I'll tell you, it does something to this old heart of mine."

"Amy's the same way," Steve said. "She's always had a fascination with the changing of the seasons. Guess she got that from you."

"Seasons." Charlie sighed. "Been through a few of those in my own life." He paused and appeared to be deep in thought. "You know, if you visit Tennessee just before the changing of the leaves, you feel cheated. Being there in the middle of it is like a gift—a second chance at life. A reprieve from the doctor after a bad diagnosis." He slowed the vehicle as they approached a fork in the road. "If the seasons of my life have to change—and I know they do—I'd rather experience it here in Tennessee than anywhere else on earth."

"Amen to that," Steve said. "Amen to that."

* * * * *

The ringing of the office phone startled Amy awake. Had she really fallen asleep at her desk again? That made the second time this morning. Still, who could blame her? She'd stayed up half the night coming up with additional plans for the build-out of the new amphitheater behind the Civic Center. She could hardly wait to share them with Steve later this afternoon. Then again, he might not be thrilled with her tweaks to his original plan. He and Dad were already on their way to town to get the supplies, after all. Well, she could always spring it on them later.

Lost in her thoughts, she almost missed the second ring of the phone. And the third. Amy yawned then answered, trying to sound as awake as possible as she spoke. "Yes, Eula Mae?"

"You have a call from a fellow who says he works for Knox County," Eula Mae's voice sounded strained. Quiet.

"Why are we whispering?"

"I don't want him to hear us. You can never trust a government official."

Amy stifled a laugh. "I work for the city, Eula Mae. Wouldn't that make me a government official? And Steve too, for that matter. He's the mayor, you know."

"Still…"

"Put the call through." When the phone rang, she answered with her most cheerful, "Hello?"

"Amy Hart?" The man's voice had a stern tone, which put Amy on her guard right away.

"Y–yes?"

"Ms. Hart, this is Fred Platt, Knox County Commissioner. I understand you're the driving force behind this outdoor theater idea?"

"Oh, well, yes." She nodded as if he could see her.

"The folks in our zoning commission heard from your mayor a couple of days back with details about your plan. Seems like a nice enough guy, but this plan of yours is riddled with flaws. We've got a lot to discuss before you can move forward."

"Riddled with flaws? How so?"

He spent the next ten minutes telling her. Something about zoning laws. Something about food permits. Something about county parks. Something about noise pollution.

Really? Noise pollution?

By about the ninth minute, Amy was ready to give up on the idea altogether. Still, she could hardly get a word in edgewise. The fellow simply wouldn't stop talking long enough.

"So here's what we're going to have to do, Ms. Hart," he said, his tone abrupt. "Someone from my department will be out to take a look at the area where you're building. At that point, we'll decide whether or not to allow you to continue."

"But—"

"And once our decision is made, you can choose to appeal, if necessary."

Sounds like you're already saying no.

By the time they ended the call Amy felt completely defeated.

If the people in the county office had their way, there would be no outdoor theater in Camelot. Not now, not ever. Then what? Once again, she would have let her friends and loved ones down.

"Just another dumb idea by Amy Lyn Hart," she muttered.

"What's another dumb idea by Amy Lyn Hart?"

Amy looked up as she heard the familiar voice. "Oh, hey, Eula Mae. We've just run into some problems with the county commissioner regarding the new building."

"Told you those government officials were no good."

"I wouldn't go that far, but I will say it's complicated." Amy tried her best to explain what she'd learned, but none of it really made sense even after the fellow's very thorough explanation. "Something about parking. And zoning laws. And noise pollution."

"That noise pollution thing is a crock," Eula Mae said. "The theater isn't going to be built in a residential area, so why should it matter?"

"Right." Amy nodded. "But he brought it up."

"Here's what you have to know, Amy." Eula Mae's eyes narrowed into slits and her voice became more exaggerated. "The sole purpose of government is checks and balances. Keeping everything in order. That's it. If they ever go too far, well then, they've gone too far." She trailed off on a tangent about her political views, sharing some rather outlandish thoughts.

"What is it with you and the government?" Amy said when Eula Mae finally paused for air. "I work for the government. Steve works for the government. We're paid with tax dollars. Sometimes I think people forget that. We're not bad people." She paused and gave Eula Mae a pensive look. "And by the way, you get paid with tax money too, right?"

"Yeah." Eula Mae groaned. "I'm such a hypocrite, working for the enemy. But the way I look at it, I'm like an internal spy. I'm here to keep things in order and flesh out any bad guys."

"We're *all* bad guys, Eula Mae, sinners in need of God's mercy and grace."

"Sorry, but I'm not gonna offer government officials mercy." Eula Mae pursed her lips, the fine wrinkles around them becoming more pronounced. "Nope. Won't do it."

Amy chuckled then leaned back in her chair. "I suppose this news from the commissioner's office shouldn't be a big surprise. I should have seen it coming. Just goes to show you I wasn't paying attention."

"I'll bet Steve was," Eula Mae said. "He's on top of this, Amy. I guarantee you. So, take a deep breath. Trust him to run the show."

"Run the show. That's funny." She chuckled. "But you're right. I can trust him." She felt her stresses lift as the words were spoken. With Steve running the town, they all felt safe, even in moments like this.

Suddenly Amy realized what the people of Camelot must have felt like with Arthur at the helm. Surely they felt safe. Secure. Protected.

She turned her gaze to the window as Eula Mae left the room. "Silly girl," she whispered. "Camelot wasn't even a real place. It's just a story."

Only now it didn't feel like a story. Somewhere along the way— perhaps due to her father's tall tales about the elusive kingdom— she'd actually started to believe that Arthur, Guinevere, and the others existed in this fairy-tale-like place known as Camelot.

Hmm. Not a bad idea, slipping off to a pretend place. Certainly a lot more appealing than hiding in the bathroom. And now with the county on her tail, she felt the urge to hide more than ever.

* * * * *

Steve and Charlie left Home Depot just before noon. After loading up the back of the truck, they climbed inside the cab and pointed the vehicle back in the direction of Camelot. Just a few yards out of the parking lot, Steve's phone rang. He turned to Charlie with a smile. "It's Amy."

Her first words caught him off guard. "Steve, we have a problem."

"Woody has smashed up the window of the Sack 'n Save again?"

"No."

"Fiona got loose in City Hall?"

"No."

"I give up. What is it?"

Amy shared an emotional tale of a call she'd received from the county commissioner regarding the building of the theater. Steve listened intently, his fists growing tighter as she talked. So, things were going to be even more complicated than he'd feared. Now what? He ended the call, whispering a hushed, "It's gonna be okay. I promise," before clicking off.

Charlie turned his gaze from the road for a second. "So what's up with my girl? Everything okay?"

Steve paused a moment before responding. He needed to collect his thoughts. "Not really," he finally said. "She just took a call from a guy who works for the county. Looks like they're going to be hovering over us while we build this theater, so we're definitely going to have to make sure everything is up to code. No slipups."

"You need a plan, Steve—for all of this."

"What sort of plan?"

"Are you asking for my advice?"

Steve paused and shrugged. "Sure. If you don't mind giving it."

"Okay, well, hear me out. I promise this will help. I've learned a lot from reading Arthur's story. The way he got people to go along with him was to invite them into his inner circle."

"The round table, you mean?"

"Yes. When you invite others into your circle, they learn to trust you. That's what you've got to do with these county officials and anyone else who wants to oppose you. It might not be easy, but in the end you'll have a win-win situation if you can make them feel included from the onset. That's only done if you agree to work peaceably with them."

"Wow. Great advice." Steve rested his elbow against the truck door and thought about Charlie's words. "I'll invite them to come to one of our rehearsals so they can see the plan in action. Then we'll work hand in hand to get the job done. By the time we're ready for our first curtain call, the county commissioner will be sitting front and center in the audience as our special guest." He hoped so, anyway.

"That a boy." Charlie grinned. "Now you're thinking. Invite their families and you'll really win them over."

"I can't wait to tell Amy the plan. She's going to think we're brilliant."

"What's this 'we' business?" Charlie said. "You tell her this was your idea. She'll see you as a hero."

Steve chuckled. "No, she'll know better. Besides, I don't think I need to play the hero role in her life. She doesn't need saving."

"Only from some of her nutty ideas." Charlie paused. "Remember that crazy lemonade-stand idea she came up with last summer— how she claimed it would raise money for the town? We've still got at least a dozen bags of sugar in our pantry left over from that flop." He laughed. "But that's my girl."

"Yep. She's loaded with ideas." Steve's thoughts shifted back to the county officials and the kinks they were throwing into the plan. Hopefully he really could cut them off at the pass and keep the peace. Otherwise, this whole plan was liable to go up in smoke.

Chapter Nine

....

Acting touches nerves you have absolutely no control over.

ALAN RICKMAN

On the day of the first rehearsal, Amy prepped herself in every conceivable way. After countless nights of studying—the acting craft, stage directions, vocal inflections, and so on—she finally felt ready. Well, as ready as one lone girl with no theater experience and a plan the size of the Smoky Mountains could feel.

She had the story down pat. No doubt about that. Watching the movie six times in a row would do that. She'd memorized every line, every nuance, every lyric. Not that the stage play matched the movie, but still, it wouldn't hurt to know the story. Yes, she certainly felt better about things, and all the more as she climbed into her car and headed out for that first rehearsal.

"Oh, help!" She whispered the words more as a prayer than anything else as she drove the half-mile from City Hall to the Civic Center, where the first several practices would take place. Once the men got the new outdoor stage built, rehearsals would shift outdoors. But for now, the Civic Center's linoleum floor would have to do.

When she arrived, she found Woody waiting for her in his car. *Hmm.* Perhaps waiting wasn't the right word. He appeared to be sleeping in the driver's seat. She tapped on the window and he startled to attention. Rolling down the window, he offered a weak, "Hi, Amy."

"Hi, yourself." Amy tried not to let her concern show, but he looked exhausted. She raised her voice to make sure he heard her. "Getting in a nap before rehearsal?"

"Started out as a prayer session," he said. "Figured we were gonna need it. Then my eyes got heavy."

"Happens to me all the time," she admitted. "You must've been tired."

"Yes. I've been staying up pretty late, looking over my blocking notes. Do we have a few minutes to talk things through before the others get here? I know we're just doing the read-through today, but I want to go ahead and knock this out. I could use your help."

"Sure, we can—"

She'd no sooner started to say "go inside and look at your notes" when Darrell's truck pulled into the parking lot. As usual, the tires were thick with dried mud, a casualty of his job as a construction worker. Pete's pest control van whipped in on his heels, the plastic cockroach on top dangling precariously to one side as he made a sharp turn into a nearby parking space. Strange. Had he been in some sort of accident? Pete was followed by Grady then a string of other vehicles.

"So much for meeting ahead of time." Amy sighed.

"Aw, that's okay." Woody chuckled as he gestured to the odd display of vehicles. "We should take it as a good sign that they're on time. They're excited about the production, looks like." He fussed with his hearing aid.

"Yeah." She glanced at the vehicles again, wondering if Gwen would show up. "Excited or just plain curious to see how I fare as a director?"

"You'll do fine, kid," Woody said, giving her a pat on the back. "Don't let them see you worked up. They're looking to you for their cues, and I don't just mean the kind on the stage. If you're nervous, they'll be nervous. So, stiff upper lip."

"Gotcha." She saluted him and then smiled.

He turned to Pete, who approached with a sour expression on his face.

"What happened to your van, Pete?" Woody asked.

"Someone attacked me."

"Attacked you?" Darrell asked as he stepped into the spot beside Pete. "What do you mean?"

"Someone shot clean through old Bugsy." Pete pointed to the plastic cockroach, a pained look in his eyes. "Now, why would someone want to do that, I ask you? What did Bugsy ever do to anyone? He's never hurt a flea."

Amy tried not to smile as the irony of that statement sank in.

The sight of a stretch limo hearse pulling into the parking lot interrupted their conversation. Amy watched as Pastor Crane swung wide the door on the driver's side of the hearse. As his feet hit the pavement, he turned to give everyone a wave. "Be right with you," he called out. "Precious cargo aboard!"

The pastor-slash-funeral director walked around the back of the car to the other side, where he opened the door for his wife. Natalie climbed out of the passenger door, her ever-growing belly leading the way as she waddled toward them. Drawing near, Natalie offered Amy a warm smile.

"Hope you don't mind that I'm here," she said. "I'm not a cast member or anything, but I couldn't resist coming along for the ride."

"Mind? Why would I mind?" Amy asked.

"Oh, well." Natalie paused, her gaze shifting downward. "I know that jealousy is a sin, but you have no idea how envious I am," she said at last.

"Of what?" Amy could hardly imagine the mild-mannered pastor's wife as anything but sweet and gracious.

"I love performing, and I'm dying to be in this show with the rest of you." Natalie pointed to her baby bump and shrugged. "But I wouldn't trade this little guy for all the plays in the world."

"Aw." Amy suddenly understood where she was coming from. "Well, if it helps any, I'd planned to ask for your assistance with something, anyway."

"Oh?"

"Yes. You're the best singer in town. I'm hoping you can help with the vocals."

Natalie grinned. "I'd be honored. I was hoping you'd say that." She paused. "Well, the part about needing my help, I mean. And I'm happy to give it."

"I'm so relieved." Amy reached out and squeezed her hand. "This is the part that's worried me the most. Well, the vocals and the choreography. I still need to find someone with dance experience."

"Just another reason why I refuse to join that-there church," Grady said as he stepped up next to Amy. "They don't allow folks to dance."

Pastor Crane shook his head. "Actually, we have no policy for or against dancing, Grady." A hint of a smile followed. "And if you have your heart set on kicking up your heels, Amy is looking for someone to choreograph the show. Might be just the job for you."

Grady muttered a few unintelligible words and then headed to the door of the Civic Center.

Natalie laughed. "I somehow doubt he'd step up to the plate. But you can count me in, Amy. Thanks for asking." She turned her attention to Pete, who stood facing his van. "Pete, what happened to Bugsy?"

"It's the strangest thing," the somber-faced exterminator said as he turned back to face the group. "He's been shot clean through, but

I haven't got a clue who did it or why. I was on a call to the Johnsons' place. They live pretty far off the main road, and I know people get a little crazy back in the woods sometimes."

A shiver ran down Amy's spine at the very thought of it. "Someone was shooting in the woods? Did you call Officer O'Reilly?"

"Not yet. I just know that while I was in the Johnsons' house, I heard a gunshot. Ran out and saw that Bugsy'd been hit." He pulled his hat off and ran his fingers through his hair. "Breaks my heart. Poor little fella."

"No doubt." Amy shook her head, troubled by the fact that someone in their general vicinity had done such a thing. So much for thinking they were safer in a small town.

They all stood together, sharing a moment of respectful silence as they stared at Bugsy. Or rather, what was left of Bugsy.

"He's a classic," Pastor Crane said, after clearing his throat. "Gonna be hard to replace him."

Pete's eyes misted over. So did Amy's, but it had nothing to do with Bugsy's demise. The overpowering aroma of Pete's uniform was enough to knock a buzzard off a hearse. Interesting irony, since she happened to be staring at one.

A nervous laugh interrupted her thoughts. "Hey, Amy, I heard a great theater joke," Pete said. "It's about a director, so I thought you might get a kick out of it."

"Um, okay. Why not." She needed a nice diversion right about now. "Let me have it."

"All right." Pete smiled and his gaze narrowed. "A stage manager says to a director, 'I have some good news and some bad news. The good news is that there is a wonderful theater in heaven—well-equipped, spacious, plenty of wing space. In fact, there's a show opening tomorrow night.'"

"The director says, 'That's awesome! So what's the bad news?' "

"The stage manager says, 'You're directing the show!' "

Pete laughed so hard after delivering the punch line that he nearly lost his breath. Pastor Crane and Natalie joined in. So did Grady and Eula Mae, who had meandered up at just the right moment.

"Very funny," Amy said when they all settled down. "You've had your laugh at my expense. Glad you got that over with."

"Oh, there's plenty more where that one came from," Pete said. "I've been looking up theater jokes online. There are dozens of them."

Overhead, a crack of thunder shook the skies. Amy looked up, startled. "Guess we'd better head inside. Hope Steve and Pop can outrun the storm."

She led the troops through the door. A couple of minutes later, Lucy Cramden entered, looking spiffy in her black leggings and oversized T-shirt with the word SUPERSTAR! written across the front. Blossom came next, the change in her hair color nearly taking Amy's breath away. Cherry red. Interesting. Next came Prissy, looking none too happy. Well, until the twins arrived, anyway. With Timmy and Jimmy on the scene, Prissy's expression brightened right away.

Within minutes the first row in the Civic Center had filled with several participants. At a quarter after five, Amy looked around, noticing several cast members still missing, including Steve. Hopefully he and her dad would be back from Knoxville soon with the supplies. She prayed the dreary weather wouldn't keep them. Still, she couldn't postpone the rehearsal. Not with so many anxious eyes boring through her. Might as well get moving.

"I brought snacks for everyone!" Caroline's happy-go-lucky voice rang out. "Cookies and punch. Got to keep the energy levels up."

"You're so sweet." Amy gave her a hug as Caroline came to the front. As she did, a rush of emotions swept over Amy. Oh, how she missed her mother. She had to believe that her mom—had she lived—would have been right here, serving up homemade cookies and filling cups with sugary punch.

Focus, Amy.

The cast members gathered around the cookie tray, nibbling and gabbing. After a few minutes, Amy turned her attention to the group. "I want to thank you all for coming," she said. "We're going to do an opening exercise and then dive right into the rehearsal. What we're going to do today is called a round-table reading. We'll put the chairs in a circle and read the script from top to bottom."

"Funny that it's called a round-table reading," Grady said. "Since we're the knights of the Round Table." He slapped his knee. "Get it? Knights of the Round Table."

He snorted, which created quite a stir of laughter in the room. Just as she got everyone settled down, Steve rushed through the door.

"Sorry I'm late," he said. "We ran into a little problem about ten miles west of Knoxville."

"Actually, Steve, being the Good Samaritan that he is, decided to stop and help an older woman change a flat tire," her father added, as he entered the room on Steve's heels.

"Aw. Nice guy." She wanted to give Steve a little wink but decided against it since so many others were looking on. There would be plenty of time to tell him later what a hero she thought he was—for saving both the town and the damsel in distress.

Steve took a seat in the front row. "Did we miss much?"

"No, actually, we were just getting started. I was about to explain what we're—"

"Sorry I'm late. Won't happen again." Chuck Manly came rushing in, still wearing his butcher's apron. He took a seat next to Steve then proceeded to tell a story about lamb chops. Amy found herself distracted at first by his stained apron and then by the sudden flurry of activity at the door. She glanced over just in time to see Annabelle racing in.

"Sorry. The manager had me on the 'twenty items or less' lane today, and you know how crazy that can be, especially when we've got a sale going on." Annabelle started talking about Sack 'n Save's latest promotional on paper products, but Amy couldn't track with her. Not with so many other things on her mind. She wanted to go over and remove Chuck's apron and then toss it in the trash. Only then she would have to touch it. Ick. Annabelle didn't seem to mind being near it. She took the empty seat next to Chuck, smiling all the while.

Gwen followed behind Annabelle, wearing her dog-grooming apron and dragging two poodles on a leash. One of them, the smaller of the two, yapped nonstop, his barks echoing against the linoleum floor.

"My client—was—running late," Gwen said between pants. "She's supposed to be—stopping by—to pick up these little guys."

Woody shook his head. "I don't care if your client is great, there are no animals inside. Not after what happened with Fiona at the audition."

Lucy rolled her eyes and grunted.

"I said *late*, not *great*," Gwen explained. "Besides, I don't have any choice. It looks like it's going to rain. You can't very well expect me to stand outside in the rain with two freshly groomed dogs, can you?"

"I don't care what you do with your logs," he said. "A little rain never hurt 'em. You still can't expect that we're going to say it's okay to bring animals into the rehearsal. It's not going to happen."

Gwen slapped herself on the forehead. "Fine. Just forget the whole thing. I'll go back to my place and you guys can keep your dumb show." She turned toward the door.

Thankfully, her client showed up at just that moment and scooped the little darlings into her arms, apologizing profusely for her tardiness. Afterward, Gwen marched to the front row, head high and lips pursed.

Amy sighed, realizing what a force to be reckoned with her old friend was turning out to be. When had things soured between them, and what could she do to fix it? Did she even want to fix it? The Bible said she needed to turn the other cheek. She'd been turning it so much lately, she felt like one of those ballerinas in a jewelry box—dizzy.

"I want to say a few words before we kick off the rehearsal," Amy said, snapping back to attention. "First, I'm so honored that you all accepted the roles you were given. I feel like everything has come together perfectly."

Off in the distance, Gwen rolled her eyes.

"And thank you for allowing me to play a dual role," Amy continued. "I'm not quite sure how I'm going to manage directing and acting, but I'm willing to give it the old college try. Thank goodness Woody is here. Otherwise I wouldn't even attempt it."

"Happy to be of service." He rose and waved his hand and then sat back down.

"Just a couple of questions before we begin," Amy said. "First, does anyone have any experience in building websites?"

Pastor Crane raised his hand. "I built the site for the funeral home. Looks pretty good, if I do say so myself. Why?"

"We need to build a site with information about the show," she explained, excitement kicking in. "And it needs to have a shopping-cart feature so people can buy tickets online."

"Never done a shopping cart before," he said. "But I'll figure it out."

"Perfect." She felt some of her anxiety lift. "And we'll have to somehow market the site to draw people in. I guess we can talk more about that as time goes on."

"I've managed to draw customers to the funeral home," he said.

That got a laugh out of everyone.

"I'm not sure they came because of your advertising, Pastor," Pete said. "Not that your site doesn't look great."

Amy chuckled. "Well, I'm grateful that you're willing to give it a try." She glanced at her notes. "Now, one more thing. We're going to need to hire musicians. We can only practice with the vocal tracks for so long. A live orchestra will make the show."

Natalie raised her hand. "How will we pay for them, Amy? Hiring musicians can get pricey."

"We have to sell advance tickets," she said. "It's the only way to guarantee we'll have the funds to pay them." She gave Natalie an imploring look. "You're doing so much already with the costumes, but I need someone who knows about music to locate musicians for us. Would you be willing to try?"

"Sure." A thoughtful look crossed her face. "I can start with my brother in Knoxville. He's a concert pianist."

"He is?"

"Yes." She gave Amy a confident smile. "Our parents raised us in a musical home. Someone was always playing an instrument or singing. And my brother got the lion's share of the talent."

"Hardly." Amy gave her friend an encouraging nod. "You have the most beautiful voice I've ever heard. You're loaded with talent. And I hear you're quite the seamstress too."

"Aw, thank you," Natalie said. "I wasn't fishing for compliments.

Just wanted to say that my brother knows other musicians...so maybe he can help us out." Her eyes sparkled. "Maybe he can even come and play the piano. That would be wonderful."

"Sounds great." Amy paused to check her notes before continuing. "Oh—many of you have been asking about Lancelot, and I'm thrilled to tell you that we've located someone who's perfect for the role. Just tied up the loose ends this morning, in fact. He's on his way. Should be here in the next few minutes." She felt a ripple of relief run through her as she made the announcement. Thank goodness this final detail had been ironed out.

"Who is he, Amy?" Blossom asked. "Someone we know?"

"No." Amy responded. "But he's connected to someone we know quite well. It's Sarge's grandson, Jackson Brenner."

"Jackson Brenner?" Annabelle looked perplexed. "That name sounds familiar."

"Maybe you've seen him in other shows," Amy said. "He's starred in quite a few over in Pigeon Forge. And before that, he did some recording in Nashville. I hear he's really, really good."

"Well, he'd better be," Grady grumbled. "That's all I'm sayin'. Since ya turned down yer own townspeople to let him play the part."

"Enough of that. Time to get busy." Woody eased his way out of the chair and faced the crowd. "Before we dive into the round-table reading, we're going to teach you some stage directions, so everyone out of your chairs. Come on up to the front of the room and join Amy for this fun exercise."

Amy watched as Pete and Lucy made their way forward. Some of the others—like Grady, Gwen, and Chuck—didn't seem as enthused.

"Never used the words 'fun' and 'exercise' in the same sentence before," Chuck muttered.

"Me neither," Grady added.

"There's a first time for everything," Pete said. "C'mon, fellas."

Amy gave him a smile, grateful for his encouraging words.

"Stage directions are a critical part of the equation," Woody explained, once everyone got into place. "So it's important that everyone pay attention. Amy's going to lead you through the process by playing a little game."

Deep breath, Amy. Here we go.

"Okay, everyone. Before we begin, I want to find out how much you already know about stage directions." Amy gestured to the makeshift stage area. "If I say upstage right, where do you go?"

Pete scratched his head. "I don't even see a stage."

"We're pretending." She gestured to the open space behind her. "I'm going to show you where upstage right would be, but let me start by telling you that stage directions are always from the actor's perspective as he faces the audience. So if I say stage right, it's the actor's right, not the audience's right. Got it?"

Grady shrugged. "Shore. Nuthin' hard about that."

"Now, back in the earliest days of theater, the stages were built on an incline but the part nearest the audience was a bit lower than the back of the stage. So if I say upstage, you move toward the back of the stage. Make sense?"

Everyone nodded.

She walked them through the various positions, feeling more confident as she went along. At the end of the demonstration, she landed at center stage and clapped her hands. "Okay. So now we'll begin our game. When I give the direction, you move." She paused long enough to move out of the way and then hollered out, "Upstage left!"

About half of the people ran to the correct spot while the others rebounded off each other as they tried to figure out where to go. After a few seconds, they figured it out and joined the others.

"Center stage!" she called out.

Thankfully everyone got that one right. Well, everyone but Chuck, who stood off to the side scratching his head with one hand and tugging at his dirty apron with the other.

"Downstage right!" Amy called out.

This time Lucy Cramden got a running start and almost took a swan dive into the front row of chairs. Thankfully, Pete caught her just before she toppled.

Poor Lucy. She looked terrified. Fortunately, nothing appeared to be broken...other than her pride, anyway. As she lingered a moment in Pete's arms, she mumbled something about her equilibrium being off. *Probably due to the overload of eye shadow*, Amy reasoned.

Just as she got control of the room once more, an unfamiliar voice rang out. "Hello, everyone. Am I in the right place?"

Amy looked up as the sultry male voice resonated across the room. Her heart flew into her throat as she clapped eyes on a man whose features would just as likely be seen on a magazine cover as in the Camelot Civic Center. From behind her, Lucy Cramden began to stutter, and Annabelle let out a gasp, followed by a little giggle.

"Wowza," Lucy whispered, her eyes riveted on the handsome stranger as she stepped out in front of Amy to take him in. "Praise the Lord and pass the knight in shining armor. It would appear that Sir Lancelot has just arrived on the scene."

* * * * *

Steve watched as every woman in the place turned in slow motion—their eyes wide and mouths agape as they took in the handsome stranger. The whole thing felt a bit like a scene from a silent movie.

Annabelle took a step back, as if the heavenly glow surrounding him was just too much to take. Lucy fanned herself with both hands, looking as if she might faint. Even Eula Mae appeared smitten, her mouth widening into a perfect *O* as she stared at him.

Not that the fellow appeared to be asking for attention. No, he seemed happy enough just to be accepted, if the shy smile was any indication. Maybe the overload of female gaping had him on his guard. It would appear so, anyway.

As happy as Steve was to see the role of Lancelot filled, he couldn't help but feel a little confused by the over-the-top reception. Jackson Brenner seemed like a nice guy, but the women in the room responded to him like some sort of movie star. What was up with that? And what was the deal with Amy? She couldn't seem to string two sentences together with Brenner standing in front of her. Strange.

Hmph. So much for playing the hero. Looked like he'd been pushed to the back of the stage. What was it called, again? Upstaged. Yep. Looked like he'd been upstaged by Lancelot, and rehearsals hadn't even started yet. He could only pray this wasn't a sign of things to come.

Chapter Ten

....

*One of my chief regrets during my years in theater
is that I could not sit in the audience and watch me.*

JOHN BARRYMORE

"Ooh-la-la!" Gwen whispered, finally shattering the silence in the room. "Is that *really* our Lancelot? If so, I definitely want a recount on the vote to play Guinevere." A giggle escaped before she clamped her hand over her mouth.

Amy rose, though her knees felt wobbly for some inexplicable reason. She made her way across the room, trying to keep her cool. So Jackson Brenner was handsome. So what? She'd been around handsome men before.

Okay, maybe not this handsome. As she drew near, his green eyes sparkled merrily. Surely he wore contacts. No one had eyes that brilliant shade of jade. She found herself a little lost in them for a second. Or two. Or three. And what kind of guy had such perfectly placed white teeth? They became all the more evident when Jackson smiled, which he seemed to do nonstop. Not that Amy was complaining—or any of the other women in the room. No, they'd all been rendered mute.

Well, all but Lucy Cramden. Her eyes widened and she mumbled something that sounded like, "I've died and gone to hunka-heaven. Someone pinch me. Oh, wait. Don't pinch me. Then I might wake up!"

Jackson cleared his throat and extended his hand in Amy's

direction. "I'd know you anywhere. You've got to be Amy. Gramps has told me so much about you."

"You mean, S–s–sarge?" she whispered.

"Yeah, Sarge." He chuckled, and the crinkles around his gorgeous green eyes deepened. "I still think it's funny that people call him that. He's always just been Gramps to me."

"Any grandpa of yours is a grandpa of mine." Lucy pushed her way between Amy and Jackson, her eyelashes fluttering so fast they nearly reached liftoff.

He gazed at her, clearly intrigued, and then directed his attention to Amy once again. She tried to keep her heart in check, but man! Something about standing in the presence of Adonis made her a little giddy. Apparently it left her speechless, as well. She couldn't seem to eke out a word, so Steve—*Oh, yeah! Steve!*—interrupted by extending his hand.

"Great to meet you. We've heard so much about you from Sarge. And we're grateful you've decided to step in and help us out. Trust me when I say we need all the help we can get."

"Isn't that what the real Lancelot did too?" Gwen asked, drawing near. "He appeared in Camelot much like a mythological hero and came up with the idea for the Knights of the Round Table. Every woman swooned...."

"Except Guinevere." Steve shook his head. "She wasn't won over in the beginning, remember? In fact, she couldn't stand him." His gaze inexplicably shifted to Amy, who felt beads of sweat pop up on the back of her neck.

Oops.

"No, it took awhile for Lancelot to sway fair Guinevere. But he won her heart in the end." Jackson smiled, and two glorious dimples appeared. If Amy hadn't known better, she would've thought a shimmering glow surrounded his head, like in that picture hanging in the church fellowship hall—the one of Moses coming down off the mountain.

Annabelle grew near, as did Blossom. Gwen pressed in even closer. Jackson looked back and forth between the women in front of him. "So, which one of you lovely ladies is the Guinevere to my Lancelot?"

Amy coughed. "I, well, I am." She offered a shy smile, unable to piece together a sentence of explanation.

The look of contentment in his eyes couldn't have been a coincidence. Neither was the fact that Steve slipped an arm around her waist and pulled her close. He sounded a bit gruff as he spoke. "My girl is going to be the best Guinevere in the land. Wait till you hear her sing."

"Hmph." Gwen rolled her eyes then returned her gaze to the newcomer, who continued to smile.

Maybe his teeth look so white because he's got a tan. That's got to be it. Amy did her best not to stare. Until those eyes—*Would emerald be a better description than jade?*—began to twinkle again.

"Well, I've been studying up on Lancelot," Jackson said as he lifted the script. "Gramps sent me that extra copy you gave him. Not sure I'll be able to pull it off, but I'll give it my best shot."

"Oh, I think you'll do just fine." Gwen's eyebrows elevated.

"Oh, more than fine," Annabelle threw in.

"Way more," Blossom added, her eyes fixed on his wavy hair.

"Well, thanks." Jackson chuckled. "And here I was worried I might get a poor reception."

"Why would you think that?" Steve asked.

"I'm not really a resident of Camelot like the rest of you," Jackson explained. "I didn't know how you'd feel about an outsider showing up and taking part in your play."

Grady grunted and turned away, muttering something indistinguishable.

"That's how it was in the story of Camelot too," Amy said, in an attempt to make Jackson feel welcome. "Lancelot came from France to join Arthur at the Round Table. He was an outsider."

"I didn't come quite that far," Jackson said. "Just from Pigeon Forge." He grinned, his Southern drawl more apparent. "No Frenchmen there that I know of. Sure hope I can get Lancelot's accent down."

"From what I've heard, you've played several lead roles," Amy said, "so I'm sure the accent won't be a problem."

"As I said, I'll give it my best shot." He paused. "Speaking of great shots, where's my grandfather, anyway?" he asked. "Running late as always?"

"I heard that." Sarge's voice boomed across the crowd. "And just so you know, I was never late to battle." He lit into a story about his drill sergeant's insistence upon punctuality and then switched gears and started talking about having the cast line up in battle formation.

"Good to see you too, Gramps." Jackson wrapped his grandfather in a tight hug. "I've missed you."

Sarge's eyes filled with tears, which he quickly brushed away. "Drop to the ground, soldier," he instructed. "Give me twenty."

Jackson dropped to the floor and did twenty of the fastest push-ups Amy had ever seen. The rest of the females gathered around him, their eyes widening in disbelief.

"Goodness, gracious," Blossom said. "I would've paid money to see this, and to think, I can watch it for free!" A giggle followed.

Off in the distance Grady continued to grumble, this time aloud. "Well, shore, he can do push-ups. Anyone his age could. But how'da we really know he can act er sing? We ain't even heard him try. I don't think it's fair to let him just waltz in here and take one of the main parts when he ain't auditioned like the rest'a us."

Chuck chimed in, voicing similar concerns.

Jackson rose and straightened his shirt, a look of embarrassment on his face. "I, um, well, I'm happy to audition. No problem at all. What scene would you like me to do?"

Woody piped up. "How about the one where Lancelot has to bare his soul to the fair Guinevere? That's the most intense scene and will give me an idea of your capabilities."

"Oh, the scene where Lancelot confesses his undying love?" Jackson reached into his briefcase and pulled out a script. "That one?"

Woody nodded and took a seat. "Sure." He looked at Amy. "You mind joining him? It will be good to hear the two of you together, to make sure the balance of voices is right."

Off in the distance Steve looked on, the concern in his eyes more than evident.

"I—I guess so." Amy took her script and entered the makeshift stage area standing next to Jackson. Maybe she'd better not look directly at him. She'd never make it through if those eyes—those mesmerizing eyes—caught her in their trap once again.

"Page forty-three," Woody hollered out. "Start with Lancelot's line at the top."

Jackson opened his script and glanced at the page, not saying anything for a moment. Or two. Or three. After a bit of awkward silence, Amy began to panic. Did he have stage fright? Maybe he couldn't act. Maybe Sarge's bragging had been exaggerated just like his war stories.

Jackson tossed the script onto a chair and flashed a confident smile. He spoke his first line and a holy hush fell over the room. His lyrical voice had the perfect cadence for the scene, and all traces of a Southern accent disappeared as he took on the role of Lancelot. Amy found herself captivated—not just by his good looks, but his posture, his expression, his tone of voice. The words he spoke to her—er, Guinevere—sounded so genuine that for a moment she forgot she was supposed to be Guinevere listening to Lancelot. No, in this moment, she was just Amy Hart, junior high-wannabe, completely and utterly swept away by Jackson Brenner, the most handsome boy in the class. The one every girl wanted to date. And marry. And grow old with.

From the back of the room, someone cleared his throat. Sounded familiar.

"Um, Amy?" Steve drew near with a concerned look on his face.

"Y–yes?"

"It's your line."

"O–oh?" She stared at the script, completely lost. Where were they again? Was it really time for Guinevere to speak?

"You're supposed to respond with the line about how torn you are between Arthur and Lancelot," Jackson said. "It's about a third of the way down the page."

How did he know that? Had he memorized the whole scene? This guy wasn't kidding when he said he'd been practicing.

She managed to speak Guinevere's lines, feeling more like a giddy schoolgirl than an accomplished actress. Still, if Jackson was disappointed in her performance, it did not show. No, as she spoke, he stayed in character. Completely and totally in character.

They finished the scene and most everyone in the room erupted in applause.

Grady's voice broke through. "Okay, so he can act. Big deal. But can he sing?"

"Let's see." Eula Mae entered the stage area and grabbed Jackson by the hand. "Come with me, if you please." She led the way to the piano, where she flipped open the music score to Lancelot's solo, "C'est Moi."

"Give it all you've got, kid," Eula Mae said as her fingers hit the keys. "These folks are merciless. You'll never live it down if you stink."

Jackson gave it his all, all right. And what he had—much to everyone's astonishment—was probably the best voice any of them had ever heard. Sort of an Andrea Bocelli–meets–Pavarotti kind of talent. Completely unassuming, though. In fact, he didn't come off as a showboat at all, only as one who truly loved to sing.

Amy did her best not to let her excitement show too much. Still, she could hardly believe her good fortune. Surely the Lord had sent Jackson to Camelot for such a time as this...to save the day, no less.

"I think he'll do fine," she said after the crescendo of his last note came to an end. "And having him here completes our cast. Yes, I think he'll do *just* fine."

* * * * *

Steve stood off to the edge of the room, watching the exchange between Jackson and Amy. He fought the temptation to interrupt them, though it took every ounce of willpower within him. What was it about that guy—that practically perfect guy—that got him so rankled? *Deep breath. Don't overreact.* Jackson leaned in close and Amy giggled. Steve felt his blood pressure rising. He glanced at his watch and was startled by how much time had passed.

"Amy." He called her name but she didn't turn around, so he tried again, this time a little louder. "Amy?"

"Oh." She turned to face him, her cheeks blazing pink. "I'm sorry. W–what?"

"It's five thirty," he said. "We've only got an hour and a half to read through the script. Don't you think we'd better get busy?"

"Right." She nodded, and the glazed look in her eyes appeared to pass. She sprang into action, clapping her hands. "Okay, everyone. Let's pull the chairs into a circle. We're going to begin with Act One, Scene One, where King Arthur is alone in the forest, hiding out because he's afraid to meet Guinevere."

Steve sighed. They would have to start with something that made him look like a wimp. Well, better to get this over with. Before long they'd move on to another scene—hopefully one where he could come out looking and smelling like a champ, not a chump.

Not that anyone would notice. No, the eyes of every person in the room remained fixed on Jackson, even as a few of the cast members pulled their chairs into place. And from the way things were going, it would probably be quite some time before life in Camelot shifted back to normal.

Chapter Eleven

....

There's nothing more boring than actors talking about acting.
JAMES CAAN

In spite of her attempts to the contrary, Amy's heart gravitated to her throat every time she gazed Jackson Brenner's way. For one thing, the man was downright beautiful to look at. Er, handsome. For another, he knew more about theater than all the other people in the room combined. And what a talent! She'd never met anyone firsthand who could sing like that. Talk about a godsend. And yet she got the distinct feeling he wouldn't rub his experience in anyone's face. No, the guy would likely prove to be helpful. And even if he didn't, he'd already lifted the morale of the group.

Well, the female morale, anyway. Some of the guys didn't look so enthused. Steve, for instance. As he drew near, she could sense the tension in the little wrinkles around his eyes. Not that she blamed him. If the shoe were on the other foot—if, say, a gorgeous, shapely Guinevere had sashayed into the room and caused the men to go gaga—Amy would probably be a little miffed too. Okay, more than a little miffed.

She offered Steve a bright smile. "I think we're ready to roll now."

"Good." His gaze narrowed, and for a moment she saw a look of pain in his eyes. Her thoughts shifted back to that wonderful kiss they'd shared the other morning, and shame washed over her. *Lord, forgive me. This relationship thing is new. I'm on a learning curve. I guess it's not okay to flirt with one guy when the one you just kissed is standing in front of you.* She sighed. Truthfully, it wasn't okay to flirt with Jackson even if Steve *wasn't* standing in front of her. How she'd allowed herself to slip, even for a moment, was beyond her.

Oh, but those eyes. And those lashes! What kind of guy had lashes like that? Were they real?

Help me, Lord.

By now, nearly everyone in the room had taken to chatting. No one seemed to be paying much attention to the matter at hand—the round-table reading. Amy called them to order once again, and before long, everyone was seated with script in hand.

"Okay, I'm sure you're familiar with the story," Amy said. "So we'll just dive right in. If you have any questions, please leave them for the end. As we read, Woody and I may stop you occasionally to give some direction."

Seconds later, they were off and running. Amy listened with amazement as Steve read the opening lines of the production. The British accent might be lacking, but the lyrical tone of his voice was not. Could it really be that he was born to act? Maybe he would give Jackson a run for his money. Sounded like he planned to try, anyway.

Amy's first lines were delivered with an undercurrent of nerves. Her voice initially trembled all over the place as she and Steve began the scene depicting Arthur and Guinevere's first meeting. But shortly thereafter, she started to relax. As the lines went back and forth, she found herself caught up in the moment, loving the sound of their two voices, the rise and fall of emotions, the beauty of the words. She could get used to this, especially the part where Steve—er, Arthur—spoke with such tenderness that she truly believed the words were written for her. Maybe they had been. If the Lord had orchestrated all of this, then she had to believe that He knew she'd one day be sitting right here, reading these lines.

Amy felt her cheeks turn warm and was grateful for the change of scene. As they reached the midsection of the story, the various other actors and actresses delivered their lines, some with more grace and finesse than others. Thank goodness Grady only had a couple of them. And thankfully Darrell seemed to take to the Mordred role with ease. Even Lucy excelled with her few lines. Amy's father seemed a little over-the-top as Pellinore, but he simmered down after the first few minutes.

But Gwen... Amy sighed as Gwen wriggled in her seat and messed with her cell phone. It frustrated Amy to see her so bent out of shape, but it frustrated her even more when she thought about how much things had changed over the years. Was there really a time, all those years ago, when she and Gwen had been best friends? They'd played dress-up and gone to sleepovers together. What in the world had happened to put an end to all that? In her heart of hearts, she missed her old friend and wondered if things would ever be different. She hoped so—prayed so.

Before Amy knew it, they were at the point in the story where Lancelot made his entrance. Out of the corner of her eyes, she watched Jackson as he delivered his opening lines. They sounded even stronger than the ones he'd shared earlier. She whispered up a prayer of thanks, grateful to the Lord for bringing him here.

For the first time, she actually felt confident in the outcome of the show. People would come...and with the caliber of talent that Jackson and Steve both provided, the audience would leave satisfied—their pockets a little emptier but their hearts a little fuller. At least that was the idea. Ultimately, the town of Camelot would rise from the ashes, financially sound and ready to face the future.

Amy found herself so lost in her thoughts that she almost missed her next cue. She jumped into her lines, feeling a little flustered. Not that anyone else seemed to notice. No, everyone in the place had his or her nose buried in the script.

Okay, maybe not everyone. Lucy, Annabelle, Blossom, and Gwen occasionally peeked over the edges of their scripts at Jackson, who, thankfully, remained oblivious. *Hmm.* She would have to keep an eye on that. No backstage romances during this play. They simply didn't have time.

Well, no backstage romances except the one between her and Steve. She couldn't stop that ball from rolling down a hill if she wanted to. Not that she wanted to. No, more than ever, she wanted to follow her heart. Surely it would lead her straight into his arms... if he would still have her, after she'd practically swooned over Jackson.

Amy found herself caught up in yet another daydream and nearly missed King Arthur's last line. Only when the others began to cheer did she startle to attention.

"We did it," Woody said with a contented smile. "We made it through the whole show."

Applause sounded across the room and Amy looked around the circle at her cast, thrilled for their time and effort and even more thrilled at their enthusiasm.

"You guys were great," she said. "I feel so..." She started to say *relieved* but changed it to "blessed." After what she hoped would be perceived as an encouraging smile, she gave some closing directions. "When we meet again on Wednesday afternoon, we'll start blocking the opening scene." She paused. "Oh, something else. We're going to need someone to choreograph the dance numbers. I've been wondering if any of you have dance experience."

An awkward silence gave her the answer she'd feared. And then, from the opposite side of the room, one lone hand went up.

"I—I used to be a cheerleader during high school back in Texas."

"Annabelle?" Amy tried not to let her surprise show.

"Yes, and I was on the drill team too. I even took ballet and jazz as a kid, so I've had a lot of experience." A sad look passed over her and she shrugged. "It's been awhile. Obviously."

"Well, I'd be honored if you would talk with me before you leave today," Amy said. "We're going to need someone to choreograph two of the numbers for sure. Maybe three."

"I'd be happy to give it a shot. I don't mean to brag, but back in the day, I was quite a dancer." A hopeful look came to Annabelle's eyes. "Sounds like fun."

"Great." One problem down, approximately ten million to go. At least Amy had a plan of action now. That helped. "One last thing, everyone. I've put together a schedule for our future rehearsals. You'll each get a copy. In fact, let me give those to you now."

She reached inside her bag and came out with several copies, which she passed around. Several of the cast members began to chat among themselves, and Amy decided to dismiss them—not that anyone actually left. No, they seemed content to visit. The guys, anyway. The women couldn't seem to tear themselves away from Jackson.

She approached the group and handed Jackson a copy of the production schedule. "I've laid out a full plan of action for our rehearsals," she explained. "That way every scene gets covered multiple times. And the musical numbers too." She pointed at Eula Mae. "We've got the best pianist in the county, and now Natalie has agreed to help our soloists with their vocals."

From across the room, Natalie gave a little wave.

"Wow." Jackson gave Amy an admiring look as he glanced down at the page in his hand. "I've seen a lot of production schedules over the years, and this is top-notch. You've thought of everything. And I like the way you've divided the music rehearsals from the drama rehearsals. That's always helpful. "

She forced back a grin. "Well, I can't take the credit. I found a sample production schedule online and emulated it. That's really the only reason I knew to start with a round-table reading."

"Well, if you need any advice from here on out, don't be afraid to ask me," he said. "I've been around the block a few times."

From across the room, Steve's eyes reflected his "Sure you have" thinking.

Gwen drew near, a smile lighting her face as she stood next to Jackson. "Speaking of going around the block, would you like someone to show you around Camelot one day this week?" she asked. "I've lived here all my life and would be tickled pink to show you off." She giggled. "I mean, to show off the town, of course. Silly me. But anyway, we'll have fun. I've got the cutest little convertible."

"Sounds tempting," Jackson said. "Of course, I came to work, not to look at the scenery." For whatever reason, his eyes riveted into Amy's at that last part. She had a few things to say about the scenery. *Wowza*, as Lucy would say. She closed her eyes and took a mental snapshot. When her eyelids sprang open, she found Steve staring at her from across the room.

Focus, Amy. Focus.

Thankfully, Pastor Crane and Natalie came over, distracting her from the confusion in Steve's eyes.

"Brent Crane," the pastor said, extending his hand in Jackson's direction. "Can't tell you how glad we are to have you here."

"Nice to meet you." Jackson shook his hand.

"Pastor Crane is the owner of the funeral home," Amy explained.

"Interesting coincidence," Jackson said.

"Yes." The pastor laughed. "I spend the weekends getting their souls into heaven and the weekdays getting their bodies into the ground." An exuberant laugh followed. "Get it?"

"Yep." Jackson chuckled. "I can't even imagine trying to balance those two. If you've taken on the role of funeral director, then who counsels the families when a loved one passes away? Wouldn't that be your job as pastor?"

"Well, I do," he said. "And sometimes Steve helps. He's really good at talking people through rough times."

"Steve?" Jackson shrugged. "The Steve who's playing King Arthur?"

"Yes." Pastor Crane nodded.

"Is he a counselor?" Jackson asked.

"No, he's our mayor." Amy hoped her voice wouldn't betray her. Steve was clearly more than that, but she didn't need to share that with a total stranger. "He's got a great heart for people."

Jackson smiled. "It's been crazy, being on the road so much. I haven't really had time to get to know people long-term. I mean, I have friends, but none that I'd spend Thanksgiving with. That's one reason I'm glad to be here with Gramps."

"We're glad you're here too," Natalie said, giving his arm a pat.

"Very glad," Annabelle and Blossom spoke in unison as they stepped up beside him.

Hmm. Looked like the fair maidens of Camelot had their eye on a certain knight. Only time would tell if he would dazzle and delight them as the real Lancelot had done. Still, Amy had a feeling that Jackson was halfway around the bend on that one already.

* * * * *

"Dealing with the green-eyed monster, eh?" Woody asked.

"What?" Steve jerked to attention.

"Can't say as I blame you," Woody said. "Looks like Romeo's making his move. Better move in to capture the fair Juliet before she jumps off the balcony and lands in his arms."

Steve's blood began to boil. So he wasn't the only one who'd noticed it. Well, he'd put a stop to this all right. Had the kisses he and Amy shared meant nothing? Why would she stand there—so close to a total stranger—drinking in his every word and giggling like that? Didn't make a lick of sense. Then again, nothing about this afternoon's chain of events made much sense right now.

He drew in a deep breath, counted to three, then exhaled. There. Much better. No point in letting his frustration get the better of him. Finally prepared, he took a few steps in Amy's direction.

He'd just reached her when she grabbed his hand. "Oh, Steve! I'm so glad you're here. Jackson was just telling me a story about Sarge that you're going to love."

"Oh?"

The edges of Jackson's lips turned up in a smile. "Yeah. Gramps came to visit us in Nashville when I was in elementary school. My grandmother was still alive back then. I was just a kid and loved to play army. He gathered all the neighborhood boys together and acted like our drill sergeant. We had to do push-ups, run laps, you name it. Then he had us hide in the bushes, to keep from being found by the enemy." Jackson laughed and Steve's tension melted. "He was always so much fun."

"You should write those stories down, Jackson," Amy said. "Seriously. One day you might have kids, and they'll need to know all of this."

"I guess." Jackson glanced at his watch then looked his grand-father's way. "Right now I think I'd better get him home. He's been looking a little...I don't know...different lately."

"What do you mean?" Steve asked. "Something we need to know?"

A look of concern settled in Jackson's eyes. "Maybe it's just because I haven't seen him in several months, but I've really noticed a change in him. He's moving a lot slower, and his stories are more scattered too."

"How can you tell?" Amy giggled then put her hand over her mouth. "Oh, sorry."

"No, you're right. It's always been hard to tell with Gramps." Jackson shook his head. "But I'm glad I'm here with him. Seems like he's at that point where he really doesn't need to be alone."

"He's lucky to have you," Steve added, feeling much better about this situation. Maybe Jackson didn't have hidden motives after all. Maybe he hadn't come to town to sweep the ladies off their feet. Perhaps he'd simply come at his grandfather's bidding.

"Oh, I'm the lucky one." Jackson grinned. "He's great. And I know I'm right where I'm supposed to be." A pause followed. "I'm looking forward to getting to know everyone. I was just telling Amy, my life in Pigeon Forge was a little different. I'm hoping that Camelot will be a place where I can really get to know people for a change."

"Oh, we're very friendly here," Amy said. "You'll see."

A niggling of jealousy distracted Steve, but he forced it away.

Lucy Cramden chose that moment to approach. A coy smile followed as she turned Jackson's direction. "Yes, we're very friendly here." An awkward pause rode on the heels of her flirtatious wran-gling, but she quickly recovered. "Jackson, your grandfather is ready to go. He sent me to fetch you."

"Yes." Jackson glanced Sarge's way. "It was great meeting all of you. I can't wait to get this show on the road."

"Show on the road. Funny." Lucy took him by the arm and ushered him across the room—out of sight but certainly not out of mind.

No, Steve had a sneaking suspicion it would be a long while before any of the women of Camelot would get Jackson Brenner off their minds. He only prayed that one woman in particular would shake him sooner rather than later.

Chapter Twelve

....

*I was planning to go into architecture. But when
I arrived, architecture was filled up.
Acting was right next to it, so I signed up for acting instead.*

GILBERT K. CHESTERTON

The following Saturday, the men of Camelot showed up at the Civic Center to begin work on the amphitheater. With Grady's hardware-store connections, the workers were equipped and ready. And thanks to a couple of Darrell's friends in the construction industry, they had heavy equipment aplenty. Amy had never seen so many bulldozers and backhoes in her life. It looked like everyone in Knox County had arrived to help.

Or hurt.

Fred Platt, the county official who had badgered her over the phone, had decided to pay them a visit as well. Oh well. Might as well head him off at the pass...or send him Steve's way. Yes, she'd be better off letting Steve handle this one. He could charm birds out of trees. Surely he could handle one lone government official.

Sure enough, Steve managed to talk the fellow through the process and showed evidence that everything would be done to code. He seemed to take it in stride, thank goodness. Then again, Steve usually managed to get people calmed down. He had that way about him.

On this particular day, ironically, the person who needed consoling was none other than Amy herself. She'd hardly slept a wink for nights. Every time she closed her eyes, another problem played itself out on the stage of her mind. And now, before another minute slipped by, she needed to address them. She waited until the county official left before approaching Steve with her list of concerns.

"Can I take you away from your work for a minute?" she asked.

"Um, sure." He looked at Darrell and shrugged. "You guys okay without me for a little while?"

"Yeah. We've got this." Darrell gestured for one of the bulldozer drivers to begin the work of digging out the area for the first row of seating. Amy found herself caught up in watching for a moment before she remembered the reason she'd pulled Steve away from the task at hand. She made a point to step far enough away that the others couldn't hear her. No point in raising red flags or causing undue concern.

"Steve, I'm worried," she managed at last.

He pulled her close and gave her a little kiss on the nose. "About what? The play?"

"Yes." She shook her head. "No. I mean, yes, I'm concerned about the play too. But there's so much I didn't think about, and it's all staring me in the face."

"The only thing staring you in the face right now is me." He gave her a little wink, which sent her heart fluttering—only she didn't feel like being cheered up. Not yet. Not with so much on her mind.

"This is important, Steve," she whispered.

"Okay, sorry." He released his hold on her and ran his fingers through his thick, dark hair. "What's got you most worried?"

"It's just all happening too fast. I'm afraid we're going to forget something, leave something out. Something important, maybe. You know?"

"No." He shook his head. "I don't have a clue. Like what? What do you mean?"

"Well, if this play is going to take place the first weekend in July like we've talked about, then everything has to be ready, and I don't just mean the amphitheater. Or the tickets. Or the programs. I'm talking about the big stuff."

"Big stuff?"

"Restrooms."

"Excuse me?"

"We have one ladies' room and one men's room inside the Civic Center. This could be a problem once the theater fills up with people. I can't believe I didn't think about it before." She began to pace, her stomach in a knot. How could she have forgotten something so important? "Building restrooms could get expensive. All of this could get expensive."

"We've already got a plan for that, Amy," he said. "The architect with Darrell's firm has already laid out a full design for bathrooms on the east side of the hill." He paused. "As for the financial, at least half the people in town have donated toward this project already. And Darrell's guys—most of them, anyway—are donating much of their time. People are lending their support. So what's next on your worry list?"

"Food."

"You're worried about food? Already?"

"Yes. No." She groaned. "Not food during the shows. I think we'll do okay with the snack bar and the medieval stuff. Ellie Parker said she's been thinking of starting a catering service out of the diner anyway. So we can cut some sort of deal with them for the meal we'll serve during the production. I'm talking about a different kind of food."

Steve still looked confused.

"We're building a theater so that people will come. And come, they will. But what will we feed them if they show up in Camelot the day before the production? Or the day before that?" She paused for breath then raced ahead. "We've only got one little diner in town with the Hardee's a few miles away. What are we going to do if three hundred people turn up the day before the show and need to eat? And for that matter, what if they drive in from out-of-state or something and want to settle in for a day or two? Where will they go? We don't have a motel. Or an RV park. And they'll wonder why we don't have other things to offer. Like shopping."

"I feel a headache coming on." Steve groaned.

"Anyway, here's what I've been thinking." She took a seat on a nearby bench. "We've got that old piece of property on the south end of town where King Arthur's Court used to be."

"The trailer park?"

"Yes. We can clean it up and use it for RVs. What do you think? We'll call it King Arthur's RV Court."

"I think it sounds like a lot of work." Steve took a seat next to her and gave her a pensive look. "But it might be possible. I just don't know if we can get it done before the show kicks off."

"We've got to try. And now that Lance has moved on, we've got that big, empty used car lot," she added. "Why not take advantage of that and use it too?"

"As another RV park?"

"No, I'm thinking we could use that space for vendors to sell their wares. You know, like an arts-and-crafts thing, with food too. That way we can kill two birds with one stone. Locals can make a little extra money selling their goods, and we can feed the guests too."

"Hmm." He shrugged. "Could work."

"Sure. It would give the people something to do when they're waiting to see the show. They can buy from Camelot residents. That might give some of those people who donated a way to earn their money back."

"Only one problem with that," he said. "Half the town is going to be busy with the show."

"Nah. Not half. There are only thirty-two people in the show. We have over a hundred more people in town who could help with the things I'm talking about."

"I like that you're thinking ahead, Amy. Wise move on your part."

"I've just been so concerned about all this that I've had a hard time sleeping. It almost feels like we're building the town from square one."

"True. But you know what? God's got this one under control. We don't need to worry."

Easy for him to say. This isn't his idea. She gave him a faint smile. "Thanks for the encouragement. I know you're busy."

"Never too busy for fair Guinevere." He leaned over and gave her a kiss so sweet that it nearly made her forget about her troubles. Nearly.

She offered up a little wave as Steve joined the other men, and then she leaned back, her thoughts reverting to the RV-park idea. A few moments ticked by, but she couldn't get a handle on things in spite of his encouragement. How could they ever accomplish so much in such a short period of time?

Amy caught a glimpse of Jackson Brenner walking up. From the looks of things, he had something on his mind that wouldn't wait. She signaled him to join her. "Everything okay?" she asked as he drew near.

"Yes." He nodded and took a seat next to her. "Just been thinking things through. I had a few ideas to share about the theater's layout. Who should I talk to about that?"

She squinted against the sunlight, looking around, and finally located Darrell standing with a group of workers. Amy pointed to him. "You need to talk to Darrell, Steve's brother."

"Will do. I think I have a few ideas that will cut back on the workload. Believe it or not, I've done a theater build-out before. This isn't my first rodeo." He gave her a wink—and for some inexplicable reason, her heart skipped a beat. She quickly reeled herself in. Amy had too much on her plate today to be swept away by this handsome Lancelot, even if he did happen to have answers to her problems.

"You okay?" Jackson asked. An inquisitive look followed. "You look a little anxious."

"Yeah." Amy nodded. "There's just so much on my mind. Steve and I have been talking through a plan to turn an old trailer park into a place for RVs. I think we're going to need it once tourists start rolling into town."

"I like it." He nodded. "Sounds like a worthy plan."

"It's such a mess, though. The weeds will have to be cleared, and who knows what we'll find underneath. I don't even know if the plumbing is intact, but I guess we'll figure that out as we go along." She sighed and gestured to the workers. "Not that I happen to have an available plumber in my back pocket waiting for this job. Every man in town is busy with the build-out of the theater."

"I know a plumber."

"Oh?" Amy's heart quickened. "You do?"

"Yes, and he owes me a favor." Jackson told her about his friend—a guy named Thomas—and before long, they had a full plan of action for the plumbing at both the potential RV park and the restroom facilities at the new theater.

"Wow, that would be great, Jackson," Amy said as he finished. She gave him a smile that she hoped would convey her thankfulness. As she did, her burdens seemed to lift. Truly, the Lord had sent Jackson Brenner to Camelot. Maybe he really was a knight in shining armor after all. Or maybe he was just a nice guy who didn't mind helping out a town in need when the situation called for it. Either way, she was plenty grateful he'd ridden into Camelot on his white steed just in the nick of time.

* * * * *

"You okay, Steve?"

Steve looked up as Caroline came over with a tray of sandwiches in hand. "Yeah. Guess so."

"Distracted by Sir Lancelot?"

Steve shrugged. "Doing my best to ignore that situation, thank you very much." He turned his gaze to Amy and Jackson, trying not to make too much of her doe-eyed look. Surely she didn't realize how her demeanor had changed the moment Jackson stepped into the scene. Not that Steve wasn't grateful for Jackson's presence. No, it looked like the guy had a lot to offer, both onstage and off. And he seemed like a nice person, to boot. Just one more reason to be concerned. Steve did his best to shake off his concerns, but this handsome stranger surely made things difficult.

"Amy's a smart girl, honey." Caroline patted his arm. "Your fears are in vain."

"Fears?"

She gave him a knowing look then pressed a sandwich into his hand. "Tuna fish. Made it just for you." She headed off to feed the other men.

Steve took a bite of his sandwich and let the sound of the bulldozers drown out any concerns he had about Amy and Jackson. For a minute, anyway. Above the roar of the machines, a voice rang out.

"Steve, can you come here for a minute?"

He turned to find Amy waving. Steve took a few steps toward her, intrigued by the excitement he saw in her eyes.

"Jackson just offered to bring in a friend to help with the RV park." She raised her voice. "A plumber."

Of course he did.

Thankfully, the bulldozer came to a halt and Steve could hear himself think once more.

"I'll give him a call in a few minutes," Jackson said. "But in the meantime, there's something I wanted to talk to you about. I had an idea."

"Oh?" Steve braced himself. Everyone was full of ideas today.

"I know you two have a lot on your mind," Jackson said. "But I thought of something that might make your jobs a little easier."

"What's that?" Steve asked.

"I've been thinking about what the real Lancelot did." Jackson offered up a sheepish grin. "Do you remember?"

"How could I forget?" Steve crossed his arms at his chest. "He swept into town, stole the hearts of the women, and wreaked havoc on the kingdom. Then he tucked his tail between his legs and went back to France. Is that what you mean?"

Jackson's eyes widened. "Oh." A pause followed. "Actually, I was referring to the part where he came up with the training program for the knights of the Round Table."

"Ah." Steve pursed his lips, feeling like an idiot.

Jackson forged ahead, that perfect white-toothed smile still blazing. "I was thinking it would be kind of fun, since I've had a little theater experience, to take the guys who are playing knights under my wing, so to speak, and teach them the ropes. Stage directions. Body language. Projection. Basic acting skills." He looked at

Steve and shrugged. "That sort of thing. I also thought it might give me the opportunity to get to know them better. And we don't have to limit this to acting skills, either. I know a lot about set construction too. I think we could get a lot done if we all work together, and I'm willing to lead the way, if you think it will help."

Shame washed over Steve. So Lancelot wasn't trying to steal the girl...at least not in this moment. He just wanted to help. Go figure.

"Jackson, I think that's a wonderful idea." Amy reached out and touched his arm. "And very generous. I can't believe you would go to all of this trouble when you don't even know us. Not really, anyway."

"Yes," Steve nodded in agreement. "I think it's a great idea. Very generous."

"Well, you've been the people who've cared for my grandfather," Jackson said, "while I've been off doing my own thing. It's about time I gave back. He needs me, but I think on some level I need him too. And heaven knows I could use the small-town life to settle me down a little. It's been pretty crazy where I've been."

"In Pigeon Forge, you mean?" Amy asked.

For a moment, a hint of sadness reflected in his eyes. But just as quickly, he brightened. "I was actually referring to my time in Nashville. I did some recording in a studio there. Tried to get an album off the ground. When that didn't take, I sang in a lot of clubs...but finally got fed up with that. A friend invited me to audition for a show in Pigeon Forge and I took him up on it. That was two years ago. I've been jumping from show to show ever since."

"And you love it?"

He shrugged. "Like I said, it gets a little wild. I'm happy to be here with Gramps. And I get the feeling he's happy to have me here."

"I am." Sarge's voice rang out. Seconds later he joined them.

"Why, I remember one weekend when Jackson was just a kid. He stayed with me and I took him camping in the Smokies. Lost the poor little guy."

"Lost him?" Amy paled. "Seriously?"

"I wasn't really lost," Jackson said. "I was just hiding out in the bushes. But a snake happened along and almost got me. Gramps came along just in time to shoot him."

"Wow." Steve and Amy spoke in unison. Steve gave Sarge an admiring look. "So your aim is pretty good, sir?"

"Always has been." Sarge reached out his hand and pointed his index finger in a gun-like pose. Unfortunately, his hand trembled uncontrollably. Jackson reached out and took hold of it, giving it a squeeze.

"This hand saved my life. I've never forgotten it."

"Shoot." Sarge laughed. "It was just a water moccasin. Wouldn't have hurt you too bad."

"Still." Jackson released his hold on his grandfather's hand. "To an eight-year-old, it was a life-or-death situation. And you were my hero." He paused and his eyes began to shimmer. "Still are."

"Aw, go on with you now." Sarge waved him off. "Go round up those knights and get to work. They need all the help they can get."

"This isn't a rehearsal day," Jackson responded. "I don't want to take them away from the construction work. Just thought I'd give them a knightly pep talk to set the stage." He paused and chuckled. "Ha. Set the stage. Funny. Didn't even mean to say that."

As usual, Amy began to giggle. Steve tried not to let her response to Jackson's little joke set him off. After all, she was just being nice to the guy. And why not? He seemed like a great man.

Maybe a little too great.

Jackson headed off to the construction area. Steve watched as he rounded up Grady, Pete, Chuck, Pastor Crane, and a couple of the other men. Not wanting to miss a word, Steve pulled up close to the group just in time to hear Jackson's pep talk.

"I want to be the first to officially dub you knights of the Round Table of Camelot." Jackson gave the fellows a nod. "And here are your first instructions."

He went on to give them the qualifications necessary to rise above every task...even construction. From there, he shared his heart about his love for theater and the impact it could have on the community. Then he veered and began to talk about his faith, honing in on the call God had placed not only on his life, but on the lives of every man in Camelot.

The newly dubbed knights hung on his every word. In fact, Pete looked downright enraptured. So did Chuck Manly. And as Jackson finished laying out their plan for the new program, the men drew close, stacked hands, and gave a cheer. This was followed by a round of backslapping. Steve watched it all, half-mesmerized and half-nauseated. For, while he wanted to join the rousing chorus of voices, he still couldn't help but wonder if Jackson Brenner's presence would serve as more of a distraction to one fair maiden in the kingdom.

No doubt about it—Lancelot had definitely taken the locals by storm. Now if only Steve could figure out how to stop that storm before it swept them all away.

Chapter Thirteen

....

I just love the hours of the theatre; I love the way it operates.
I always say that when you're doing a play
it's like getting a shot of B-12,
and when you do television for a long series
you need a shot of B-12.

GAVIN MACLEOD

"Steve, you're the mayor."

Steve winced as he heard Eula Mae's voice. He turned away from the window, where the early morning sun peeked through the blinds and sent ribbons of sunlight across the room. "Yes, I am."

She took a couple of steps in his direction, closed the blinds with a *clack*, then crossed her arms and stared him down. "Don't you think you should wear a suit every now and again?"

"Why?" He dropped into the chair behind his desk, wondering what had brought this on. Not that he wasn't used to it. He got this speech from Eula Mae at least once a month.

"Well, you're representing our fair town, and we want to put our best foot forward, especially with those government officials chasing us like dogs after a rabbit. You don't want to end up on the end of someone's keychain."

"Um, okay."

"And since we're talking about canines, can I ask why you look so scruffy all the time?"

"Scruffy?" Steve ran his palm across his chin, feeling the stubble. "Hmm. Well, you know how it is, Eula Mae. I shave, but my five-o'clock shadow shows up at noon. Besides, it's the trend to be a little scruffy-looking these days. Some people like it."

"Even if you're the mayor?" The elderly woman squared her shoulders and gave Steve a sideways glance. "I tell you, if I was the mayor, I wouldn't let my hair get long like that. And I'd drive to Knoxville and buy a suit."

"I own a suit. I wore it to Maggie Sampson's funeral, remember?"

"I wouldn't wear those sandals, either," Eula Mae said, pointing at his feet. "They're not professional. Don't you own any dress shoes? Or boots?"

"Jesus wore sandals," he countered.

She responded with a glare.

"Is there anything about me you wouldn't change?" Steve's patience took a dive.

"Hmm." She looked him over. "Well, I probably wouldn't change the hair color. It's a nice shade of brunette. But when that fella from the county comes prancin' in here, he needs to see that we're taking our jobs seriously."

"I do take my job seriously." Steve raked his fingers through his hair, wondering if, indeed, it did need a trim before the county official returned for round two of the interrogation.

"Well, then, stop showing up to work in blue jeans," she said. "And see if you can find a real dress shirt to put on sometime." She took the time to remind him about how men used to dress back in her day. Finally she paused and gazed at him, as if awaiting a response.

Steve narrowed his gaze. "There are some things I just don't understand about you, Eula Mae. You claim to hate government officials, but you seem to adore me. When you're not slicing and dicing me, I mean. I would think you'd be happy that I don't look like the rest of the pack. I'm an individual."

"Hmm." She continued to stare but said nothing.

Steve paused, deep in thought. Something about her expression didn't ring true. He began to put two and two together. "I'm starting to think you have something else up your sleeve."

"Oh?" Her gaze shifted to the window.

"It's not the county officials you want me to impress. Am I right?"

She plopped down into a chair across from him and stared him down. "And if I admit you're right, then what? Will you think I'm meddling in your personal life?"

"Eula Mae, I don't know what I'd do if you *stopped* meddling. So go right on and tell me. I'm a big boy. I can take it."

"I think you're nervous."

"About this conversation?" he asked. "Maybe. A little."

"No. And not about the play, either. Or that theater you're building. You're a nervous wreck that Jackson Brenner has swept into town to save the day. And I think a grown man should be able to admit when he's nervous."

Ah. "Well, nothing like cutting to the chase."

"I knew it." She slapped his desk with her open palm. "You're jealous of him. Admit it."

Steve shrugged but didn't respond. *Jealous* wasn't exactly the word he would have used. *Frustrated* was more like it.

"I'll have to admit, he's a handsome guy." Eula Mae sighed. "Those eyes of his could see right down into a woman's soul. And those broad shoulders! Who has shoulders like that? I haven't seen such a sturdy fellow since Jack LaLanne." She paused and seemed to drift off in her thoughts. A curious smile brightened her face as the conversation began again. "And have you seen his hair? I usually don't like highlights on a man—you know how I am about such things—but they really work for him."

"If this is supposed to make me feel better, it's not working." Steve turned and gave Eula Mae a stern look that he hoped she would not ignore.

"Right." She grinned. "I forgot I was supposed to be making you feel better. Got distracted."

"Obviously." Steve cleared his throat.

"So what are you afraid of? Just spit it out."

He did his best to stifle the groan that threatened to erupt. "It might sound weird, but I'm concerned that this whole Camelot thing is going to turn out to be strangely prophetic."

"Prophetic?" Eula Mae's brow wrinkled. "Ah. Meaning that Lancelot will eventually steal Arthur's woman?"

"Yeah." Steve rose and walked to the window. He separated a couple of the blinds, and a sliver of sunlight came jutting through. Steve squinted through the tiny slit and glanced out at the parking lot. He watched as Woody's Mustang buzzed by, going way too fast.

"Just because it happens like that in the musical doesn't mean it's going to happen in real life," she said. "Your story is going to have a different ending."

"How do you know that?" He turned from the window, wishing he'd never opened up in the first place. *Is it getting hot in here?* "We don't have any way to predict the future. And even if we could, I wouldn't want to know."

"I can feel it." She pointed to her heart. "Besides, even though Jackson is rugged and handsome and really, really buff doesn't mean that Amy has noticed any of that."

Steve groaned. "Again, I have to ask…is this supposed to be making me feel better?"

"Hey, can I help it if the guy is captivating? You have to take that up with God. He's the one who created him. He's also the one who gave Jackson those great cheekbones and bright white smile."

"I'm sure he paid to have his teeth whitened," Steve said. "For that matter, I think his tan is fake too. I've never really seen that skin color before, have you?"

"Whatever." Eula Mae grinned. "The point is, there are always going to be beautiful people in the world, and we can't help looking at them. But in the end, most are just a distraction."

"Are you saying that Amy's distracted by him but not really interested?"

"Well, she'd have to be a fool not to be interested." Eula Mae giggled. "I mean, would you not be interested if Miss America walked in and took a fancy to you?"

"I'd like to think I'd turn my head and look the other way."

"Think again." Eula Mae chuckled. "As I said, we can't help staring at those who are physically appealing. And man, is Jackson physically appealing." She seemed to drift away for a moment but shook her head and came back to the conversation. "But remember, Steve, real beauty comes from the inside. Amy sees that in you. We all do." She paused and gave him a motherly smile. "And just for the record, you're not too shabby-looking either. Except for that ridiculous stubble on your face and that shaggy hair."

"Thanks a lot."

"No, really." She nodded. "You're a handsome guy, Steve. If you don't believe me, just ask Gwen."

"Ugh." He sighed. "That's not exactly the person I'm trying to attract."

"I know, but it just proves my point. She finds you extremely handsome. I've heard all about it."

"She does?"

"Sure."

Steve shook his head, uncomfortable at the very idea. "She's pretty but definitely not the kind of girl I'm looking for. I like a more natural girl, not one who spends hours every morning plastering on makeup and spraying her hair."

"So I guess Blossom's out of the question then." Eula Mae laughed and slapped her knee. "Sorry, I couldn't resist. That girl goes through a bottle of hair spray a day. And Lucy Cramden is pretty heavy-handed with the Mary Kay. Not that she's your type anyway."

Steve chuckled. "I'm sure that dozens of woman in Camelot are beautiful, but the only gorgeous woman I've ever known is...." He sighed.

"Yep. I'm a beauty queen inside and out!" Eula Mae laughed. "Can't help but admit it. Then again, I suppose you were really talking about Amy, not me. She is a thing of beauty, to be sure. A real Camelot princess, through and through."

"And I can tell Jackson notices." Steve felt his jaw tightening. "That's the hard part. I want him to know she's mine."

The wrinkles between Eula's Mae's eyes deepened as she frowned slightly. "Does *she* know that?"

"Well, I've…" *Kissed her. Told her that I care about her.*

"Have you told her that she's the best thing that's ever happened to you?" Eula Mae's gaze narrowed. "Have you told her that the stars don't come out at night until you've seen her? That the sun doesn't rise in the morning until you've whispered her name? Have you written her a song?"

"A song?" *Good grief.* "No."

"Well, you'd better get busy, then. Women like to be wooed, and I have a feeling Jackson is the type to woo her. I think a nice love song would do the trick. Chances are pretty good he's crafting the second verse of his as we speak. She can already hear his melody in her head, and that's not a good thing. Not if you're going to stand a chance."

"But I'm not a songwriter."

"Doesn't matter. Just make something up. That's what Woody did." She clamped a hand over her mouth. "Oops."

"Woody?" *No way.*

Eula Mae giggled, and her wrinkly cheeks turned the prettiest shade of pink. "That old fool's been in love with me for years. I'm surprised you haven't noticed it."

"Um, no. Sure haven't."

"He's a great actor. Always has been. But he's drawn to things of beauty." She winked and gestured to her wrinkled face. "Do you think for a minute he'd look twice at another woman—Lucy Cramden, for instance—when he could look at this instead?"

Don't say a word, Steve.

"I think not." She giggled. "He's drawn to me just like Amy and the other girls are drawn to Jackson." Her expression shifted. "But, anyway, don't fret. Jackson is just a handsome distraction. You're the real deal."

"What does that make you?" Steve asked. "A beautiful distraction to Woody?"

"No." Eula Mae shook her head. "I'm the real deal too." She gave him a playful wink. "And if you ever want to know how he really feels, ask him to sing a verse or two of 'Eula Mae's Star Song.'"

She walked out of the office humming an unfamiliar tune, and he plopped into his chair, deep in thought. As he did, several of Eula Mae's words came rushing back at him.

"Okay," he spoke aloud, "so Jackson Brenner is a thing of beauty."

"Um, he is?"

Steve looked up, stunned to find Amy standing in his doorway. He flinched. "Oh, hey, I…"

She leaned against the doorjamb. "Steve, is there something I need to know?"

He felt his cheeks grow warm. "No. Absolutely not."

"Well, that's good." She laughed. "Had me worried for a minute there." A smile lit the room, drawing him to his feet. "You ready to go to rehearsal?" she asked.

"With your hand in mine," he offered, "I'm ready to fly to the moon."

Not exactly a song…but a step in the right direction.

* * * * *

Amy stared at Steve, trying to figure out where he was headed with that "fly to the moon" statement. Kidding around, most likely.

No, as he swept her into his arms for a memorable kiss, she had to conclude that he wasn't kidding around. The fiery passion left little to her imagination.

"Wow," she said when the kiss ended. "I don't know what you and Eula Mae were talking about in here, but if it prompted this, I'd like to hire her to counsel you every day."

"She's pretty witty," he said, "in her own oddball sort of way."

Amy chuckled. "Must've said something to get you stirred up."

"The only person who gets me stirred up is you," he whispered.

"In a good way, I hope," she echoed. "Because I somehow manage to get everyone else worked up in a not-so-good way with most of my crazy ideas."

"Oh, you get me stirred up in a good way, I assure you."

Steve pulled Amy close once more and planted a kiss on her lips that answered any lingering questions she might have about his feelings for her, whether she happened to be crazy or not. And right now, wrapped in his arms, she decided she would gladly trade every moment of sanity for one more sizzling kiss like that.

Chapter Fourteen

....

If all the world's a stage...I want better lighting!

ANONYMOUS

Just three weeks after the first rehearsal, Amy drove to the Civic Center, her Jeep Liberty loaded with props and costume materials. Her mind reeled with thoughts and ideas related to the show. Much progress had been made, especially in the last couple of rehearsals, but they had a long way to go before this musical could debut. A shiver ran down her spine as she considered what the critics might say if they stumbled across a rehearsal. And critics weren't the only adversaries on her mind. She pondered Steve's suggestion that they invite Fred Platt—the county official—to a rehearsal. *Why would we want to do that? So he can see what screwballs we are?*

"Rome wasn't built in a day," she reminded herself as she made the familiar drive. Indeed, all good things took time to build.

Oh, but they had come a long ways, hadn't they? She smiled, thinking of the more humorous moments in their last rehearsal— say, the part where she and Steve had learned the choreography to "What Would the Simple Folk Do?" And the moment when Grady had—thanks to Jackson's gentle coaching—finally spoken his lines without a serious twang. Yes, with Jackson at the helm, most of the other knights were in pretty good shape too. Better than she'd dared hope, actually. And the work they'd done on the set pieces took her breath away. Camelot was starting to look like a real place.

She giggled, realizing, of course, that it *was* a real place. Her home. Her own private kingdom. A town worth saving.

Thank goodness for progress. And the theater build-out was coming along nicely too. She whispered up a prayer that Camelot would stay the course. And that she would have the stamina to see this thing through, even if she hit a few bumps in the road.

Amy pulled into the parking lot of the Civic Center, deep in thought about today's upcoming rehearsal. They'd finally arrived at the one scene she'd most dreaded—the lusty month of May. Today she and Annabelle would officially pair up the knights and ladies-in-waiting to begin choreography. Another quick prayer helped quiet the anxiety over their decision. Who should be paired with whom? It could be catastrophic if she mismanaged this scene. Maybe Woody should be involved in the decision. Yes, surely he would know.

As Amy slipped her car into PARK, she paused to whisper a prayer of thanks that things would continue to go smoothly. Across the parking lot, Steve got out of his truck and waved. Her heart did a little flip-flop thing as she remembered their last kiss. *Mmm.* Every day her heart entwined a little more with his. Sure, he hadn't really opened up and shared his feelings in full. But his kisses spoke volumes. Right? Surely the words would come in time.

Amy had just started in Steve's direction when something caught her eye. Officer O'Reilly pulled his patrol car into the parking lot and stopped. Strange—the good sergeant usually parked his car in front of the diner or in the City Hall parking lot. Sometimes he sat perched just beyond the bend in the highway, hoping to catch would-be speeders. *Hmm.* Must be some reason he'd shown up here today.

Amy approached and peered through the open window of his patrol car. "Joe, what's up? Something happen?"

"Not yet."

Steve drew near, slipping his arm around Amy's waist. He gave O'Reilly a curious look. "What do you mean?"

O'Reilly shook his head, his eyes narrowing. "I've been keeping a close eye on Woody."

"Woody? Why?" Not quite what Amy had expected him to say.

"He's got no business driving that old car of his," O'Reilly said. "The inspection's been out for years, and it won't pass emissions testing. Not even close."

She sighed. "I know. But Joe..."

"Don't 'But Joe' me. The man is a hazard on the road. Besides that, he can't hear a thing. If an ambulance went blazing by him, he'd never know it. I've given him dozens of warnings, but he's just not taking any of them seriously."

"We're planning to buy him a new hearing aid," Steve said. "We're going to vote on it at the next city council meeting."

"But until then, the man can't hear a train coming around the bend. And he obviously can't hear my siren. I've tried stopping him on three different occasions when he just whizzed right past me. If it had been any other officer"—Joe shook his head—"he'd be in jail right now for evading arrest. That's all I've got to say about that. And the few times he did stop, I found myself in a predicament."

"What kind of predicament?" Amy asked.

"He's got a couple of outstanding tickets on file. One for speeding, another for the registration and inspection issues. But he refuses to pay. Says he doesn't have to."

"Refuses?" Amy sighed, wondering what possessed Woody to be so stubborn.

"Is it the money?" Steve asked.

"No. The old guy's got a lot of money. It's not that. He's just set in his ways. And he seems to have some sort of issue with authority figures. Said he wants proof that I clocked him going eighty in a forty-five. That kind of thing. He doesn't have a leg to stand on, and I think he knows it. But he still won't deal with it. Just prideful and stubborn."

Amy released a breath. "I don't know what to tell you, Joe. I will talk to him, though. Maybe I can get through to him."

"Someone needs to." O'Reilly fidgeted with his badge. "Because I'm going to have to put out a warrant for his arrest if he refuses to take care of the tickets."

"A warrant?" *Yikes.* Amy swallowed hard. "Does he know that?"

"I tried to tell him, but, again, he didn't believe me. Told me to take it up with his attorney."

"Does he have an attorney?" Steve asked. "I don't know of any in town."

"Who knows?" O'Reilly sighed. "I just know that he's a crusty old soul who's getting on my nerves." He muttered something under his breath about a few others in Camelot who also got on his nerves. "He thinks he's above the law, and that's never good. Frustrates me to no end."

"You're right." Steve shook his head. "He's got to take care of this."

"So I can count on you to say something to him?" Joe gave him a hopeful look.

"I'll do my best."

"Thanks. I'm counting on it." With a nod of his head, Joe slipped his car back into gear and headed out to the road.

As the officer disappeared around the bend to the east, Amy looked at Steve and released a slow breath. "It's like a soap opera around here, isn't it?"

"Yep." Steve chuckled. *"As the Stomach Turns."*

Amy laughed. "No kidding. Definitely filled with quirky characters."

"We are an interesting lot. No doubt about it."

She nodded. "Yes. A lot of *what*, I'm not quite sure." She paused, choosing her words carefully. "If anyone had told me I'd be working with a cast like this…" Her words drifted off as she found herself distracted by something off in the distance. "Um, Steve?"

"Yeah?"

She gestured across the parking lot. "Is it my imagination, or are Sarge and Jackson unloading a mule from the back of that trailer?"

Steve squinted and put up his hand to block the afternoon sun. "Hmm. Yep. Looks like a mule to me."

Amy squeezed her eyes shut, hoping to erase the image. When she opened them again, Jackson was leading the animal down a ramp and heading their way.

* * * * *

"Sarge, what in the world?" Steve stared at the stubby swaybacked mule, dumbfounded. "You brought your donkey to the rehearsal?"

"Well, sure." Sarge shrugged and squinted his eyes. "Don't look so surprised."

Steve had barely started collecting his thoughts for a response when a squeal of tires in the distance alerted him to Woody's arrival from the west. Driving way too fast, of course. He pulled into the spot next to Amy and got out of the car, moving as slow as molasses. What a strange contrast.

"What have we got here?" Woody asked as he joined them. "Acting out the stable scene from the Christmas story or something?"

"No." A look of confusion registered on Jackson's face as he faced Woody. "Gramps said you guys needed B-52 for the jousting scene. I questioned him about it, but he was adamant."

"Wait." Steve shook his head. "Jousting...on a donkey?"

Jackson shrugged. "Seemed a little odd to me, but that's what he said—that you and Amy specifically asked for the donkey."

"Jackson is going to ride my mare, Katie Sue, for his jousting scene," Sarge said. "I'll use B-52. Things might go a little easier on my backside if I do." He rubbed his rear and headed back to the trailer, returning with a mare that had to be older than Methuselah. The poor old thing appeared to be nervous around people too. The minute she saw Woody, she began to stomp and whinny. And by the time Lucy, Annabelle, and Blossom had arrived, the skittish mare looked as if she might just take off running across the parking lot. Not that she could really run—not in that shape.

Steve watched it all, mesmerized. How would Amy deal with this? Had she and Woody really told Sarge to bring a donkey? If so, why? Hopefully they had a plan. He glanced her way and immediately picked up on the look of terror in her eyes. Nope. She didn't have a plan.

An approaching car caught his eye. Steve looked over to see an unfamiliar white SUV. The fellow who climbed out of it was just as unfamiliar—a scrawny guy wearing a baseball cap, T-shirt, and jeans, with a camera hanging around his neck. Steve instantly went on the alert.

Apparently the others sensed a problem with this fellow as well. Everyone stopped talking as the man drew close.

Steve gave him a nod. "Can we help you?"

The fellow nodded. "This the group putting on that play?" He glanced at a scrap of paper in his hand. "The Camelot Players?"

"Camelot Players?" Steve shot a quick look Amy's way, and she gave him a frantic nod. Hmm. So, she'd named their ragtag group. Interesting. "Um, yes. That's us. The Camelot Players."

"Good." The fellow reached inside a worn bag and came out with a notepad. "Got a few questions for you."

"Are you from the county?" Woody interjected. "'Cause if you are—"

"No. Well, not officially." The guy rubbed his nose. He looked around, his brow wrinkled but focusing on Lucy Cramden, as she approached with a hatbox in hand. "I–I–I–choo!" Several dramatic sneezes followed. "Sorry." He wiped his nose on the edge of his sleeve after the last one. "Don't know what came over me."

Steve shifted his weight and gave the man another once-over. He didn't look familiar at all. Who was this guy? "Excuse me. Who did you say you are, again?"

The fellow offered a crooked grin. "Name's Mickey James. I'm with the *Knox County Register*. Heard you all were doing a play, so I came to write about it. Hope you don't mind a few pictures." He started messing with the lens cover on his camera.

"Well, I guess that would be okay." Steve paused to think about it. "We can use all the PR we can get, but I'd like to see whatever you write before it goes to print. I'm the mayor of Camelot. Steve Garrison." He extended his hand, and the reporter gave it a firm shake.

"Sure thing. Since you're the mayor and all, would you like to give me a quote for the article?"

"Be glad to. Just let me think about what I want to say, okay?"

"You've got it." Mr. James lifted the camera and squinted through the lens. Turning toward the mule, he snapped a couple of photos and then chuckled. "I've seen a lot of plays over the years, but I don't recall one starring a mule."

"Still trying to figure that one out myself," Steve said, before laughing. "I'll let you know when I've got the full story on that one."

He didn't have time to think about it right now, however. As

Amy and Woody introduced themselves to the reporter, the parking lot began filling with vehicles, including Pete's van. Poor Bugsy still clung to the top, tattered and torn. Steve could practically see right through him. Still, the forlorn plastic bug hung on for dear life.

Just then, Steve heard dogs yapping. He turned to see that Gwen had arrived. She approached the group, looking frazzled and smelling like dog shampoo. Of course, the doggy smell might be coming from the trio of large hairy monsters attached to the leashes she held in her hand. They pulled her halfway across the parking lot before she got control of them.

"Sorry, Woody." Gwen fought to maintain her hold on the leashes. "I know how you feel about having animals at the rehearsals, but I didn't have any choice. These boys need a walk before they get picked up. But don't worry, I'll put them back in the grooming truck until their owners arrive. Anyway, I wanted to come over and let you know I'm here. Didn't want you to start without me."

The largest of the dogs, a golden retriever, drew near B-52, sniffing his ankles. Another one of the dogs—was that a Rottweiler?—headed straight for the mare with a menacing look on his face. What really took the cake, though, was the boxer. He went crazy, diving under everyone's legs and nearly flipping poor Lucy Cramden upside down in the process.

"I don't understand this." Gwen did her best to hang onto the leashes but ended up with a couple of them wrapped around her ankles. "Boxers are usually such a docile breed. I have no idea what came over him. Come here, Buddy. Be a good boy."

The dog refused to obey. Instead, he focused on the large hatbox in Lucy Cramden's hands, nudging it and yelping nonstop. Gwen continued to struggle with the leashes, finally freeing her ankles so she could walk properly.

"Call off your beast, Gwen," Lucy said. "Get him away from me, you hear?"

"Honestly, I have no idea…"

At that moment, the overly excited dog leaped in the air and knocked the box out of Lucy's hands—and Fiona came flying out.

What happened next left Steve in a state of confusion. Gwen lost her grip on the leashes and all three dogs took off after Fiona like hounds on a hunt. B-52 went into panic mode and began to squeal. Katie Sue—God bless the old, dear mare—began to take quick steps toward Pete, which startled him and caused him to drop the sandwich he'd been holding. As soon as Fiona smelled the food, she changed directions, heading straight for Pete. Unfortunately, the three dogs followed, scaring the wits out of Pete, who took off running. At this point, the dogs went crazy. So did Fiona, who apparently had a penchant for bologna and cheese on wheat. The reporter came alive as the parking lot vibrated with activity. He began to snap photographs nonstop. *Wonderful.*

In the middle of the chaos, Blossom walked up, still wearing her apron from the salon and looking pretty winded. She'd switched her hair color again, this time settling on jet black. Interesting. And a little creepy. "Sorry I'm late, y'all," she said with a sigh. "I…" Her words drifted off as she took in the chaotic scene before her. She snapped to attention. "Would've been here soon, but I had a hair emergency."

"Hair emergency?" *Your own, perhaps?* Steve gave her a curious look, still more than a little distracted by the canines now running in circles and chasing the ferret with the bologna sandwich in her mouth.

"Yeah." She pulled off her apron and sighed. "A perm gone wrong. Please don't ask for details. Just trust me when I say that I had a bona fide reason for being late." She looked around. "Looks like I'm just in time for the action."

"You can say that again." Steve had barely gotten the words out when Woody reached down and snatched up Fiona, who lost her hold on the bologna sandwich. She began to cry out in that high-pitched shriek of hers, but the real action took place on the ground at Woody's feet, where the three dogs lapped up the remains of her precious meal.

"Oh, my poor baby!" Lucy raced to Woody's side and gathered up Fiona. "What have they done to you?" She glared at Gwen. "If they've hurt her, I could sue."

An ugly argument ensued between the two women, which got the reporter more excited than ever. He reached for his notepad, leaned against one of the nearby cars, and began to write at a steady pace. Amy looked on, her face pale. Steve could only imagine what she might be thinking.

In the midst of this chaos, Eula Mae showed up. She took one look at the dogs and let out a whistle, and they all fell into line. Thank goodness. They knew an authority figure when they saw one.

"Come get your beasts, Gwen," Eula Mae called out, her voice ringing with confidence.

Gwen pulled herself from the argument with Lucy and grabbed the pups by their leashes, pulling them toward her van. Hopefully she would come back without them. In the meantime, they had a lot of work to do.

Eula Mae approached Steve, her eyes narrowed in suspicion. "Hey, boss…"

"Yes?"

She lowered her voice and pointed to Mickey James. "Who is that fellow?"

"Just a guy who works for the paper in Knoxville. He wants to do a story on us."

"Paparazzi, huh?" She began to fuss with her hair. Seconds later, a look of concern settled onto her face. "Wait a minute. How do you know he's really with the paper? He could be anyone."

"He showed me his media badge."

"Anyone can get one of those. I could get one if I wanted to." She stared the fellow down. "You know what I think?" she whispered.

I'm sure you're going to tell me.

"I think he works for the county." Her brow wrinkled and her voice lowered further. "Or maybe even the state. Yep. That guy's a spy, sent here to check us out. Could be he works for the feds. He looks like the type to spy on innocent citizens."

"A spy?" Steve laughed aloud. "You've got a great imagination, Eula Mae."

She tugged at his arm. "Not so loud, boss. He's going to hear you. He's probably got one of those high-powered microphones on him, attached to a miniature tape recorder. I saw one in a movie once."

"Let him record us," Steve said. "This is Camelot, a place where we wear our flaws and imperfections on our sleeves. We've got nothing to hide."

"Can I quote you on that?" Mickey asked, joining them. He reached for his camera.

"Sure. Why not?" Steve posed for a shot with Eula Mae, who ducked under his arm and took off sprinting.

"I don't need my face plastered on the front page of the newspaper," she called out. "So you go on and write that story, mister. I won't be a part of your little scam. No sir."

Steve looked at the reporter and shrugged. "Guess she's a little camera-shy."

"No problem. I see people like her every day. Sort of a crazy old broad, isn't she?"

Steve chuckled. "Guess you could say that. But she's our crazy old broad and we love her." He bit his tongue the minute the words escaped. *Oops.* Would *that* make the headlines?

Woody approached with his script in his hand. "What in the name of all that's holy are we going to do with that mule? And Sarge's old mare isn't fit for a jousting scene. She's not fit for anything except being put out to pasture. Don't know what the nutty old guy was thinking."

"So..." Mickey began to scribble. "You think the Sarge has a few screws loose?"

"A few?" Woody laughed. "That's the understatement of the century. We could fill the hardware store with that many loose screws!" He laughed all the way into the building.

Sarge came walking by, pulling B-52 on a rope. "C'mon, old fella. Hope you've got enough life left in you to take down Lancelot. That's the plan, anyway."

"He's going to take down Lancelot?" Mickey asked, eyes growing wide. "Seems a little extreme."

"Yeah, that's us. Extreme." Steve chuckled and patted Mickey on the back. "Before you make any rash judgments, though, come inside and watch us rehearse. Chances are pretty good we'll give you all the story you'll ever need."

"I'm counting on it," Mickey said, tightening his grip on his camera. Mumbling something about tomorrow's headline, he followed Steve into the Civic Center.

Chapter Fifteen

....

Acting isn't really a creative profession.
It's an interpretative one.

PAUL NEWMAN

Amy tried to collect her thoughts as she followed Steve and the reporter into the building. Somehow the idea of having someone from the media here felt a little unsettling. Still, she couldn't blame anyone but herself. Calling her little troupe of actors the Camelot Players had been rash, at best. And now that they had both a mare *and* a donkey tied up to the flagpole out front, things had gotten even more complicated. What was Sarge thinking? Seriously. A donkey? For the jousting scene?

"Hey, Amy. Do you have a minute to talk?" Jackson smiled as he stepped into place beside her.

"Sure. What's up?" She slowed her pace, allowing the others to pass them.

"Just wanted to update you on the plumbing issues," he said. "The RV park situation isn't as bad as you thought. The pipes were in pretty good shape. We're talking minimal work to get water flowing out there. I thought you'd want to know."

"Jackson, how can I ever thank you?" She put her hand on his arm and gazed into his eyes. "Seriously, you've made all of this so much easier on me. You've been such a…" Really, only one word made sense. "A godsend."

"Thank you." He offered a shy smile. "But I'm the one with the advantage here. I've made so many new friends…." His words drifted off as he gazed into her eyes. "Anyway, I've had a wonderful time getting to know all of you. And I want to get to know you more."

"O–oh?" Her comfort level suddenly took a plunge.

"I mean, the whole town. I'm thinking about staying permanently."

"No way." Her heart flip-flopped.

A dazzling smile followed, garnering her full attention. "Well, sure. Who knows how long the show will run. Maybe we'll be playing these roles for years to come. But, regardless, my grandfather needs me, and I need to settle down for a while. Stay put in one place."

"And Camelot is the town for you?" She tried not to focus on his gorgeous green eyes, but what could a girl do? She couldn't exactly look off in the distance with someone standing directly in front of her, could she? Besides, they drew her in, casting some sort of spell.

He nodded, his eyes never leaving hers. "Camelot is definitely the place for me."

Is that some sort of subliminal message, or am I reading too much into this?

"I'm—I'm so glad," she managed. "It might not be quite as exciting as the real Camelot, but we have our share of characters, for sure."

"Including Gramps." He chuckled. "I'm so sorry about the misunderstanding with the animals. I should have known better than to bring that donkey. I'll be happy to take them back to his place before we get started, if you think we'd be better off."

Amy paused to think before answering. She didn't want to hurt Sarge's feelings, after all. "Nah. It's okay. As long as they don't eat the daisies in the flower bed, we'll be fine. Besides, it's great fodder for the journalist. Heaven only knows what he might make of it."

"That's what worries me, actually." Jackson laughed. "But if you're okay with it, I'll relax."

"What can we do at this point but forge ahead?" Amy said. She entered the building and found Grady, Chuck, and Pete hovering over the set pieces they'd been working on. Jackson shared with a great degree of excitement about the progress they'd made.

"Wow." She let out a whistle and walked around the medieval castlelike structure. "Guys, you're the best. How did you ever get this much done so quickly?"

Grady turned twelve shades of red and Chuck's gaze shifted.

"Shoot, twern't nuthin' to it," Grady said. "Just slapped t'gether a buncha stuff from my hardware store. Boards 'n' paint, that's all yer lookin' at."

"Yes, but what you've done with it is magnificent." She turned to give him an admiring look. "Who did the painting?"

Chuck looked up with a smile. "Never knew I had an artistic side till now," he said. "But I've enjoyed it. Painting is a little like butchering a hog." He went on to explain, in detail, the similarities. Amy cringed more with each word. "It's all art," he said. "Set design and slaughtering—same thing."

Hardly. But Amy wouldn't fault him for the comparison. No, not when she happened to be staring at the beginning of what could be a lovely set. If Chuck was capable of this kind of work, he could compare butchering to painting all he liked.

"It's all Jackson's doing, anyway," Pete said. "He was the one who told us what to do. We're just coloring in the lines he drew for us, basically."

"Nice lines." Amy felt her cheeks warm as the words slipped out.

"Thank you." Jackson gave her a winning smile, followed by a little wink.

Oh my. She fought to still her heart.

Thankfully, Pete interrupted her thoughts. "Hey, Amy, I've got another joke for you."

She braced herself. Pete's jokes had been getting a little old over the past few weeks.

"How many actors does it take to change a lightbulb?" he asked.

Amy shrugged, clueless.

"Just one." He erupted in laughter then managed to get himself under control to deliver the punch line. "They don't like to share the spotlight. Get it? Share the spotlight?"

"I get it." Amy tried not to groan. "I get it."

Pete slugged Jackson in the arm. "Didn't mean any harm by that, my friend. If all actors are like you, they're a pretty good lot."

"Thanks." Jackson reached for a paintbrush. "Now, let's get to work. I think we can finish painting this castle before rehearsal begins. If we hurry, that is."

Amy watched the men work for a second, until she heard Natalie's voice ring out. "Hey, Amy, I hate to interrupt, but I have something to talk to you about."

She turned to find the pastor's wife standing behind her, holding an armload of costumes.

"You know, the church has a ton of costumes from old Christmas and Easter productions," Natalie said. "So Caroline and I got to thinking that we might be able to save a little money on costumes if we recycle some of these robes into medieval attire. What do you think?" She held up one that looked a bit like a bathrobe.

Amy gave it a close look, afraid to voice her opinion. Maybe they could make it work...with a miracle from on high.

"I'm a pretty good seamstress," Natalie said. "And Caroline is too. I've printed some pictures of costumes from the web and think we've come up with a way to transform these. Would you be willing to let us give it a try?"

"To keep from having to pay for new costumes?" Amy nodded. "Of course. And in case I haven't mentioned it, Natalie, I couldn't have done this without your help on the vocals. The guys are sounding great on their songs."

"So are you," Natalie whispered then gave her a wink. "We couldn't have found a better Guinevere if we'd searched the whole land."

A rush of emotion swept over Amy as she whispered her thanks. "Just pray today's rehearsal goes as smoothly as the vocal rehearsals have gone," she added. "I've got a bad feeling about this one."

"I'll be praying," Natalie said. "You know what the Bible says: the Lord won't give us more than we can bear."

"He must think I can stand a lot." Amy offered up a weak smile. The last few weeks, though fun at times, had presented her with one of the toughest challenges of her life. Was she up to the task? Only time would tell. For now, she felt a little...discombobulated.

And all the more so as the reporter snapped a photo of her pulling her hair up into a messy ponytail in preparation for the rehearsal. Lovely.

Natalie turned back to Caroline to discuss the costumes and Amy glanced across the room once more. Her gaze settled on Steve, who gave Jackson a friendly slap on the back. *Good. It's about time those two became friends. They have so much in common.*

After a quick glance at her notes, Amy clapped her hands. Much as she had been dreading this scene, it could wait no more. "Time to get started on the lusty-month-of-May scene," she called out. "Annabelle's been working on the choreography, and I think you're going to like what she's come up with."

"I know I will." Lucy Cramden giggled. "Been waiting for this for weeks."

"This is going to be so much fun!" Blossom's cheeks flushed, and Chuck gave her a nod.

Chuck looked plenty nervous. For that matter, so did the rest of the guys. Grady, lowering his paintbrush, looked downright ill, in fact.

Annabelle stepped to her place, front and center, raising her voice to be heard above the crowd. "Okay, I think I'll start by pairing up the knights and ladies," she explained. "So let's see…" She looked over the candidates, trying to come to a logical decision. "I'll be dancing with Chuck."

The happy butcher smiled with delight, all hints of concern now gone. Amy couldn't help but think this duo would fare well. She also wondered if Chuck would get a few extra dance lessons on the side.

"And what about Lucy and…" Annabelle looked back and forth between Grady and Pete. "Pete."

Amy would've thought Pete had won the lottery, judging by the look of joy on his face at this announcement. He moved into place beside Lucy with a genuine smile.

To her left, Amy heard someone muttering. She turned in time to find Lucy eyeing not Pete, but her father. "I'll give this my best shot." Lucy rolled her eyes. "Even if I did end up with the wrong partner."

The look on Pete's face nearly broke Amy's heart. Poor guy. How long would he go on trying to get Lucy to notice him?

"Prissy, I think I'll pair you up with both of the twins," Annabelle said. "It might make for a fun scene if they were fighting over you."

Timmy and Jimmy seemed to like this idea a lot. They elbowed each other to get closer to the beautiful teen, and she looked on, all smiles.

"Next we'll have Grady and Blossom," Annabelle added. She looked back and forth between the forty-something hairstylist and the country bumpkin hardware-store owner, likely wondering what sort of duo they'd make. Amy had to wonder, herself.

Oh well. No time to worry about that now. Surely Blossom would forgive them for this selection and play along.

"Charlie, you and Sarge will be in this scene as well," Annabelle said. "And Darrell too. You'll be taking turns, dancing with each of the ladies at the maypole."

"Dancing, eh?" Sarge rubbed his hip. "Gonna have to double up on my arthritis meds if I'm supposed to dance."

"We'll take it easy," Amy explained. "And if it proves to be too much, you can sit out this scene."

"Sit out, my eye." He shook his head. "No, thank you. I've never been one to sit out a challenge. Why, I remember back in Vietnam—" And off he went again, sharing another war story. Thankfully, he ended it quickly with the words, "So I won't be quitting, even if you tell me I'm the worst dancer you've ever seen. I'm not a quitter. No, sir."

Amy contemplated his strong reaction. Apparently Sarge, like so many others, had finally settled into his role in this production. And how wonderful to see his "I won't give up, no matter what" attitude.

"We'll run through the lines leading up to this scene and then begin to choreograph the song," Amy said.

Annabelle nodded. "I've got it all worked out. No worries. But I'm not quite done placing people yet, Amy." She paused. "Eula Mae, I'd like you to help me out, if you will."

"Need me to pick up something from the store?" Eula Mae's eyes lit up. "Is there some sort of sale going on over at the Sack 'n Save that I've missed?"

"No, silly." Annabelle chuckled. "I want you to dance in this song like the other ladies are doing."

"Excuse me?" The older woman took a step back. "You're not trying to put me in this play, are you? I agreed to be the rehearsal pianist. But I don't act or sing. No way, no how."

"You never mentioned anything about dancing," Annabelle said. "And we could use more women. We'll be using the vocal track to rehearse, so we won't need you on the piano." She pointed to the stage area. "It's important that we fill the gap. Woody, Sarge, and Charlie are without women."

"Not for long." Eula Mae grinned and headed straight for Woody. She looked at the crowd. "Eat your heart out, ladies. I'm staking my claim." She slipped her arm around Woody's waist and gave him a little kiss on the cheek.

Amy looked on, stunned. Eula Mae and Woody…a couple? How had she missed that?

Annabelle looked her way with a wink. Wow. So Annabelle had known all along. Well, some people were just more intuitive than others.

"Caroline, I'd like to bring you into this number too," Annabelle said.

Caroline paled. "Oh no, thank you. I gave up dancing years ago when my husband passed away. I couldn't possibly."

"But we need all the women we can get."

"C'mon and join us, Caroline," Amy's father said. "It'll be fun."

She reluctantly stepped up beside him, looking none too sure of herself.

"Okay, Amy," Annabelle said with a grin. "You're in this scene too. In fact, you're the lead dancer."

Yikes.

"You'll start out by dancing with Steve." Annabelle pointed Steve's way, and he responded with a look of terror in his eyes. "Then, midway through the dance you'll switch partners and end up with Lancelot. Er, Jackson."

Amy felt her stomach rise to her throat. She'd known this moment would come, of course. But switching partners felt a little too...symbolic.

Not that she really had time to think about it. Eula Mae came over and grabbed her by the hand. "If I can dance, honey, you can dance."

Amy looked into Steve's eyes and offered a little shrug. He responded by pulling her close and placing a kiss on her forehead—for everyone to see. Apparently Eula Mae wasn't the only one staking a claim today.

Gwen stood on the sidelines, her expression growing tighter by the moment. "Excuse me, Annabelle. But where do I—?"

"Oh, I'm glad you asked." Annabelle clasped her hands together. "This is where it gets fun. You start the dance with Jackson but end up with Arthur. Er, Steve." She giggled. "In other words, you and Amy switch partners in the middle of the dance and never go back to the way things started. If that makes sense." She paused to roll a strand of her long hair around her index finger.

Gwen's expression brightened. "I start with Jackson"—she looked his way with a coy smile—"and end up with Steve?"

"Yes, that's right."

"Couldn't have planned this any better myself." The blond beauty sashayed over to Jackson, who looked over at her with a welcoming smile.

Amy wanted to raise her hand in protest, but she couldn't really change the script even if she wanted to. If this was Annabelle's vision for the dance, so be it. She could live with it...for now.

"Okay, let's get started." Annabelle turned to her motley crew of dancers and began to demonstrate the steps. In spite of her some-what fluffy size, she looked really good. Now for the tough part—getting the others to look that good too.

Amy looked on as Annabelle led the knights through their steps. Okay, so maybe Grady wasn't a dancer, but he certainly gave it his all. She could imagine her dad, Woody, and Sarge looking like knights in their costumes, but they danced more like those wooden toy soldiers with knees that refused to bend. Pete did a fair job. So did Chuck. And Jackson...wow. The guy could dance. The one who caught her eye, however, was Steve. He looked so handsome as he moved around the floor, following Annabelle's lead. Yes, this was going to be nice. Very nice, indeed.

"Now we're going to add in the ladies," Annabelle said as they finished. "You'll start with a little curtsy like this." She demonstrated and nearly toppled over. Thank goodness, Chuck appeared beside her, offering his arm. She flashed a smile brightly at him. Well, until the reporter began to snap pictures. Then she returned to her "all business" attitude. "Let's all try that together, ladies."

Another curtsy followed, which Amy tried to emulate. It felt a little silly at first, but after awhile, she got the hang of it. And by the time all the steps had been given, she decided she rather enjoyed dancing. And who better to share the moment with than Steve, the one who'd captured her heart? Yes, as she gazed into his eyes, she had to admit that the Lord had orchestrated this dance just for the two of them.

Well, the two of them and Jackson Brenner, who caught her eye from across the room and gave her a little wink. After settling the fluttering in her heart, Amy turned her attentions, once again, to Steve. Her leading man.

* * * * *

Steve spent the first few minutes of the choreography rehearsal wrestling his stomach out of his throat. Something about dancing— either privately or in front of a crowd—made him a little nauseated. Why, oh why, had he given that reporter permission to take pictures of the rehearsal?

After a few minutes with Amy in his arms, though, Steve began to relax...enjoy it, even. Her perfume nearly drove him crazy. What was that? Something new? Regardless, he could hardly think straight. Not that a man with a beautiful woman in his arms should be able to think straight. No, he should just still his thoughts and enjoy the moment. If he could.

Far too soon, the moment arrived when Steve had to switch partners. He released his hold on Amy and watched as Jackson took her in his arms. *Ugh.* This might be tougher than he'd first imagined. Feelings of possessiveness swept over Steve as the music began once again. Gwen took hold of his hand and off they went, tripping the light fantastic. Or just tripping. He couldn't quite get the hang of it with his new partner. Things just weren't the same with Gwen in his arms.

"Hey, you stepped on my foot."

"What?" Steve startled to attention. "Oh, sorry."

"It's okay." Gwen clutched his hand even harder and gazed into his eyes with such tenderness that it almost stopped him in his tracks. "I'm so glad it worked out this way, Steve," she whispered in his ear. "This is a lot of fun."

"Mm-hmm." He didn't dare say more. For, while he'd finally started to enjoy the idea of dancing, the only partner that made sense was the one who seemed to be having the time of her life in Jackson Brenner's arms on the other side of the room.

To his right, Steve heard a little giggle. He looked over to see Eula Mae and Woody doing a fancy spin. The giggle quickly turned to a shout as Woody tripped and went sprawling on the floor. As he landed, he let out a cry loud enough to bring the rehearsal to a halt.

"Woody!" Eula Mae knelt down beside him. "You okay?"

"My—my arm." He grabbed hold of his right elbow and flinched.

The reporter drew near, snapping pictures. Steve gave him a warning look then moved in Woody's direction. "Do you need help up?" he asked as he knelt down next to him.

"Hmm." The older man shook his head. "Can't seem to move this arm." He groaned then looked Eula Mae's way. "I told you I had two left feet."

"Let me look at that arm." Jackson dropped to his knees at Woody's side. "I worked as a paramedic for a while just out of college." He began to examine Woody's elbow, which looked oddly out of shape. Steve felt queasy just looking at it.

Apparently so did Woody. He looked a little green. "Hurts all the way down into my hand." He released another groan. "Hope I haven't broken anything."

"Oh, you've definitely broken something, no doubt about that," Jackson said. He looked over at Steve, his eyes filled with concern. "I'd feel better if you called 911."

"Oh, no need for that," Woody said. "I'll drive myself to the doctor."

"You will not." Eula's Mae's firm voice rang out. "For once in your life, listen to reason, you stubborn old man. You're in need of medical care, and you're going to get it. Besides, you can't drive your car in this condition. It's not possible."

Woody, who seemed to be enjoying this attention on some level, started looking a little pale. Steve reached for his phone and dialed 911. He explained the situation to the woman on the other end of the phone, who responded with a couple of questions.

"They want to know about your overall health," Steve said.

"Why the devil do they need to know about my finances?" Woody said, growing paler by the moment. "It's my arm, not my pocketbook."

It took Steve a minute to figure out where this conversation was headed. "They said *health*, not wealth."

"Oh." Another grimace followed before Woody responded. "Well, I'm on medicine for blood pressure and I have a pacemaker."

"You do?" Eula Mae grabbed his hand. "Why didn't you tell me?"

"What's to tell?" he asked. "I got it in the '90s. But I'm in fine shape. Or I was, anyway. But I'll tell you the truth—if you put me in an ambulance, my pocketbook will be in worse shape than my elbow, so will one of you please just drive me to the doctor?"

"You need a hospital, not a doctor's office," Jackson said. "This is a bad break. It might require surgery."

"Still, I would think one of you fine citizens would drive this old fool to the hospital," he said. "What do you say? Can we skip the ambulance?"

Steve posed the question to the woman on the other end of the line, who asked several questions of her own about Woody's current condition. In the end, she agreed that he was stable enough to ride in a car to the hospital.

As he ended the call, Steve knelt down next to Woody. "Okay. I'll take you myself. I want to keep an eye on you."

"I'll go with you," Jackson said, concern registering in his eyes. "But in the meantime, we need to stabilize that arm."

He spent the next couple of minutes doing just that, using some cloth strips torn from one of the older church costumes. Afterward, Jackson dove into the most powerful prayer Steve had ever heard, pleading with the Almighty for Woody's healing. By the end of it, most of the ladies in the room had tears in their eyes.

"C'mon now, Woody," Jackson said, pulling a chair his way. "We're going to start by getting you into a chair and then we'll see if you can stand. If you can't, we'll carry you out."

"Carry me out, my eye," Woody said. "I'm walking out of here like a man." He gave Steve a don't-you-dare-pick-me-up look.

As Steve rose and released a pent-up sigh, Mickey drew near with camera in hand. Steve elbowed him back with a gentle nudge. Still, he could hear the rapid click of the camera in spite of his warning.

Several of the men helped Woody into the chair, where he sat for a couple of minutes looking as if he might topple. Then, over a period of several minutes, Steve and Jackson helped him to a standing position.

"Is it my imagination, or is the room spinning?" Woody asked.

Steve was just about to insist he sit back down, when Woody chuckled. "Just kidding. Get me to the car, fellas. And by the way, let's ride in my Mustang. If we've gotta go to the hospital, let's go in style."

"But…" Steve started to argue about the inspection being out but thought better of it. Hopefully by the time they got to the parking lot, Woody would agree to go in Steve's truck. If they could get him into it. *Hmm.* Maybe the Mustang would be better after all.

Nearby, Eula Mae's eyes filled with tears. A couple of the other ladies looked as if they might join her in an emotional meltdown.

"Don't worry now," Woody said with the wave of a hand as they led him from the room. "You just get me to a doctor and he'll patch me up in no time. I'll be back tomorrow, for sure."

Steve didn't have the heart to tell him that he wouldn't be back tomorrow. Or the day after that. From the looks of things, Woody was down for the count. And the Camelot Players had just lost the only director who really knew anything about putting on a show.

Chapter Sixteen

....

Acting is not about being someone different.
It's finding the similarity in what is apparently different,
then finding myself in there.

MERYL STREEP

The morning after Woody's accident, Amy settled onto the sofa with a cup of coffee in hand. She reached for the *Knox County Register*, and her eyes widened in disbelief as she read the headline: CHAOS REIGNS IN CAMELOT. She squeezed her eyes shut then opened them, reading it again. Yep. Same headline as before. She skimmed the article, horrified at what she found written there. Okay, so most of it was true, but did that reporter have to take advantage of them in such a public way?

"Dad!" she called out. "Dad, have you seen this?"

Seconds later he appeared in the doorway, nibbling on a piece of bacon. "What happened? Is the house on fire?"

She pointed to the paper, her heart pounding wildly. "Look what that reporter did. He's...he's ruined us."

Her father swallowed the rest of the bacon and took the paper from her, his gaze shifting to the headline. A deep sigh followed, and he tossed the paper on the desk. "You've got to admit, we gave him a lot to write about. Impeccable timing on his part."

"Still." Amy rose and paced the room. "He didn't have to lay it all out there like that. Seems a bit brusque, don't you think?"

"Maybe. But you know what they say in Hollywood."

"What's that?"

He gave her a knowing look. "Publicity is publicity. And this is free publicity for the play. Front page, no less. People are bound to be curious after reading what a bunch of screwballs we are. They'll come see the show just to find out if what he's written is true."

"And when they find out it is?" She leaned against the arm of the sofa and forced back the tears. "Then what?"

"Then we work double time to prove we've got the goods," he said. "Not that it's really anyone's business. We're a team, Amy. We stick together no matter what. Right now our main focus is on Woody."

"True."

"Have you heard anything about his condition?"

"Steve called me on his way into work about ten minutes ago. He said they've set Woody's arm but are keeping him in the hospital under observation for another twenty-four hours because of his blood pressure. It was pretty high last night, I think. But at least he didn't need surgery. That's a huge relief."

"Of course." Her father paused. "Should we go see him?"

She shook her head and dropped into the recliner. "No, Steve said the doctor wants him to rest." A lingering pause followed. "I'm just sick over the fact that Woody's in pain. And how in the world can I direct the show without him? I'm so clueless."

"You know how Woody is," her father countered. "He'll show up at the rehearsals even if his arm is in a cast."

"Probably." She paused, deep in thought. "But it's not just the directing that has me upset. Dad, this is my fault. All of it. Every single bit. Don't you see?"

"Your fault? You shoved him down on the floor?"

"No. I'm just saying that this play was my idea. If I hadn't come up with it, Woody wouldn't have been there. If he hadn't been there, he wouldn't have fallen. So it all goes back to me."

"You're overanalyzing this, honey." Her father shook his head. "Just like you always do. And if we're going with your theory that the one who conceptualized the idea is at fault, then we would have to conclude that Henry Ford is ultimately responsible for what happened to your mom."

"What?"

"Well, sure. He's the one who designed the Model T and basically got the whole automobile industry started. And if automobiles hadn't been invented, your mother would still be with us."

"Dad." She shook her head, finding his logic completely skewed.

He gave her a compassionate look. "Honey, you had a great idea. We'll never regret putting on this show." A chuckle followed. "Well, maybe on the night of the dress rehearsal, but even then we'll think it's a good idea. And Woody loves it. You've given him a reason to go on. You have no idea how much he's needed this. And I'll go a step further and say that he's eating up the attention this broken arm is getting him. So don't fret. You do that far too much."

"Fretting is my middle name." She sighed.

"Then change your name." He gave her a serious look. "Because fretting—worrying—is senseless. And it's a sure sign that you're trying to hang onto something that's not yours to hang onto. So let it go."

"I wish I could figure out how to do that," she said. "Letting go isn't as easy as it looks."

"I know." His eyes began to glisten. "If anyone knows that, I do."

"I know that, Dad. I'm sorry."

His cell phone rang, and as he glanced down at it, the corners of his lips turned up. He dabbed at his eyes and muttered, "I, um, I need to get this."

"Someone calling about Woody?"

"No, um…" He shrugged and answered with a gentle "Hello?" before disappearing into his bedroom.

Very odd.

Not that Amy really had time to be worrying about her father's phone calls. No, with another city council meeting this evening, she really had only one thing on her mind—staying on top of her work and making sure the county officials didn't stop them in the meantime.

She picked up her phone and called Steve at work to let him know she was on her way. Eula Mae answered on the third ring, her voice sounding a little muffled.

"H–hello?"

"Eula Mae? You all right?"

"Oh, I'm…" The older woman sniffed. "Just missing Woody."

"Aw." Amy's heart went out to her. "Take the day off and spend it with him. We'll get along fine without you, and it will make you feel better."

"The doctor says he needs to rest."

"Well, he can rest with you by his side. And I'm sure he'd love the company."

"He won't let me come." She sighed. "Said he doesn't want me to see him in a hospital bed. Stubborn old fool. He's worse than Sarge's mule."

"I might have to agree with you there," Amy said. "I thought maybe this situation might soften him a little."

"Hmph. Besides, I hate to leave the office because there's so much going on around here. You coming in soon?"

"Yes. I'm on my way now. I was just calling to let Steve know."

"He walked over to the diner to pick up some donuts. I think he felt sorry for me."

"Ah." She paused. "Well, what's going on over there that I need to know about?"

"What *isn't* might be a better question. Probably better if you wait till you get here, though. Then we can talk."

"I'll be there in a few minutes."

"Good. I think you and Steve and I had better hash a few things out before tonight's city council meeting. Trust me. There's a lot brewing."

"Lovely."

Amy hung up the phone and hurried to get ready. After grabbing her purse, she knocked on her father's door then waited a moment for him to answer. Nothing. "Dad?" She peeked her head inside.

He looked up from his cell phone. "Yes, honey?"

"I have to leave for work now."

His gaze shifted back to the phone in his hand. "Okay. Have a good day. See you at the meeting tonight."

"Right." She gave him another quick glance, trying to figure out why he looked like he'd been caught with his hand in the cookie jar. Strange. But just another in a long line of odd happenings of late.

She made the drive into town, for the first time noticing the flowers blooming along the highway. Had she really been so busy that she'd overlooked the transition from spring to summer? Crazy. She wanted things to slow down, for life to go back to normal. Somehow she had the feeling "normal" was a thing of the past. Just a setting on the dryer, as her mother used to say.

After arriving at City Hall, Amy made her way to Eula Mae's desk. She found her on the phone, whispering what sounded like sweet nothings. Well, if you could call it whispering. Woody must surely be on the other end of the line, because her words of love were actually shouted.

"Sorry, Woody," Eula Mae hollered into the phone. "I have to go. Amy's here now." After a lengthy pause she repeated, "*Amy*, not gravy. And stop talking about food. You'll get your breakfast soon enough, and in the meantime I'll make a couple of calls to see if they can locate your missing teeth."

Eula Mae ended the call and looked at Amy with a smile. "Poor old guy. I guess they took his teeth away while he's on the morphine. I'm thinking that's why he doesn't want me down there. He's embarrassed."

"Aw, can't say as I blame him," Amy said. "But if you really care about him…" She gave Eula Mae a pensive look. "And I'm assuming from your reaction to his accident that you do…then why would he care if you see him without his teeth?"

"Personally, I would never let the woman I love see me without my teeth." Steve's happy-go-lucky voice chimed in.

Amy turned to face him, doing her best not to laugh. "Oh?"

"Mm-hmm." He pulled her close, pretending to be toothless, and gave her a kiss on the cheek. "See how awkward that is?"

Amy laughed. "Very. But I'll still love you even when you are old and toothless." *Whoa. Did I really just say that out loud?*

Steve's eyes widened. "I'm taking that to the bank," he whispered in her ear.

As he loosened his hold on her, Amy stepped back, her face hot with embarrassment. Her words had been presumptuous, considering that Steve had never really opened up and shared his feelings with her. Not really. Had she blown it by using the *L* word so soon?

Off in the distance Eula Mae cleared her throat.

"I hate to break up this little lovefest, but we're on government property. Don't think we're supposed to be smooching in here. It's probably against the law or something."

"Guess that kiss you and Woody shared last Friday afternoon in the storage room will have to stay a secret, then." Steve gave Eula Mae a peck on the cheek. "And don't tell anyone I just did that, either. I don't want to be ticketed for impulsive kissing."

Her wrinkled cheeks flushed. "Heavens. I wouldn't dream of it."

"I thought so." Steve laughed. "But speaking of Woody, how's he doing today? When I left the hospital last night he was sleeping like a baby. Talking in his sleep too."

"About the Mustang or me?" Eula Mae asked.

"Neither. Something about the play, actually. He was giving stage directions."

"Figures." A hint of a smile creased the edges of Eula Mae's lips. "I've already talked to him four times this morning. He's as ornery as ever." A giggle framed her next words. "He is a mess under the best of circumstances, but he sounds so funny when he's on medication. You wouldn't believe some of the nutty stories he told me on the phone just now. Sounded more like Sarge than Woody."

"How long is it going to be before he's up and around?" Amy asked. She held her breath, hoping for a positive answer...not just for the sake of the show, but for Woody's sake as well.

"He can't drive until the cast is off," Eula Mae said. "So I'm his designated driver till then." She grinned. "I've been dying to get my hands on that Mustang for years."

"Well, while we've got it, let's get that old car fixed up so it passes inspection," Steve said. "And try to locate those traffic tickets he got from O'Reilly. I've heard all about them. Three times, no less."

"Me too." Amy shook her head. "I guess this is as good a time as any to help out a brother in need. Might ease my conscience a little too."

"Ease your conscience?" Eula Mae gave her a funny look. "You feeling guilty about something?"

"About everything. If I hadn't come up with this idea—"

"Stop right there." Steve put his hand up. "You do this guilt trip thing a lot, and this time I'm not going along for the ride. Sorry."

"Excuse me?"

"Not going there," he repeated. "You didn't do anything wrong."

"But…" She bit back the words.

"No buts. Woody was at that rehearsal because he wanted to be."

"Heavens, yes." Eula Mae practically beamed. "Why, this musical is the highlight of his life. I've heard all about it." She giggled. "And besides—not that I'm saying his accident was a good thing, mind you—but with Woody in the passenger seat, I'll have a captive audience for the first time in years."

"Mm-hmm." Amy narrowed her gaze. "So that's how it is."

"That's how it is." A girlish giggle erupted. "I can't believe I'm saying this out loud. Our relationship has been years in the making. Years. And for the longest time I couldn't admit it to anyone but myself."

"So what made you open up?" Amy asked. "How did you both finally decide to confess your feelings?"

A shimmer of tears filled Eula Mae's eyes. "I think we've both known for ages…but we're both so stubborn and set in our ways. When you've been alone for years, it's hard to admit that you have a need for someone else. You'd rather have folks think you're self-sufficient." Her gaze shifted to the floor. "But I'm not self-sufficient. Not even close. It's all an act. The reality is, I want to experience love again before I die. Firsthand, no holds barred. So I'm putting it all out there with Woody."

Amy grabbed Eula Mae's hand. "Well, I'm glad you are. And it couldn't happen to two nicer people." She followed her words with a warm embrace.

From across the room Steve gave her a little wink, causing her heart to flutter.

See? He might not say it, but he shows it.

"Thanks, honey." Eula Mae returned her squeeze. "And just for the record, I'm glad to see you two have finally come to your senses. I would've hated to see you waste as many years as Woody and I did." After a pause she reached down and picked up a couple of pink sticky notes from her desk. "I hate to change the subject, but we've got some serious wrangling to do before tonight's meeting."

"What's happened?" Amy asked.

"Well, everything was so chaotic yesterday, we decided not to bother you with it."

"We?" Amy looked at Steve, her heart rate quickening. "This is something you know about too?"

"Yeah." His expression shifted, and she could read the concern in his eyes. "Some guys came through town yesterday afternoon just before the rehearsal, asking several of our residents about their property. They want to build in the area."

"Build what?"

Steve sighed. "One of them said he wants to build an outlet mall. He already talked to Grady about that vacant lot next to the hardware store. That property's been in Grady's family for years and they've never wanted to build on it because of the view. Now he's thinking about selling. Or so he said."

"Ugh." A shiver ran down Amy's spine. "Can you even imagine all of those beautiful trees being cut down?"

"No. But that's only half the story," Eula Mae said. "The other fellow wants to build a movie theater in town near the diner." Her eyes lit up. "Not that I'm totally opposed to that idea. Sure would beat having to drive to Knoxville to see a show."

"Still…" Amy shook her head, her thoughts tumbling. "I don't know how I feel about all of this. An RV park is one thing, but malls? Movie theaters? What's next, a sports stadium?"

Steve shrugged. "We have to be realistic. The more people we draw in, the more we'll need to accommodate them. We're talking about a huge change to our little town here. Far more than just a theater."

Amy groaned. "I've created a monster."

"Don't look at it that way," Steve said. "It's a happy monster, at least for now. It hasn't gobbled us up just yet. And the way I see it, what those investors want to build is nothing compared to what God is building *in* us, so we have to keep that in mind."

"What do you mean?" Amy asked.

"Don't you see? He's put all of this together. And he's built our little community into a real family—one we can be proud of."

"I know." Amy paused to think about his words. "You're right, and I'm really not complaining, trust me. It's just that so much is happening so fast. Sometimes I feel like I got the cart before the horse, as my grandpa used to say. And I don't mind admitting I'm a little worried about the final outcome here. If all these newcomers sweep in and buy up our land, it's just a matter of time before—"

"I'm with Amy," Eula Mae interrupted. "I'd rather err on the side of caution. We need to bring this up at the meeting tonight and ask everyone not to do anything rash. I, for one, don't want the town sold off inch by inch. Could be we all wake up one morning to find out it's owned by strangers."

"Maybe," Steve said. "But it's not our place to tell folks what to do with their own land. You know? We have no control over that, no matter how strongly we feel about it."

"It's going to be tempting for those who could use the money," Amy said. "And can you even imagine how those people from the county are going to react if we're in a continual state of building? It's going to be a mess."

"Not necessarily," Steve said. "It's like your dad told me weeks ago. We've just got to continue to befriend the people from the county—let them know we're all on the same team. Like Arthur did with the knights. Everyone respected everyone...."

"And in the end he lost everything." Eula Mae clamped her hand over her mouth. "Oops. Guess I didn't need to point out that part."

"I was going to say—and maybe I'm just being idealistic—that I think there's room for all of us to get along." Steve leaned against the desk. "We've prayed and asked God for a solution to save our town. Now along come these businessmen. Maybe they're an answer to prayer. So I don't want to jump the gun and assume they're all bad. And I'm doing my best to befriend Fred Platt, the county commissioner."

"Okay." Amy nodded. "I'll do the same. And I'll try to keep a positive outlook too. It's not like we don't have other things to focus on right now." She couldn't help but feel happy as she thought about the production. "We're making progress on the show. I feel it. Things are really moving along."

"Four more weeks," Steve said with a grin. "That Fourth of July debut should be quite a party."

"Whoa. Four weeks." As she spoke the words, her confidence slipped away...until Steve pulled her into his arms.

"God created the world in six days. Surely we can pull off a show in four weeks."

"So you think putting on a show is like creating the world, eh?" Eula Mae chuckled.

"Sure," Steve responded. "I see a lot of similarities. We're building a set. Creating characters. Learning how to live together, work together." He paused. "Reminds me a lot of creation, in fact."

"I guess that would make Camelot the Garden of Eden," Amy said. "Well, at least until the outlet mall and movie theater go in. Then there's no telling what it'll become."

Eula Mae moved toward the hallway. Turning back, she gave a little wave. "Well, look on the bright side, you two. At least we don't have to name the animals."

"Name them, no," Amy said, doing her best not to laugh. "Live with them...yes."

* * * * *

Steve watched as Eula Mae disappeared down the hallway. "She's quite a character, isn't she?"

"They all are. But they're *our* characters, and I'm thankful for that. I don't know what I would've done without them these past few weeks. Seriously."

"Me either. They've been great. Seems like we're all closer than ever, and that's a good thing." He paused, his thoughts shifting. "Speaking of the people we care about...I know the timing might not be the best, but there's something else I wanted to talk to you about."

Amy looked at him with alarm in her eyes. "What?"

"This is totally off the subject. At least, I think it is." He lowered his voice, just in case Eula Mae decided to make an unannounced entrance. "I'm worried about Caroline." He swallowed back the fear that rose as he spoke the words.

"Oh?" Amy leaned against the desk and gave him an inquisitive look.

"Yes. She's been acting odd lately. I don't think she's feeling well." He shook his head. "I wish things would slow down long enough for me to keep a better eye on things. I know my mom's worried about her. She called again last night, asking all sorts of questions."

"What kind of care do you think Caroline needs? Is she sick? I've noticed she hasn't been herself lately."

"I don't know." Steve raked his fingers through his hair, wishing he could push back the fears that rose up every time he thought about Caroline's illness. "That last lupus flare lasted for months. I don't ever want her to go through anything like that again." He wanted to add, "It nearly killed me to see her so weak"—but didn't.

"Maybe this isn't health-related," Amy said. "Maybe..." She shrugged. "I don't know. Maybe she's not adjusting well to the changes our little town is going through. She's lived here all her life. Could be she's not happy with the direction things are going."

"Hmm." He paused to think about that. "I'm not sure. But I'll ask her tonight before the meeting. Hopefully she'll tell me." A shrug followed. "That's the weird thing. She used to tell me everything. Lately, she's just been...what's the word?"

"Aloof?"

He chuckled. "Okay, aloof. Not exactly a word I use every day, but it's fitting. I don't know what to do when the women in my life are...aloof."

"Don't worry, sweetie pie!" Eula Mae's voice rang out as she entered the room once more. "I'll never be aloof. You know me. I'll always speak my mind. Won't leave anything to the imagination." Her gaze narrowed. "Which reminds me...you never did get a haircut. Do you need to borrow a few bucks to go to the barber's office?

'Course, I don't earn as much as you do. You know how those government people are. They never pay very much, and they keep most of it for taxes anyhow. But I'll be happy to contribute to the cause if it will get that hair trimmed to a reasonable length before those government officials sneak in here and write you up for giving a poor first impression."

Steve groaned. "Eula Mae, sometimes I wonder why I put up with you."

"Funny." She chuckled. "I was just thinking the same thing about you." She headed back to her desk and plopped down in her seat, muttering something about how scruffy he looked.

Steve looked at Amy and rolled his eyes. "I can never catch a break, can I?"

"This isn't about catching a break, young man," Eula Mae interjected. "It's about becoming the best man you can be."

Turning his attention back to Amy, Steve realized he was staring at the only woman in the world who could possibly make him the best man he could be. And he would tell her that…just as soon as the time was right.

Chapter Seventeen
....

So I was determined to use my last two years in college
doing something I thought I would enjoy, which was acting.
And it was probably because there was girls
over in the drama school too, you know?

JAMES EARL JONES

The following morning, Steve awoke with a thousand thoughts rolling through his mind. All night long he'd tossed and turned, trying to work through the three hours of conversation that had taken place at last night's city council meeting. It turned out the fine folks of Camelot had a lot to say about the would-be entrepreneurs and their plans. Some—like Sarge—were for it. Others, like Gwen, were dead-set against it, for fear the strangers' influence would destroy the homey feel of the town.

And some—like Steve himself—still didn't know what to make of it all. Sure, the building process would interrupt the town's easygoing flow. But, really, what else could they do? If hundreds, possibly even thousands, of tourists showed up for this play, they would need accommodations, food, entertainment...the works. Right? And wasn't the whole idea to save the city from financial downfall? Perhaps the Lord had arranged all of this to bring in revenue. He could only hope.

A hot shower didn't do much to calm Steve's nerves. Neither did a bowl of cereal and a banana, his usual breakfast. And the fact that Caroline wouldn't answer her cell phone didn't make him feel much better about things, either. He decided to stop by her place on his way into town. As he drove, he made a couple of calls, including one to Amy to see if she had ordered Woody's hearing aid. He couldn't help but smile as he reflected on the response he'd gotten from city council members when he'd suggested the town cover the cost as a gift to Woody for his help with the play. Their resounding "Yes!" had brought joy to his heart. At least one thing had gone well at the meeting.

As Steve pulled up in Caroline's driveway, his cell phone rang. He glanced at it, knowing before he even saw the number who it would be. Darrell. Again. A lengthy conversation followed, not unlike the ten or twelve before it. Things at the theater build-out site were moving right along, but not without some degree of frustration on Darrell's end. Nothing much Steve could do about that. The construction stuff was a little out of his league.

About five minutes into the conversation, someone beeped in. Steve sighed as he glanced at the number. "Darrell, I've gotta go. It's the county commissioner."

He quickly switched gears, trying to sound as businesslike as possible. Eula Mae would have been proud of his attempt, anyway. Not that he could really squeeze a word in edgewise. On and on Mr. Platt went, listing the issues he'd found on the recent inspection.

"Well, yes, that's right," Steve said when the fellow paused for a breath. "I saw the form. And I just heard from my brother, so I'm aware…"

The commissioner cut him off, sounding terse. So much for winning him over with the friendship approach. Maybe God had something different in mind for this fellow.

"Yes, we do have a couple of electrical problems. And we've got someone working on that today. We've also got someone on the plumbing problem. But—" Steve never had a chance to finish. Instead Mr. Platt went on and on, talking about forms. Paperwork. Holdups.

When the conversation ended, Steve found himself battling a headache.

He looked up to see Caroline standing beside the car, still wearing her housecoat and holding the morning paper in her hand. She mouthed the words, "What's going on?"

Steve got out of the car and gave her a hug, determined to put the conversation—and the town's woes—behind him. "G'morning."

"Good morning to you too," she said. "I was starting to wonder if you were coming in. You've been out here twenty minutes."

"No way." He released his hold on her and glanced at his watch. "I guess you're right."

"Everything okay?" She gave him a motherly look.

"There's just so much happening at once." He'd leave it at that.

"The theater?"

He sighed, trying to decide how much to share. If something really was going on with her, she didn't need to be fretting about the construction issues. What could she do, anyway? *She could pray.* The words flitted through his mind. Yes, she could pray. Hadn't Caroline's prayers gotten him through most of the other hurdles he'd faced in his life?

Before he could say anything, she patted him on the arm and began to share. "I know a little," she said. "Darrell called this morning, wondering if I'd seen you. He's plenty worked up. Sounds like he's run into all sorts of complications. And did he tell you about that guy from the county?"

"Yes. Fred Platt. That's who called just now." Steve began to walk alongside her up the driveway toward the house. "But I really don't want you worked up over this. Not right now."

"Why not now?" she asked. "What do you mean?"

"Well…" Did he dare broach the subject? "You've just seemed a little out of sorts lately. I've been concerned."

"Ah." Her gaze shifted to the ground. "Well, don't worry about me, honey. I'm fine." She glanced up with the hint of a shrug. "I'll let you know if I'm in trouble. I promise."

"Okay."

"You've got bigger fish to fry right now, anyway," she said. "Tell me what's going on with this guy from the county. How can I pray?"

"How much time do you have?" He released a sigh, feeling the tension in his shoulders. "Might take awhile."

"I have a couple of hours till I have to meet up with Natalie at the church. We're still working on costumes." She grinned. "You coming early to rehearsal today to try on yours?"

"I'll try. I'm going to get Woody's car worked on while he's not looking."

"You're a good boy." A contented smile followed. "Your mama raised you right."

"Yes, she did. But she had a little help from a good friend."

Caroline beamed.

They entered the house together and she led the way into the living room. She settled into her recliner then looked his way. "Okay, out with it. Spill the beans about the guy from the county."

Steve took the spot on the sofa across from her. "It's just red tape on top of red tape. That's all. Nothing God can't handle."

"He's pretty good with ripping up red tape," she said. "But be specific. If I'm going to pray, I want to get it right."

He told her every detail, right down to the parts he felt sure would trouble her most.

"So he's saying we might not be up to code in time for the performance?"

"Yeah." Steve felt the wind go out of his sails. "But don't tell anyone, okay? I don't want to have to push the date back. Not yet. Not till we know for sure."

"The Bible says that our prayers are powerful," she said. "But they're even more powerful when we're in agreement. Want to pray now?"

He nodded then listened in as she began a heartfelt conversation with the Almighty, pleading for His mercy and intervention. For as long as Steve could remember, Caroline had been intimate with God. Her prayers sounded very much like ordinary conversation. Regular, everyday chatter. In fact, about halfway into her prayer time, he wondered if she'd switched gears and was talking to him. No, she was still praying. A sense of stillness came over him as she continued. Truly she had the right idea. God was big enough to handle all of this.

When she finished, she folded her hands in her lap and a look of happiness settled on her face. "Well, that's done. Tell me what else is on your mind."

"What else?"

Her gaze narrowed. "You can't hide anything from me. That construction business isn't the only thing you're struggling with."

"O–oh?"

"Yes. I've been concerned about you. This is a lot for one person to handle. But I'm referring to something else a little more personal."

"Ah." He'd anticipated this conversation for a while now.

"I know when you're bothered by something. There's something happening between you and Amy."

"Not really something bad, if that's what you mean." He sighed. "Honestly, I think the problem is on my end. I'm insecure, maybe? I don't know. Does that make me sound like a wimp?" He squared his shoulders and sat up a little straighter.

"You're the farthest thing from a wimp," she said. "You've more than proven that you're made of tough stuff. And your tenacity made your mom tough too. I honestly think she would have given up, if not for you and your brother." She paused, her gaze unsettling him. "So tell me what's going on with Amy."

"I love her."

A smile lit Caroline's face. "Well, I've known that much for years. Congratulations for catching up."

He smiled. "I mean, I love her, but I'm trying to figure out how to tell her that."

"Have the words 'I love you' crossed your mind?"

"Very funny." He paused. "I'm just in unfamiliar territory."

"Well, maybe 'I love you' isn't the best jumping-off point, then. Tell me how she makes you feel."

"You sound like Eula Mae. She told me I should write Amy a song."

"Maybe." Caroline grinned. "But it helps to voice what you're thinking and feeling before coming up with a melody line. So, spill it. If you're comfortable with that, I mean."

"Hmm." He paused, his thoughts coming alive as the memory of his last kiss with Amy surfaced. "Well, you know how sometimes you're driving along and come to the crest of a hill? You go sailing over, picking up speed as you come down the other side."

"Sounds like Woody." Caroline chuckled. "I've seen him do that a hundred times on the hill leading into town."

"Exactly." Steve forged ahead. "Perfect analogy. I've been over that hill going too fast myself. I remember exactly what it feels like. Even if you brake, you don't always slow down enough to stop the adrenaline from kicking in. For a few crazy seconds you feel like you've lost control, like you're going too fast. Like you're flying, even. Your heart jumps into your throat. But it's an undeniably exciting feeling. *That's* what I feel like whenever Amy walks into the room."

Caroline smiled. "I know that feeling well. Falling in love is amazing. If you don't believe me, just ask your mom."

Steve paused, realizing she must be talking about his stepfather. Definitely not his real father...not that he wanted to broach that subject. Not today.

Or maybe he did. His insecurities really went back to his dad, anyway. Didn't they?

"What's really bothering you, Steve?" Caroline's words interrupted his thoughts. "It's written all over your face. You're troubled by something. There's more to this than what you're saying. I'm trying to read between the lines."

"How do you learn to trust again? I think I still have some issues related to my dad. In some strange way, I think his actions have had me a little stuck. Maybe I'm afraid of telling Amy that I love her because I'm afraid that one of us is going to end up hurting the other."

"You're making assumptions," Caroline said. "And none of it is based on fact, just on fear."

He sighed.

"Steve, what happened with your dad stinks—for your mom, for you boys, and now for Amy. It was hard walking your mom through that. And sometimes I think you boys had to grow up so fast that you never got to relax. That's what you need to do now. Relax. Be yourself. Let go of whatever is holding you back and jump in headfirst. Amy's worth it. You're worth it."

A long pause followed. Steve turned his attention to the bird-house outside the window, where a cardinal lighted and began to nibble at the feed. Seconds later, the bird flitted away. Seemed symbolic, really. It might just be easier to fly off and avoid the problem. Well, not that his relationship with Amy posed any problems. No, the minute he thought of her, his heart came alive. It wasn't Amy. This was—this was all about him. And he needed to jump the hurdle. Hadn't she let it slip that she loved him? Okay, so maybe her words "I'll still love you even when you are old and toothless" weren't the stuff romance novels were made of. But they sure beat anything he'd said to her…so far.

"Okay," he said at last. "I'm going to do it."

"You are?"

"Yes." Steve rose and began to pace the room, the music in his heart now blaring. "This afternoon, before the rehearsal, I'm going to figure out a way to tell her what I'm feeling." The craziest sensation swept over him as he contemplated doing so. Joy. Nerves. Peace. "I've waited long enough. Today's the day."

* * * * *

Amy arrived at the Civic Center an hour early so that she could check on the progress of the theater and meet with Natalie and Caroline to iron out costume details. She was greeted by men in hard hats, along with the sound of bulldozers going strong. Even Jimmy and Timmy had shown up to help. Prissy looked on, a wide smile on her face.

"Wow." Amy shook her head, unable to believe the transformation. As she looked at the beginnings of a new stage and the nearly completed seating area she found herself overcome with emotion.

Jackson greeted her, his work clothes dirty and soaked in sweat.

Not exactly Lancelot material at the moment, but the look of satisfaction on his face made up for it. "Pretty amazing, isn't it?" He gestured to the would-be stage. "Just think, in less than a week we'll have our first rehearsal up there."

"Can't wait. I can almost hear the orchestra now."

"Speaking of the orchestra, I heard from Gramps that you found all the musicians you needed."

"Well, mostly. We're still looking for a cello player."

"I'm sure he—or she—will turn up." He brushed the dirt from his hands. "Just in the nick of time, if the Lord works in His usual way."

"I never could figure out the eleventh-hour thing," Amy said. "Why is it that God usually chooses to wait till the very last minute to let things work out?"

"I'm not sure. I just know that it's a test of our faith when we're not sure how things are going to come together. And it's always just a miraculous feeling when it does." He paused and gazed at her. "Speaking of which…"

"What?"

"Can I ask a question?"

"Sure." She gave him a cursory glance.

"Well, talking about the eleventh-hour stuff reminded me of the city council meeting last night. I know I'm not really a resident here, but I have a vested interest—both in my grandfather and…well, in you."

"Me?" She sucked in a breath, wondering what he meant.

"I just wanted to make sure you're okay after last night's meeting."

"It was rough." Amy sighed. "And it's obvious that everyone in town has his or her own opinion about strangers coming in and buying up the land." She shook her head. "Can't say I blame people for getting worked up. I'm a little unnerved myself. Things are moving too fast, and I'm completely to blame. I got this ball rolling down the hill, but I'm afraid it's going to end up crushing us."

"Well, before you get too carried away with that thought, remember that you prayed about the decision to put on the play." He paused and gave her an intense look. "You did pray about it, right?"

"Of course."

"Okay. Then here's how I feel about that. If you prayed and God gave you the peace to move forward, you didn't exactly get ahead of Him. And if you didn't get ahead of Him, you're probably tracking with Him."

"Tracking with Him?"

"Moving step by step with Him holding your hand."

"Ah." Amy looked down as she felt Jackson take hold of her hand. He gave it a squeeze then gazed at her with tenderness in his eyes.

Off in the distance, Natalie approached with a wave. Jackson released his hold on Amy's hand.

"Hey, Amy." Natalie placed a hand on her blossoming belly "Thanks for coming early. I don't think this will take long."

"No problem. You have an outfit for me to try on?"

"Three, in fact," Natalie said. "Caroline is inside ironing the dress for the wedding scene. I think you're going to love it."

Natalie turned her attention to Jackson. "Hmm. We'd planned to have you try on your costume as well, but you're a little…"

"Grimy?"

"Yeah. That's putting it mildly."

"I need to run home and take a quick shower; then I'll come right back. I think the guys can do without me for a while."

He waved at Darrell, who hollered, "Thanks for your help!"

"No problem."

As he took off, Amy reflected on his words. She had prayed about this. And God would see it through.

Going inside the Civic Center, she met up with Caroline, who greeted her with a warm hug. "Hello, darlin'."

"Hello yourself," Amy said. "You're in a good mood today."

"I am." Caroline flashed a suspicious smile. "Feeling mighty good, in fact."

"I'm so glad to hear that." She gave the older woman an inquisitive look, trying to figure out what Steve had been so worried about. Caroline seemed fine today.

Natalie and Caroline reminisced about the fun they'd had putting together the costumes and then showed Amy some of their handiwork. Amy looked on with amazement as they showed off the various pieces they'd sewn.

"Honestly, ladies, I don't think they could have been any nicer if we'd ordered them from a costume company."

"Aw, well, thanks." Natalie grinned. "I'm glad I'm able to contribute."

"And I'm sure these costumes are going to make you all look like kings and queens." Caroline beamed. "So let's try on a few, shall we? We'll start with the dress you'll be wearing in the first scene." She and Natalie followed Amy into the ladies' room with their arms loaded with costumes. The ladies chattered so loudly, their words reverberated around the little room. Not that Amy minded. No, their conversation had a homey feel to it. And Caroline's bubbly voice put her at ease, as always.

Amy changed into the lovely blue gown, mesmerized by its beauty. "Wow," she said, looking at her reflection in the mirror. "Breathtaking."

"Yes, you are." Caroline gave her a little kiss on the cheek. "But I suppose you were talking about the dress."

"Yes, the dress." Amy gave Caroline's hand a squeeze. "But thank you."

"I'm so glad you like it." Natalie fidgeted with one of the sleeves. Seconds later, she withdrew her hand and placed it on her tummy. "Oh!" She grabbed Amy's hand and pressed it to her belly. "Do you feel that? He's doing a somersault."

"That's crazy." Amy pressed her palm against Natalie's rounded midsection, amazed at the activity coming from within. "I've never felt anything like that before."

"Me either." Natalie giggled. "Not until a few months ago, anyway. To be honest, I wasn't sure what to expect with our first baby. This is all new territory for me."

"Oh, honey, this is going to be the best experience of your life," Caroline said. "Trust me."

The three women stood side by side, their reflections in the mirror showing off the vivid differences between them all—Natalie, with her extended belly; Caroline, with the soft wrinkles around her eyes and salt-and-pepper hair; and Amy, with her long blond hair, decked out in medieval attire. How different...and yet how much the same.

"When you find that man you love," Caroline said to the reflections in the mirror, "the rest is just gravy."

Natalie giggled and put her hand on her tummy. "Gravy, huh?"

"Yep." Caroline began to hum the melody to "I Loved You Once in Silence."

Amy's heart soared. She wrapped her arms around Caroline's neck and whispered, "I'm so glad you're feeling better."

"Well, me too, honey. Now, let's get you into that second dress."

Amy tried on the soft pink number, loving it even more than the first. She especially liked the shimmering fabric.

"Looks great with your eyes," Caroline said. "Steve is going to flip when he sees you in this dress."

Amy felt her cheeks grow warm.

"Okay, ready for the crème de la crème?" Natalie asked. "Want to see the wedding dress?"

Amy glanced at the clock. "Do we have time before the rehearsal starts?"

"Sure. It won't take long. I just need to pin up the hem." She brought in the most beautiful white Renaissance dress Amy had ever seen.

"Oh, Natalie, it's gorgeous. Just takes my breath away."

"Thank you."

Amy slipped the gown over her head and laced up the front. While Caroline knelt to pin the hem, Natalie drew near with a headpiece in hand.

"I made this by hand," she said. "Do you like it?"

"Like it?" Amy could hardly believe her eyes. The delicate beading...the shimmering jewels... "Natalie, I'm floored."

Natalie pinned it on, moving slowly but surely, and humming all the while.

"Wish we had a bigger mirror so I could see the train on this dress."

"There's the big one in the foyer," Caroline said, taking her by the hand. "Let's go take a look."

They entered the main room of the Civic Center and headed straight for the full-length mirror in the front hall.

"Wow." Amy stared at her reflection.

"'Wow' is right." Jackson's voice rang out from behind her.

She turned to see him cleaned and dressed in jeans and a T-shirt. His eyes widened as he took in the dress. "You look...amazing."

Amy's cheeks grew warm. "Didn't Natalie do a fantastic job?"

"She did." His gaze remained riveted on her gown—and then her face. A smile teased the edges of his lips, and she wondered why he grew silent.

"Looks like you got here just in time, Jackson," Natalie said. "Let's get you into that jousting costume before the others get here."

He disappeared in the direction of the men's room and Natalie's voice called out behind him. "Your costumes are marked with your name. Let me know if you need any safety pins or anything, and come out when you're done."

Moments later, Amy was completely blown away as Jackson entered the room dressed in his royal-blue doublet. In that instant, she found herself transported. This really was Camelot. She was a princess, dressed in royal attire, waiting for the prince to take her by the hand.

Hmm. Only one problem.

Wrong prince.

Chapter Eighteen

....

Acting is a form of confusion.

<small>TALLULAH BANKHEAD</small>

Amy swallowed hard as Jackson took a step in her direction. His eyes sparkled as he extended his hand. "If I didn't know better, I'd think I was looking at the real Guinevere."

"Oh?" *Do I take his hand, or...* She took it then allowed him to spin her around like a princess at a ball. She could almost hear the music in her head as everything began to twirl.

Almost. After a few seconds of daydreaming, other thoughts kicked in.

Where's Steve? Why isn't he here? He knew we were supposed to come early today. Oh, yes. He's working on Woody's car.

Amy stopped dancing, the music in her head slowly fading. How sweet of Steve, to give his whole day fixing up that old Mustang for his friend. He was a real prince, the stuff legends were made of. And she would wait for him, symbolically and otherwise.

Still, Amy could hardly breathe as Jackson released her and gave a royal bow. She responded with a curtsy, playing along so that none of this would seem too real.

"So, what do you think of my getup?" Jackson asked, pointing to his costume.

"You look like the real deal," she said. "I half expected you to come charging across the field on a horse."

He grinned. "That's coming up in today's rehearsal, right? If we can find a real horse, anyway."

"Yes. We're definitely rehearsing the jousting scene today. I've put it off for too long." Amy took another look in the mirror, examining her dress once more. "It's kind of fun playing dress-up." She turned, her skirt making a lovely swishing sound. "Haven't done anything like this since I was a kid. I always wanted to be a princess."

"You always *have* been," Caroline said, drawing near with a box of straight pins in her hand. "From the moment I first met you, I knew you had the makings of royalty."

Amy's breath caught in her throat. She turned with a strained smile, hoping to keep the conversation moving forward.

A camera flash caught Amy off guard. When had the reporter gotten here?

"Hey, Guinevere and Lancelot, give us a smile." Mickey's jovial words seemed genuine enough, but the click of the camera contradicted it. *Ugh.* Would they end up on the front page again? "Get a little closer, you two," he said. "Give us a pose." Mickey drew near and situated them, putting Jackson's arm around Amy's waist.

Deep breath, Amy. It's just a picture.

Still, as the reporter gestured for her to lean her head against Jackson's broad shoulder, Amy felt her stomach flip. When Jackson gazed into her eyes, however, she calmed down and felt her tensions lift. The music began to play in her head once again, its melody strangely compelling.

Yes, something about this particular Lancelot really cast a spell on her, whether she wanted to admit it or not. And if the music in her head didn't stop playing sooner rather than later, she might just find herself...what was the word? Ah yes. Captivated.

* * * * *

Steve rushed through the door of the Civic Center, concerned about the time. He'd spent half the day getting Woody's car worked on and, eventually, inspected. A few complications had threatened to bring him down, but he'd risen against them. All with one thought in mind: he had to get to Amy. Had to tell her how he felt. Once the words were spoken, he could breathe easier. How hard could it be anyway—to tell a woman he loved her?

As he entered the room, Steve's gaze fell at once on the woman who consumed his thoughts. She was dressed in the most beautiful wedding gown he'd ever seen. Talk about the perfect moment. Her beauty took his breath away.

Until he realized she was standing arm in arm with Jackson Brenner, dressed in an over-the-top knight-in-shining-armor getup.

Everything Steve had spent the day thinking about—pondering, praying about—shot right out of his head. Suddenly he could only see Guinevere and Lancelot, arm in arm. As a couple. Alarm bells went off in his head and his heart, though he fought to silence them before his expression gave him away.

"Glad you could join us." Natalie approached Steve. "I've got your Arthur costumes ready to try on. Which do you want to see first?"

He didn't even stop to look. Grabbing one, Steve slipped into the men's room, his thoughts in a whirl. He tried not to think about the look of contentment on Amy's face as she posed for the camera with

Jackson in her arms. Steve couldn't help but feel a twinge of guilt. Not that he could blame Jackson. No, the guy was genuinely good.

Just like the real Lancelot.

Great. Now I'm starting to believe the legend.

He put aside all conflicting thoughts as he put on the first costume. Unfortunately, it didn't fit quite like he'd hoped. The shoulders were too wide, dwarfing him. And those stupid tights… Amy could call them pants if she liked, but they still looked and felt like little-girl tights to him. Still, he couldn't go bare-legged, could he? No, he'd better forge ahead. Against his better judgment, he eased into them.

Might as well get this over with. Steve made his way back out into the main room, stunned to see that most of the cast had arrived. *Great. Nothing like showing off your skinny tights-covered legs to the ladies.* From across the room, he kept a watchful eye on Amy and Jackson. She offered him an inviting smile, and his heart lifted. *See? You have nothing to worry about.*

A familiar voice sounded behind him. Feminine. Gentle. Sincere. "Wow, Steve. At moments like this, I really believe you were born to be a king."

He turned to find Gwen staring at him.

"You think?" He caught a glimpse of his reflection in the mirror.

"I think." Her words reflected the same kindness he now saw in her eyes.

"Even with these ridiculous…" He pointed down at his legs, unwilling to say the word.

"Mm-hmm." She nodded then shifted her gaze to his face. They stood close enough to touch, neither of them saying a word. And then he heard a familiar voice.

"Did you miss me, everyone? The lost sheep has returned to the fold."

Steve turned to see that Woody had entered the room, his arm in a sling. The cast members began to cheer. A couple of the women —Amy included—erupted in tears.

Woody's put his uninjured hand over one ear. "Why is everyone shouting?" He pointed to his new hearing aid. "Sounds like you're all amplified a hundred times over."

"We're just so happy to see you here, Woody." Amy wrapped him in a tight hug. "I'm glad you're okay."

"Just a broken arm. Nothing major. And please stop hollering at me. I'm not deaf." He stuffed his fingers into his ears, a pained expression on his face.

"Are you still going to be able to play the part of Merlin?" Annabelle asked.

"Yep. We'll figure out a way," he said. "I'll manage. Been looking forward to it."

"Caroline and I have already got that figured out," Natalie said. "If you can go without your sling for the scenes when you're onstage, we'll make the sleeves of your costume long enough and full enough to cover the cast."

"They're pretty good at the costume thing." Steve gestured to his doublet as proof.

"You're not gonna get me in those girly tights, though," Woody mumbled. "Can't believe they talked you into it, Steve."

He groaned. "They're not tights. They're pants."

"Mighty tight pants," Woody muttered. "But I don't suppose we have time to be talking about costumes right now, do we? Don't we have a show to put on in just a few weeks? Why are we all just standing around? Let's get to work, people."

"Yes, we've got to work on that jousting scene." The corners of Amy's lips curled up in a smile. "Sarge, are the animals here?"

"Yep." He chuckled. "Brought Katie Sue and B-52, too!" A round of laughter followed. "But seriously, they're out in the trailer."

"Well, give us a few minutes to change out of these costumes," Amy said, "and we'll get this ball rolling. I think we'll run the jousting scene in the field off the parking lot. If the noise from the construction isn't too loud, anyway."

Steve followed Jackson into the men's room, making light conversation as they changed back into their street clothes.

"How does it feel to be king?" Jackson asked, hanging up his costume.

"Pretty good, I guess." Steve offered what he hoped would look like a convincing smile. Still, he couldn't let go of the unsettling feeling that gripped him every time he thought about Amy and Jackson, arm in arm.

He gave himself a quick glance in the mirror and was startled to see the weariness in his eyes. This whole thing—the play, last night's meeting, Caroline, and the situation with Amy—was apparently taking a toll on him.

Jackson slapped him on the back. "Amy's calling us. Better get out there. Never want to keep a woman waiting."

"Guess you're right." He buried the sigh that threatened to erupt and followed Jackson into the Civic Center. His heart quickened as he saw Amy dressed in her usual jeans and T-shirt. Hopefully he would have a few minutes with her before the rehearsal began.

But he'd no sooner taken a step in her direction than she reached for her clipboard.

"All right, everyone. Outside. Pronto!"

She led the way across the parking lot and into the field on the south end of the property, chatting with Woody all the way.

Steve watched as Jackson and Sarge unloaded the mule and mare from the back of the trailer. A better man would've offered to help. Take Pete, for example. He headed over to offer assistance. And so did Darrell. And Grady.

Steve sighed then took a few steps in their direction. Thankfully, they didn't need him. Sarge led the mare to the field and Jackson followed behind with the mule on a short leash. Would've made for an interesting photo op. Where was that reporter when you needed him? Oh yeah. Taking pictures of Lucy, Annabelle, and Blossom.

"C'mon, everyone," Woody called out when the camera stopped clicking. "Let's get busy on that jousting scene."

Steve glanced across the parking lot at Jackson, wondering if the idea of riding the horse while carrying a sword made him nervous. No, the guy looked as cool as a cucumber. Figured. He probably taught fencing lessons on the side. Or raced horses.

Amy took charge, script in hand. "Okay, in the jousting scene, Lancelot faces three of Guinevere's finest horsemen." Amy turned to Grady, Sarge, and Pete, who all looked a little green. Steve didn't blame them.

"The scene starts with Sir Lionel," Amy said. "Pete, that means you're riding first. You will be followed by Sir Dinadan. Grady, that's you. Then comes Sir Sagramore. Sarge, you're Sir Sagramore. You're the one who…" She paused and looked at the script. "Oh. Hmm."

"What is it, Amy?" Sarge asked.

"Well, according to the script, you're the one who goes last. You die and then you're prayed back to life by Lancelot. That means you have to fall from the horse—er, mule—and pretend to be dead."

"Hmm." Sarge shrugged, rubbing his hips. "If I fall from B-52, I *will* be dead. Won't even have to act. A'course, that might be problematic for the second show. And the third. And so on." He chuckled.

"I'll take the part of the dead knight," Pete said. "Don't mind a bit. I'll do my best to fall soft. And slow."

"Just be careful, Pete," Steve said, his alarm growing. "We don't need any more broken bones."

"Yes, please be careful," Amy echoed. She turned to Sarge. "Since you and Pete swapped, that means you're up first."

"Are we practicing with real swords?" Sarge asked.

"No." Amy shook her head. "Definitely not. I hadn't really thought about what to use for rehearsal, to be honest. This whole scene has eluded me, which is why I've put it off till now."

"Oh, I know...." Grady went to his car and returned with a couple of fishing poles. "Here ya go, Amy. Perfect for fightin'."

Steve looked on as Grady handed one to Jackson and the other to Sarge. Then he watched, with his stomach in his throat, as Jackson climbed aboard Katie Sue and Sarge mounted the mule. Not that the stubborn animal had any intention of running. Oh no. He seemed content to stand in one place. Forever, apparently.

A gentle swat on the hip from Sarge sent B-52 shooting across the field. Not exactly in the right direction, but at least he was running. Sarge whooped and hollered and finally got the animal turned around. At this point, he and Jackson barreled down the field toward each other, pretending to stab their opponent with a fishing pole. Jackson very nearly succeeded. In fact, he came a little too close, to Steve's way of thinking.

Off in the distance, Blossom, Annabelle, and Gwen cried out, "Get him, Lancelot! Get him!"

"Aren't they supposed to be cheering for Sir Lionel?" Steve asked, pointing to the script. "Someone needs to remind them."

"Oh, that's right." Amy turned to the girls and gave them instructions. Gwen's smile quickly faded.

Sarge climbed off the mule, all smiles. "Well, that was a blast. Haven't had that much fun since I rode a donkey into town back in Vietnam." And off he went on another war story.

"Thanks, Sarge," Amy said, interrupting him. "Okay, Grady's turn."

"Y'all know I'm not a churchgoer," Grady said, climbing aboard B-52. "But I sure could use some prayer right about now." He managed to get the mule in place, though he nearly slid off a time or two in the process.

Steve looked on, wondering how this would end. He watched as Jackson's horse took off across the parking lot and headed straight for Grady, who looked a little pale as he hung on for dear life. B-52 kicked into gear once again and took off running. At the last minute, Jackson threw out his fishing pole and caught Grady's cap.

"Oops. Sorry, Grady," he said.

"Enough already," Steve called out. He took a few angry steps in Amy's direction. "He's being too rough. Lancelot—I mean Jackson."

"What?" She looked his way, confusion registering in her eyes. "You think so?"

"Yes. These other men don't have the…" He hated to say the word. "Skill. They don't have the skill that he does."

"Are you going to let me direct this scene, or would you like to take over?" Amy's tight expression clued him in to her frustration.

"You're working with men here, Amy. You don't understand how crazy this could get if you're not careful."

"Steve, don't be silly. Everything is fine."

"I'm just saying you shouldn't plow ahead without thinking it through. It could get dangerous, especially when we trade in those fishing poles for real swords. Remember that line near the end of the play— 'Might doesn't always mean right'? Well, that applies in this situation."

"You're quoting lines from the play at me?" she asked.

"If that's what it takes. Just trying to put things into perspective." He paused to calm down then carefully chose his words. He lowered his voice to make sure no one else heard. "We need to move carefully. We don't need another accident."

She turned her attention back to the group, clapping her hands. The mist of tears in her eyes gave away her anger. "Let's keep this thing moving." She faced the cast and plastered on a smile. "Okay, guys. Enough jousting. Let's move on to the garden scene, the one where Guinevere and Lancelot declare their undying love."

Ugh. Steve turned away from the crowd, wanting to put an end to this rehearsal here and now. Still, with so many people depending on him, what else could he do but stick around and watch the woman he loved declare her affections for another? Steve had to admit, the idea of Amy and Jackson quoting the mushy lines from the play made him nauseous. Even if they were just acting.

Oh, how he prayed they were acting.

* * * * *

Amy released a breath and counted to ten, trying to put Steve's words out of her mind. *What is his problem?* Did he not realize they only had a few weeks to pull this thing together? She'd put off the jousting scene till now, knowing it would be the toughest one in the show. And yet the rehearsal had gone pretty well. Better than expected. No one had gotten hurt. Why had he created such a scene?

"You ready, fair maiden?" Jackson appeared at her side, the kindness in his eyes calming her at once. "I've been working extra hard on this scene."

"I–I'm ready." She looked at Woody, nerves suddenly getting the best of her. "Are we rehearsing this one outside?"

"Might as well," Woody said, pointing. "Use that bench. It will make a great prop."

Amy took a seat on the bench and released a slow, steady breath, letting go of her angst and preparing for the scene ahead. This would be a tough one. Tougher still with Steve looking on.

"Okay, let's start at the top," Woody said. "Jackson, pick up at the line where you're telling Guinevere how much you love her. Start behind the bench, then work your way around to the front and take a seat next to her."

Amy closed her eyes for a second, getting her bearings. She did her best to ignore the clicking of Mickey's camera. As Jackson's lines began, she found herself caught up in them. How wonderful would it be to have a man speak those intimate words over her...for real. Was such a heartfelt speech really possible from a man's lips, or did all men dance around the "I love you" issue as much as Steve did?

Stop it, Amy. Focus.

As his lines continued, Jackson approached the front of the bench. He sat so close she could feel his breath on her cheek as he spoke his lines. His words held her spellbound, his enunciation perfect, his volume exactly right. More than anything, she loved the cadence of his voice—the rise and fall as he delivered his lines—the genuine emotion he poured into the heart and soul of the character. Something about the lines felt so compelling. By the time he reached the "If Ever I Would Leave You" opening, Amy found herself completely caught up in the moment.

Until she glanced across the field at Steve and saw the pain in his eyes. Then she just felt...confused.

She rose from the bench and slipped her hands into the pockets of her jeans. "We'll have to stop there, Woody. The music CD is inside."

"That's okay. We'll run through Arthur's soliloquy," Woody said. "Steve, c'mon up here and let's get this scene going."

Steve rose and, with everyone looking on, delivered his lines perfectly, every word heartfelt. As Amy listened to his compelling speech—the one where he offered up forgiveness to Guinevere and Lancelot for betraying him—her emotions got the best of her.

Unfortunately, she didn't really have time to process any of this. Off in the distance, an approaching vehicle caught her eye. And when Fred Platt, county commissioner, got out of the car, she realized the other scenes she'd planned to rehearse would very likely have to wait till another day.

Chapter Nineteen

....

As in a theater, the eyes of men, after
a well-graced actor leaves the stage,
are idly bent on him that enters next.

WILLIAM SHAKESPEARE

Fewer than ten minutes after the county commissioner interrupted the rehearsal, Amy dismissed the cast. What would be the point of continuing, with Steve in such a strange mood and Fred Platt consuming so much of his time? No, she'd rather pack it in and go for a drive. Only then would she be able to clear her thoughts and think. And pray. Maybe she still had time to get God's perspective on all of this before she opened her mouth and said something she'd later regret.

"Walk with me?" Jackson asked, drawing near. "I've got to put Katie Sue in the trailer."

"Sure." She stepped into place beside him as he guided the mare across the parking lot, beyond Lucy's powder-puff pink car, and past the pest control van.

At first Jackson made small talk. But after a while he shifted gears. "You okay?" he asked, giving her a sideways glance. "You seem a little..."

"Stressed?" Amy sighed. "It's okay. You can say it. You won't hurt my feelings."

He nodded and patted the horse on the rump to get her to walk up the ramp to the back of the trailer. "Yeah. Stressed. Guess that's the right word. Just don't seem yourself." The horse let out a whinny but made her way into the trailer. That job done, Jackson turned to Amy. "Was there something wrong with that scene we acted out? Are you upset by my performance or something?"

"Good grief, no." She groaned, wondering why he'd even ask such a thing. "Just the opposite. I thank God every day that you've come to Camelot, trust me."

"You do?" He quirked a brow and a boyish grin lit his face. "That's good to hear."

Immediately her stomach felt queasy. "Oh, I didn't mean...well, you know. Glad for the sake of the play."

"Ah." His eyes never left hers. "Just the play?"

So she hadn't been imagining it. He really thought he stood a chance with her. Surely he realized she and Steve were...

What were they, after all? Would you really call it "boyfriend and girlfriend" at their age? And could you call it that if you weren't exactly getting along? Steve seemed to be upset at her today. And she...

She needed time to think. Something felt off, and she had to chew on it for a while.

"I have to get out of here, Jackson," Amy said. "We can talk more tomorrow. But right now I need to take a drive."

"Gotcha."

She turned on her heels and headed for her car on the far end of the parking lot. As she passed Steve, she offered up a little wave. He responded with a nod but didn't say anything. So strange. Oh well. Hopefully nothing a bubble bath and a good night's sleep wouldn't cure. After a long drive in the hills.

As she pulled out of the parking lot, Amy's gaze shifted to Pastor Crane's hearse. It seemed oddly ironic, since everything inside of her— the feelings she'd shared with Steve, her hopes for a great production, her plan to save the town—suddenly felt like it had died. Her hopes had been buried alive, swallowed up in an instant.

She pulled out of the parking lot and onto the highway, her breathing coming a little easier as she rounded the first bend in the road.

For as long as Amy could remember, driving had served as her cure-all for life's ills. The backwoods of Tennessee could lift the spirits of anyone, even the weepiest woman. And that's what she was right now. Weepy.

She turned off toward town, the winding road bringing a strange sense of relief. And when she turned off onto Merlin Circle, her pain lifted. Really, was there anywhere on earth where the contrast of colors was more vivid? Was she the only one who noticed it? The trees practically hugged her on Merlin Circle. They were so close together they almost made her feel a part of them.

Amy continued to drive as the road stretched out in front of her for a spell. Then, just as quickly, she hit a winding patch. She contemplated how much her life felt like that road, taking her places she never dreamed she would go. Okay, some she didn't exactly *want* to go to—but she learned something about herself at each stop along the way. Some spots were higher than others, some were lower. But they were all part of the journey. And for some odd reason, today the journey seemed longer—and tougher—than ever.

* * * * *

Steve watched as Amy pulled away in her car. She hadn't even said good-bye. Okay, she'd tried to communicate with him through a wave, but he'd… Steve sighed. He'd ignored it, his heart too heavy to respond. What he should have done—what he'd do next time—

was sweep her into his arms and kiss her soundly, then share every thought in his head about how she made him feel.

Well, how she made him feel on a good day.

Today, he just felt…jealous. Yes, *jealous* was surely the word. And now he had to face the added frustration of a lengthy conversation with Fred Platt. Perfect. Just what he needed to wrap up a wonderful afternoon. What would happen next? An incoming storm? A newspaper headline announcing the doomed production?

He looked up just in time to see Mickey talking to the commissioner with his writing tablet and pen in hand. Oh no. He would have to head this thing off at the pass, and quick. Steve took a few determined steps in their direction, interrupting their conversation with a brusque nod. "Fred, I'm all yours. Would you like to go inside?"

"No, let's walk around back. I need to point out a few remaining concerns. It won't take long this time, I promise."

"Okay."

Steve spent the next ten minutes talking through Fred's short list of concerns, including a spot for handicapped parking and a wheelchair ramp. Not quite as bad as he'd anticipated, really, and things he'd already put on his to-be-addressed list, anyway.

By the time they arrived back in the parking lot, most of the ladies had gone. Sarge and Jackson stood next to the horse trailer, talking and laughing.

"I'll be in my car, filling out some paperwork," Fred said. "Will you be around for a few minutes, in case I have any more questions?"

"Sure, I'll hang around." Steve glanced at his watch: 6:39. "I need to talk to a couple of the guys, anyway. We've got a lot going on around here."

From across the parking lot, Pete gave him a wave. "Steve, do you have a few minutes?" he called out.

"Sure." Steve headed toward the pest control van, his gaze shifting to poor Bugsy, who still clung to the top as if his life depended on it. Maybe it did. As he drew near, Steve couldn't help but notice that Pete appeared to be flustered. "You okay? You look a little... I don't know. Ill?"

"Ah. Well, I, um..." Pete's sigh spoke volumes.

"Spit it out."

"All right. I want to talk to you about...well, women."

"Ugh." Steve groaned. "Do we have to?" *Today, of all days?*

"Just need some advice. Do you mind?"

"What kind of advice?"

"I'd rather talk privately," Pete said. He gestured to his van.

"Sure. I guess." Another glance at his watch followed. Steve climbed into the pest control van, the aroma nearly doing him in. After a few minutes, however, he became acclimated to the odor. Mostly. From the passenger seat—with the window rolled down, anyway—he could barely smell it anymore.

From his spot in the driver's seat, Pete turned his way. "I feel so ridiculous talking to you about this. Don't know why I even bothered you, now that we're in here. I feel like an idiot."

"No, it's okay." Steve squirmed in the seat; the springs were giving him a little trouble. "What's up?"

Pete's face contorted. "It's Lucy."

"Lucy Cramden?" Steve felt his curiosity pique. "What about her?"

"I've tried every which way to get her attention, but she's just not seeing me. Sometimes I think I'll have to perform some sort of miraculous act to get her to focus on me. She's only got eyes for Charlie Hart. My gut tells me he's not interested in her. Otherwise, I wouldn't even dare to hope. But still..."

"I hear ya."

"Don't know what else I can do." Pete slumped over the steering wheel, a look of defeat on his face. "Guess she's just not interested. Either that or she's just distracted."

"I hear ya."

"You said that already." Pete gave him a curious look. "You okay?"

"No. To be honest, I'm having a few female problems of my own." Steve started to open his mouth to share about Amy but stopped himself. No point in stealing the conversation away from Pete. Besides, what would he say?

"You are?" Pete gave him a compassionate nod. "Feeling a little insecure with Jackson on the scene?"

"Not sure 'insecure' is the right word. He's just so stinkin'..."

"Perfect?"

"Yeah." Steve sighed. "I feel like an idiot even saying it, but the guy is just too perfect. There's got to be a chink in his armor somewhere."

"And you're going to find it?"

"I keep looking for one. Can't seem to find anything—not yet, anyway." Steve watched through the open window as Jackson continued chatting and laughing with Sarge, who couldn't seem to stop smiling. "Everyone loves the guy. He's great."

"Only..."

"Only, I don't. Which is wrong. I'm supposed to love everybody. Can't really call myself a Christian if I don't. But..." His gaze lingered on Sarge, who climbed into the passenger seat of his vehicle, letting Jackson take the wheel. "See there? See what a great grandson he is? Always making things easier on others. Always has the solution for every problem. Has a great attitude. Generous to a fault."

"Yeah. He's a great guy." Pete gestured out the window at Grady, who approached the van with an inquisitive look on his face. "Looks like we've got company. Do you mind?"

"No, I guess not."

Grady opened the sliding door on the side of the van and climbed inside. A couple of minutes later, Chuck joined them. Then Darrell.

"What's happening in here?" Darrell asked as he climbed inside. "A party?"

"Hardly," Pete said. "We're talking about women."

"Ah." Darrell's expression brightened. "I like the subject matter."

"That's because you haven't had your heart broken yet," Pete said, slumping again over the steering wheel.

"Yeah," Steve echoed. He turned his attention to the window, watching as Jackson and Sarge pulled away. After a moment's pause, he looked at the other men and shrugged. "Eula Mae says I should write Amy a song."

"A song?" Pete appeared to be thinking about that.

"Yeah. She says women need wooing and I'm apparently not very good at that."

"Hmm." Grady cleared his throat. "Well, since y'all brought up the subject 'a women and all, I've got a couple 'a questions."

Steve turned back to look at him. "Like what?"

"I can't stop thinkin' 'bout that scene you just acted out," Grady said, the furrows in his brow growing deeper.

"The forgiveness scene?" Steve asked.

"Yep." Grady nodded. "Seems like Arthur really loved Guinevere. And Lancelot too."

"Right." Steve nodded. "He did."

"And he forgave them. In spite of what they did to him."

"Yes." Steve bit back his thoughts on that issue. Grady would have to bring this up, today of all days.

Grady exhaled and shrugged. "I don't get that. If someone took off with my girl, I'd knock his head off. I wouldn't forgive 'im. What'd make a person wanta do that?"

"Love." Steve and Pete spoke the word in unison then looked at each other and shrugged.

"Love?" Grady didn't look convinced.

"I know you're not a churchgoer, Grady," Steve said. "And I don't mean to preach, so don't take this as a sermon. I just see so many similarities between the story of King Arthur and the story of God's love for us."

"What do you mean?"

"Well, you said it yourself. It was his deep love for those who broke his heart that triggered his forgiveness. Same with God. It was His deep love for us—the ones who sinned and broke His heart—that triggered His forgiveness."

"I'm not followin' ya," Grady said. "How did I hurt God's heart?"

"We all do it, Grady." Steve chose his words carefully. "We put ourselves first. We forget how much God has done for us and chase after things that we think can bring us fulfillment. In a sense, I guess you could say we've cheated on God like Guinevere and Lancelot cheated on Arthur. And God chose to offer forgiveness, even when it didn't make sense."

"Ah." Grady appeared to be in thought. "Wonder why He did that. I probably would've just wiped 'em out."

"Me too." Steve nodded. "Arthur had a choice in how he reacted, and he chose to sacrifice his pride and forgive."

"Compassion isn't a sign of weakness," Darrell threw in. "God loves us even in our sin."

Even as his brother spoke the words, shame swept over Steve. He didn't have time to think about it, though, because a rap on the door caught his attention.

"Lookee there," Grady said. "It's Woody and Charlie. Hope they don't mind a little sermonizing."

Steve sighed. Had his impassioned response to Grady's question really come across as a sermon? If so, he'd been preaching to himself more than anyone else.

"Probably wondering what we're doing in here," Darrell said. He opened the side door and gestured for them to climb inside.

"Smells like an exterminator's convention in here," Woody said, waving his free arm. "If we're having a meeting, I can think of a thousand other places I'd rather hold it." He let out a sneeze. Then another. And another.

"Hey, now." Pete shot him a warning glance. "Don't be knocking my business. I don't criticize your directing skills."

"Sorry." Woody climbed in then looked around for a place to sit.

"Somebody move that container over for him," Pete said. "Just be careful while you're doing it. Don't want to risk any leakage. That stuff's pretty potent."

"So what are you guys talking about, anyway?" Charlie asked, climbing in behind Woody. "Everyone looks so serious." He pulled over a box and sat on it.

"Women." All of the guys spoke in unison.

"Ah." A suspicious smile crossed Charlie's face. Very interesting.

Apparently Pete noticed it too. His eyes narrowed and his brows seemed to thicken.

"Women are a mystery, aren't they?" Charlie said. "Like mythical beings, really. They bring such joy to our lives."

Pete squirmed in his seat, and for a moment Steve thought the two men might have words over Lucy Cramden. He didn't have long to think about it, however. From across the parking lot, something caught Steve's eye. He watched as Fred Platt got out of his car and took a couple of steps toward the Civic Center. Just a few feet shy of the building, Mickey joined him and the two men began to engage in conversation.

"I smell trouble." Steve shook his head, wondering what he could do to stop the situation from snowballing.

"That's not what I smell." Darrell pinched his nose. "Pete, I've gotta give it to you. Don't know how you work with these chemicals all day long. I think they're frying my brain."

"Really? I don't even notice it anymore." Pete shrugged.

Steve leaned out the open window, hoping to distract Fred from Mickey's prying questions. "Over here, guys."

Fred nodded and walked toward the van, with Mickey following close behind. Darrell opened the side door once again, gesturing for the two men to join them.

"Are we gonna fit in here?" Fred asked, looking around. "This van is packed out."

"Shore." Grady moved over. "We can always make more room."

"What's so hush-hush?" Mickey asked as he climbed inside. "Big story brewing in here?" His nose wrinkled and he sneezed. "Smells like something else brewing, actually."

"Women," Grady said. "We're talkin' 'bout women."

"Oh." At once Mickey's face tightened. "Not sure I'd better stick around, then." He shifted as if ready to bolt.

"Oh no, you don't," Chuck said, taking hold of his arm. "You've meddled in our lives for weeks now. It's about time we got to know you too. If you've got a story about women, we want to hear it."

Mickey sighed. "Don't think so. I'm a closed book."

"Time to open it, then," Steve said. "You're in good company, man. Trust me. Your stories are safe here."

"Which is more than we can say about our stories in that newspaper of yours," Woody muttered.

"Out with it," Pete said.

Mickey started reluctantly. Slowly. He spoke of a broken marriage and an attempt to reunite with his estranged wife. By the end of his conversation, Steve felt like applauding the man for opening up and sharing his heart in such a vulnerable way.

Chuck took it from there, offering advice and talking about his blossoming relationship with Annabelle. Steve listened in, amazed by the depth in his voice. He also found it interesting that Chuck, a butcher, could articulate his thoughts about women so beautifully.

Then Grady took over, surprising everyone with his announcement that he'd had his eye on Blossom for months. Who knew?

Woody went next, confessing his love for Eula Mae and sharing that his time in the hospital had only served to cement his feelings. Steve had to smile as the older man added a few additional thoughts on where he planned to take her for their honeymoon, should he work up the courage to pop the question. Disneyland. Wouldn't that be interesting?

Then Pete spoke up, his voice trembling as he shared about his affection for Lucy Cramden. He occasionally glanced back, as if to ask, "Charlie, are you listening? You have a problem with all of this?"

Ironically, Charlie Hart sat in utter silence, not saying a word but his gaze shifting out the window. Steve couldn't help but wonder about his unwillingness to join in. Very odd. And very unlike Charlie, who usually talked more than most of the other men put together.

Fred Platt didn't have anything to say either, though the pained expression on his face spoke volumes. Steve had a feeling there was more to the man than he realized. Far more.

"Anything you want to add, Fred?" Steve asked finally.

The county commissioner shrugged. "I've got a great wife. Two kids. But we've separated a couple of times. My wife says I'm married to my job."

Mickey grunted. "Ironic. My wife left me because she said I was married to my job. So that's not the answer. I've come to the conclusion that work is a great filler till love comes along."

Steve found himself caught up in listening to the men and wanting to—what was it Grady had called it again? Oh yes. Sermonizing. He wanted to sermonize. To tell Mickey that there was a love greater than the one he'd experienced in his broken marriage, one that wouldn't fail him. Still, with his heart in his throat, he could barely manage a word, let alone a whole speech.

"So let's go back to that idea Eula Mae had," Grady said, interrupting Steve's thoughts. "She said Steve should write Amy a song."

"Yeah." Steve shrugged. "But I'm no songwriter."

"Neither am I," Chuck threw in. "But maybe if we all worked together, we could come up with a song—not just one for Amy, but for all our girls."

"All our girls?" Pete sighed. "I can't even get mine to look twice at me."

"Well, maybe she will after she hears us sing this song we're going to write." Chuck nodded. "It could work."

"Wait." Pete shook his head. "Now we have to sing too?"

"Sure, why not?" Chuck laughed. "The ladies will have to give us an *A* for effort if we write 'em a song and sing it." He paused. "Just have to think of the perfect time to do it. Timing is everything." Chuck began to hum an unfamiliar tune. "You got any paper in this van, Pete?" he asked when he stopped. "An idea is coming to me."

Pete reached under his seat and pulled out a clipboard with several invoices on it. "Don't think it's terribly romantic to write a song on a Contract Killer Pest Control invoice," he said. "Let me see if I can find a scrap of blank paper." He rummaged around and came up with an old church bulletin, which he passed Chuck's way. "Just use the page inside that they leave blank for sermon notes."

"Okay." Chuck took the page. "I'm thinking it needs to be something really romantic." After a few seconds of silence, he groaned. "Nothing's coming to me."

"Give me that stupid piece of paper," Mickey demanded. "I never claimed to be a songwriter, but I've written a poem or two in my day. And I am a reporter, you know. We do know how to write."

"Great idea!" Grady said. "It's 'bout time you did sumpthin' helpful 'round here."

"I like the idea a lot," Pete added. "Mickey, you're the perfect choice. Just add something really flowery and nice to sway the women, okay? Our lives—well, our hearts—are dependent on it."

"No pressure." Mickey scribbled a few words then scratched through them. Then jotted a few more. And a few more. His wrinkled brow spoke of a deep concentration level, but no one dared interrupt him. "What do you think of this?" he asked at last. He proceeded to share what he'd written, his words lyrical and romantic. Steve could hardly believe something that beautiful could have come out of the hard-edged reporter.

"It's great," Chuck said. "Sounds like a song from a radio."

"Do I detect suspicious behavior inside this vehicle?" The voice from outside the van startled Steve, who jerked and rammed his elbow into the door. He looked over to see Joe O'Reilly standing there in his police uniform with a curious look on his face.

Steve spoke through the open window. "Hey, Joe."

"Hey yourself. Everyone all right in there?" Joe leaned forward, clearly curious.

"Talking about women," Pete explained. "Decided we'd all stay in here till we had 'em figured out."

Joe grinned. "Hope none of you have any plans for the next twenty or thirty years. Should I call out for a pizza? Maybe order breakfast while I'm at it?"

"Good idea." Steve laughed. "I'm getting plenty hungry in here. What about the rest of you guys? Want to head over to the diner for something to eat?"

A rapid succession of yesses followed.

Darrell opened the side door of the van, and one by one the men climbed out.

"I hate to be rude," Joe said, "but you fellas smell like you've been baptized in pesticide."

"We have," Pete said. "And we're better men for it."

"Amen to that," Chuck said. "Feel like I've been reborn."

"I feel like I need a shower." Grady paused, his gaze shifting up to Bugsy.

Steve joined the men staring at the gaping hole in Bugsy's side. It seemed strangely symbolic. "Do you suppose we'll ever figure out what happened to him?" he asked.

All of the men grew silent. Grady even removed his cap.

Pete exhaled loudly, his eyes growing misty. "The way I look at it, it had to be a woman who did this to Bugsy."

"A woman?" Steve looked Pete's way, dumbfounded. "Why do you say that?"

"Because..." Pete brushed at his eyes with the back of his hand then looked Steve in the eyes. "Only a woman could leave a fella *that* torn up."

Chapter Twenty

....

Acting is not a mystery. There's nothing that I
know that other actors don't know.
We all act, we're all actors, we all know the same thing.
The only thing that separates us is experience.

Vincent D'Onofrio

Less than a week before the show was set to open, Steve found himself shifting into overdrive. Between his work at City Hall and the final plans for the build-out of the theater, he'd hardly slept a wink in days. Not to mention the Camelot rehearsals, which—due to technical difficulties—had taken twice as long as anyone had expected. Who knew the sound and lights guys would have such a big challenge with the outdoor theater setup?

Still, as the hours tilted forward and opening day drew nearer, one thing remained abundantly clear. They would—and could—do this. With the Lord's help. And it was the Lord Steve leaned on, as never before.

Midafternoon on Monday he pulled into the parking lot of the Civic Center, surprised by all the other cars. In fact, he'd never seen the place so crowded. In the field to his right, Grady and Chuck worked to section off areas for additional parking. Come Friday night, they were going to need it. He hoped. In the chaos of preparing for the show, only one lingering question remained. Well, one critical question. Would the people come? Would folks really show up and support their tiny town by attending performances? Sure, they'd sold a couple dozen tickets, but most of those were to locals. Could they really sustain this effort, or would the whole thing be in vain?

Don't think like that, Steve. Keep a positive mental outlook.

He had to do that, for both his sake and Amy's. Over the past week or so, she hadn't been herself. He'd never seen her so stressed out. Steve had kept his distance, in part because of her ever-growing moodiness and in part because she seemed to prefer the distance. He prayed it would end soon.

Charlie pulled into the parking lot behind Steve, taking the spot next to him.

Is that a woman in the car with him?

Sure enough. And not exactly who he might have imagined. As soon as the realization settled in, Steve got out of his vehicle and walked over to the passenger side of Charlie's truck. Opening the door, he called her by name. "Caroline?"

She gave him a shy smile. "Hey, honey. Charlie was good enough to stop by and pick me up. I didn't feel like driving today."

"You're not feeling well?" Steve leaned against the truck. "Why didn't you tell me? You know how concerned I've been."

"Oh, it's not that," she said. "I just thought it would be nice to ride with someone else for a change." A smile turned up the edges of her lips. "Now, where is Amy? Natalie and I were supposed to meet with her to redo the hem in her wedding gown. Have you seen her?"

"Not yet." Steve shook his head, now turning his gaze to Charlie.

"Amy's been pretty emotional," Charlie said. "Thought I saw her crying in church yesterday. You know how private she is, though. Wouldn't let anyone know even if she was upset."

"I think she's just exhausted," Steve said. "And feeling the weight of all of this because she suggested the idea in the first place."

"She knows we're not holding her responsible if this thing doesn't fly," Charlie said. "I'm not sure why she takes on so much responsibility."

"She's always been like that," Steve said. "For as long as I can remember. She gets these ideas, dives in headfirst, then beats herself up when things don't work out." He paused, reflecting on his words. "But we have nothing to worry about this time. It's going to work. We've done our part. Now it's time for the Lord to do what only He can do."

Charlie smiled. "Amen to that. It takes faith to step out and build something, even before you know it's going to work."

"This whole thing has been a faith move—for the community and for us as individuals," Steve said. "I think God's watching closely to see if we falter at the last minute. That's why we've got to keep on keepin' on, even when things get tough. And from what I've heard from Woody, the final week of rehearsals can get plenty tough."

"Hope we're up for the task," Charlie said.

"I'm going to head inside and look for her," Caroline said. "Maybe I can cheer her up." She headed off in the direction of the Civic Center.

Pete pulled into the parking lot next and got out of his van, a look of excitement on his face. "Did you see what's going on in town?" he asked. "Haven't seen this much frenzy since Woody drove through the plate-glass window of the Sack 'n Save."

"Are you talking about the RV park?" Steve nodded. "It's almost done. Eula Mae set up a phone line for people to call for reservations. We have a handful coming in Thursday. That's when we'll set up the tents in Lance's parking lot for the vendors. We're expecting quite a few of them, so there will be food and shopping for our tourists. I expect it will grow over time."

"Yes, and did you see all of the goings-on at the diner?" Pete asked. "Ellie Parker is on a roll, adding more booths and turning the storage room into a workspace for their new catering business. She's got great plans for the food for the show. I've never seen her so excited."

"That's the point," Steve said. "I haven't seen our townspeople this energetic for years. It's like we've had an injection of hope. And hope is a good thing. It's what we've been lacking around here for the past few years. Your daughter had a good idea, Charlie. She really did."

"Yep." Charlie smiled, his eyes twinkling. "Gotta agree with you there. Putting on this play has been great for all of us. And I like what you said about hope. I'm a firm believer in looking ahead to better days." He glanced across the field in the direction of the Civic Center.

"Speaking of better days..." Pete grinned. "I had a little talk with the Lord about Lucy Cramden after church yesterday."

"Oh?" Charlie and Steve spoke in unison.

"Yep. He told me to be patient. That good things come to them that wait. So I'm waiting."

Off in the distance, Eula Mae's voice rang out. "Yoo-hoo! Steve. I need to talk to you."

"Sorry, fellas," he said. "When Eula Mae calls, I don't dare delay."

Charlie laughed. "She's got you whipped."

"Yep. But I've learned to live with it."

"Good preparation for marriage, I suppose," Pete said.

Steve thought about those words as he crossed the parking lot in Eula Mae's direction. How could he even begin to think about marriage when the woman he loved had distanced herself from him?

"Steve." Eula Mae gestured for him to come to the door of the Civic Center.

"What's up?"

"We need to talk." Her strained whisper was barely audible.

"Why are we whispering?" he responded, his voice lowered to match hers.

"Because…" She gestured with her head. "That county official is still out in the parking lot. You never know. He might have the whole place bugged."

"Bugged." Steve chuckled as he echoed the word. "We've got a pest-control expert on hand, Eula Mae, so we can take care of that in a hurry."

She didn't seem to get his joke. Her expression didn't soften. "I'm just saying, the fellow could be a spy," she whispered.

"No, Fred is a great guy," Steve said. "And I invited him to come to the rehearsal today. Besides, I've got good news. He stopped by the office earlier and dropped off the paperwork from the county."

"Have you tested it for traces of poison?" Eula Mae whispered. "That's how they get you, you know. You touch it and then put your hands to your mouth, and…*wham*. You're dead."

"Eula Mae, you're not listening. We passed the inspection. We've been given an eleventh-hour stay. They're not shutting us down. We've been cleared to have the performance. We're good to go."

"Oh." She released a breath. "Well, I'm still whispering."

"Why?"

"Woody just pulled into the parking lot and is headed our way." She glared at Steve. "You had to go and buy him a hearing aid."

"Well, sure." Steve nodded. "What's wrong with that?"

She lowered her voice a bit more, her gaze darting out to the parking lot. "I liked him better when he couldn't hear me."

"Why is that?"

"Because." She shook her head. "I was always muttering things under my breath whenever he got me riled up, and now he can hear every word."

"What have you got to be riled up about?"

"Not sure." She sighed. "Just feel like I'm on the slow boat to China with that man. We're like the tortoise and the hare. I'm the hare, in case you're wondering. And now things are more complicated than ever because he can actually hear what I'm saying." She glared at Steve. "See what you've done? You've taken the zing out of our romance."

"Well, I didn't mean to take the zing out of your romance, Eula Mae." Placing a hand on her shoulder, he said, "But just so you know, Woody's head over heels in love with you."

"Oh?" A smile lit her face.

"Yes, and he's not whispering about it," Steve said. "In fact, he's been shouting it at the top of his lungs. So you might as well stop muttering and tell him how you feel."

"Someone talking about me behind my back?" Woody's voice rang out.

Steve turned and smiled then gestured at Eula Mae. "Yes, we were talking about you. But I think it might be a good thing if someone started talking *to* you, instead." He gave Eula Mae a gentle nudge in Woody's direction.

She sighed and then whispered, "I don't know what to say."

"Sure you do," Woody said, pulling her close. "Just tell this crazy old fool that you love him, and we can get on with the show."

Steve began to walk away just as Eula Mae let out a little giggle. Looked like the zing hadn't really gone out of their romance after all. Now if he could only figure out how to put it back into his own.

* * * * *

Amy paced the new theater, her mind reeling. *Set pieces. Check. Theater build-out. Check. Well, except for the restrooms, but they're*

*coming along nicely. Costumes. Check. All but Pellinore's, but that's
okay. Natalie will get that done.*

Natalie. Hmm.

The last time she'd seen Natalie, the poor woman had been
unable to stand because of her swollen feet. Still, with Caroline's
help, she finished up most of the costumes.

Thinking of Caroline reminded Amy of Steve, of course. He'd
been acting so strange lately. A little distant, even. Then again, she
hadn't gone out of her way to rekindle their romance. Her thoughts
had been on one thing only—the play.

"The play's the thing," she reminded herself.

"No, the *people* are the thing," Caroline said, drawing near. "But
I understand what you're saying. And I do have to admit that putting
on a play can be consuming. We've more than proven that. It's taken
its toll on quite a few people."

Amy tried not to let her dismay show. Still, Caroline had just
deflated any enthusiasm she might've mustered up moments before.
Unfortunately—or fortunately—she didn't have time to dwell on it.
Pastor Crane approached, concern etched in his brow.

"Everything okay?" Amy asked.

"Yes." He nodded. "We had three funerals this week, and poor
Natalie's run ragged. Have you seen her?"

"Yep." Caroline nodded. "She's inside ironing Arthur's wedding
doublet. Looks like she's ready to pop, so I made her sit down to do
the rest of the ironing."

"She's not due for three more weeks," he said, "but she's
miserable."

"Pretty common in the last month," Caroline said. "Make sure
she puts her feet up when you get home tonight."

"I've been massaging them for her every night." The sweetest look passed over him. "I do what I can. Sure can't carry the baby for her."

"Wait a few weeks, and you'll be able to do that," Caroline said. "But by then, Natalie probably won't want to let go of him. Trust me on that."

Something about this conversation made Amy feel a little...odd. Sad, even. What would it be like to have the man you loved walk you through a pregnancy? To have him kneel at your feet and massage them, speaking words of love over you?

"A penny for your thoughts." Jackson's voice stirred her from her thoughts.

"Oh, hey." She offered a weak smile.

"Hey yourself. Getting excited?"

"Yes." She paused. "I was just about to ask how things are going with ticket sales on the website. We've been so worried about what will happen if the town is overrun with people, we've never stopped to consider the opposite."

"What do you mean?" Pastor Crane asked.

"What if no one comes? What if we've done all of this and can't sell any tickets?"

"We're already selling tickets," he said. "I checked the website last night; we've sold a couple dozen."

"To residents," she countered. "Probably."

Pastor Crane reached out and put his hand on Amy's arm. "Have faith. God's got this one covered, Amy. Deep breath."

"It will all work out. You'll see," Caroline reassured her. "Although if you could come inside when you're free, we could see to the hem of your wedding dress and that would be one less thing to think about." She smiled at Amy and waited for her nod before turning back toward the Civic Center.

As Caroline and Pastor Crane walked away, talking about Natalie's delicate condition, Amy couldn't help but feel pretty delicate herself. Not just frazzled. More...run-down. Exhausted. She prayed she would make it through these next few days.

"Did you happen to check the weather report?" Jackson's voice interrupted her thoughts.

"No. Why?" Amy gave him a curious look.

"Well, there's a storm front coming in from the northwest. It's supposed to hit us in a couple of days."

"No." She dropped into the seat, defeat setting in.

"It's just a storm, Amy. It will pass." He took the seat next to her.

"No, it's not just a storm," she argued. "It's another in a long line of interruptions to my plan to put on a show." She'd no sooner uttered the words "my plan" before conviction settled in. "I mean, God's plan."

He reached over and took her hand, giving it a squeeze. "Yes, it's God's plan. And because it's His and not ours, we can rest easy in the fact that He's got the details ironed out. Even the part where the storm rolls in. So do what Pastor Crane suggested. Take a deep breath."

His gentle gaze distracted her momentarily. Why was he always so...nice? Why couldn't he just be snippy every now and again? Why couldn't he avoid her, like Steve was doing? Did he have to show up every time she needed someone to hold her hand and offer words of comfort?

Shaking off her thoughts of men—Jackson in particular—Amy rose. "I've got to gather the troops. We were supposed to start ten minutes ago." She quickly made the rounds, inside the Civic Center and out, rounding up her cast and crew. After giving a few last-minute instructions to the techies and musicians, Amy gathered the cast together to pray. Her excitement grew as she saw them all in their costumes for the first time. They might be a ragtag lot, but they sure cleaned up nice. Even Chuck, the butcher, looked like a million bucks in his knightly attire.

Instinctively, she looked to Steve to lead them in an opening prayer. Would he still be willing? His warm smile convinced her that he would. And sure enough, his powerful words to the Lord gave her just the courage she needed to move forward. *We can do this, Lord. But You've got to help us. Otherwise, it's just going to be a big mess.*

After the prayer, Annabelle led the others in a warm-up, starting with toe touches. Amy chuckled as she watched her father attempt to touch his toes.

"It ain't happenin'!" he called out. "Either my legs are getting longer as I age or my arms are getting shorter. Either way, I can't reach the ground anymore."

Amy laughed. For a moment, anyway. A few seconds later, something distracted her. Looking at Annabelle in her soft blue gown, Amy had to conclude the obvious. The store clerk might've started out as a size eighteen, but the dress now hung on her like a sack of potatoes. Looked like this choreography gig had more than energized her spirit; it had taken off a few pounds. Maybe more than a few.

"Annabelle, when you get a minute, let's talk." Amy flashed an encouraging smile.

When the warm-up period ended, the cast members were sent to their places backstage and Annabelle approached Amy with a look of concern in her eyes.

"Is everything okay?"

"Oh yes." She offered a relaxed smile. "No biggie. Just wanted to suggest that you stop in to see Caroline and Natalie before you leave today. You'll need to change out of that costume so they can take up the seams."

"Take up the seams?"

"Well, sure. It's falling off of you."

"It is?" Annabelle looked down. "Crazy. I've been so busy, I didn't notice." She tugged at the waistline, which hung loose. "Guess you're right."

"If we don't take it up, you'll be tripping all over yourself. Might as well take care of it now." She paused and smiled. "And by the way, you look great. Love the new hairstyle."

"Oh, thanks." Annabelle grinned. "It was Blossom's idea. You know how she is. She's been wanting to experiment on me for years, but I wouldn't let her. But something about this show gave me the courage to try new things, so I decided to let her go for it."

"'Go for it,'" Amy echoed. "I like those words. They seem pretty fitting right now, don't they? That's what we're all about to do— go for it."

And go for it, they did. The next two hours were spent wriggling and winding their way through Act One. Talk about ups and downs! Just about the time Amy thought she could catch her breath, another catastrophe hit.

They'd just taken a break to eat dinner when Gwen came running Amy's direction. "Amy, come quick!" The pained expression on Gwen's face, coupled with her breathless words, left nothing to the imagination. Something terrible had happened.

Turning on her heel, Amy followed her across the stage to the back, where she found Sarge in a heap on the floor. Jackson knelt on his right and Steve on his left. Steve worked feverishly, checking his breathing and pulse.

"I called 911," Gwen said, her eyes filled with tears. "They're on their way."

"What happened?"

"I'm not sure. He was acting a little funny all morning." Gwen shrugged. "Saying some odd things and looking a little lost. But with Sarge, it's kind of hard to know...ya know?"

"Right." Amy nodded but didn't say more for fear of hurting Jackson's feelings.

"Then, just before you called us to break for dinner, he started talking kind of crazy. His words were slurred. And the next thing I knew, he said he had to sit down. But there wasn't time to sit. Down he went." Gwen's eyes filled with tears.

Steve looked up, and Amy could read the concern in his eyes. "I'm pretty sure it's a stroke. I hope the paramedics get here soon."

"Is—is he breathing?"

"He's breathing and his pulse is steady," Steve said with a nod. "But I'd feel better if—" Off in the distance a siren pealed out, and Amy sighed with relief. Minutes later, two paramedics pushed their way through the crowd and went to work on Sarge right away. One of them spoke into the walkie-talkie on his shoulder. In the meantime, the entire cast gathered around, many of them ushering up quiet prayers. Steve asked everyone to step back, his voice commanding authority.

One of the paramedics ran toward the ambulance, returning with a stretcher. Within minutes Sarge was situated on it, his eyes closed and an oxygen mask firmly in place.

"Where are you taking him?" Jackson asked. "I want to come with you."

"You can follow us," the paramedic said. "Hope you're up for a drive. He needs to go to the medical center in Knoxville."

Jackson's eyes widened and he nodded.

"Do you want me to go with you?" Amy asked.

"I..." He shook his head. "No. Amy, you've got to stay here and keep going. This rehearsal is too important. If the second act doesn't get knocked out, we don't have a show."

"What good is a show when the people in it are hurting?" Amy felt the tears rise.

"I'll go with him, Amy." Gwen gave her an imploring look. "If you're okay with that."

"Of course."

She stepped back, watching as the paramedics continued their work. In the midst of the struggle to elevate the stretcher, Sarge seemed to jar awake. For a moment, he looked as clear-eyed as a youngster ready to head outdoors to play. His lips began to move beneath the oxygen mask, and he grabbed at it, pulling it loose. His lips continued to move, the words faint...barely distinguishable.

"Didn't—mean—to—do—it." Each strained word sounded weaker than the one before it. Sarge's eyes fluttered closed once more.

"Do what, Gramps?" Jackson asked, leaning over the stretcher. "You didn't mean to do what?"

Sarge's eyes popped open once again, and the oxygen mask trembled as he tried to grip it. "Didn't—mean—to—shoot—"

"Shoot?" everyone echoed.

"Shoot who?" Jackson asked. "Gramps, who did you shoot?"

The old man's eyes grew wide and his next words rang out, clear as a church bell on a Sunday morning.

"Bu–Bugsy," he said, the spark now gone from his eyes. "I—shot—Bu–Bu–Bugsy."

Chapter Twenty-One

....

Acting is like a high wire act. Your margin for error is very slim.

CHRISTINE BARANSKI

Amy looked over the programs for the show, frustrated by the typos she found there. "These will have to be redone."

"You think?" her father asked, looking over her shoulder. "They look pretty good to me."

"Look how Eula Mae spelled Grady's name." She pointed to the word *G-r-o-d-y* and winced. "And she only put one *n* in Annabelle's name. These are little things, but we'll need to get them ironed out so no one gets offended."

"Speaking of people getting offended, what's going on with Pete and Lucy Cramden?"

She gave her father a curious look. "What do you mean?"

"Well, the other day when we had our Come to Jesus meeting in the pest control van, Pete looked pretty upset."

"Wait." He'd lost her. "Come to Jesus meeting in the pest control van? What are you talking about?"

"Oh." He clamped his mouth shut and said nothing.

"Dad, c'mon. What are you talking about?"

"Well, a bunch of the guys—mostly Steve and Pete—wanted to get together to talk about women."

"Steve...wanted to talk about women?"

"Yeah." Her father smiled. "He's crazy about you, you know."

"No, I don't know." She paused. "Well, about half the time I know, and the other half I'm trying to figure out if he knows I exist."

"He knows. He's just shy. Like King Arthur. In case you haven't figured it out, you've typecast him, Amy. Steve is a great leader—a wonderful mayor and genuinely kind to everyone he meets, just like Arthur was. He's just not as good as some people at opening up and sharing. In some ways I think he's too kind, if such a thing is possible."

"I guess." She paused, her thoughts shifting to memories of Steve pouring his heart out for others. "He's a great guy, Dad. I just wonder if this relationship of ours is going to fizzle out. Things have been so strange lately."

Her father drew near and gave her a hug. "Relationships are tricky things, honey. One of these days, when things settle down, you and I can have a real heart-to-heart about what makes a relationship work. But today is not that day. We've got a dress rehearsal in a couple of hours."

"Yes." She glanced at the clock on the wall. "Still need to take care of about forty-five things before leaving. There's so much to do."

"I'm headed out to, um…" He paused and shrugged. "Well, I've got a few things I need to do too. See you there. Okay?"

"Sure." As she watched him leave, Amy tried to figure out what he was up to. Maybe he planned to pull some sort of prank during the rehearsal. She'd heard a couple of rumors indicating the guys were up to tricks. She prayed they'd forgo any antics and just focus on the show.

Her cell phone rang and she smiled as she saw the number. Jackson.

"Hello?"

"Hey." He sounded positive. Upbeat. "Wanted to let you know Gramps is doing a little better today. They've got him talking a little bit. And he ate some Jell-O."

In the background she heard Sarge's voice: "I hate Jell-O. Can't a fella have some real food?"

She laughed. "Well, tell your grandfather that we're all praying for him." She wanted to add, "And ask him why he shot Bugsy!" but refrained. Hopefully he would come clean in time.

"He feels your prayers." Jackson's tone changed. "And he's grateful. I—I am too." A pause followed. "Honestly, I don't know what I would have done if you—and I mean all of you—hadn't been here to walk him—us—through this. I hate to see him suffer, but there's some consolation in knowing that he's got a good support base, praying and caring."

"We do care," she said. "We love your grandfather, Jackson. And we…" She stopped herself short of saying "We love you, too."

"Camelot is more than a myth," Jackson said. "I see that so clearly now. It's a real place, with real people who would lay down their lives for others. Just wanted you to know how grateful I am. And grateful to the Lord for bringing me to such a place."

She'd just started to respond when Sarge's voice rang out from the other end. She couldn't make out his words, but he sounded passionate.

"Gramps wants to know if the show will go on," Jackson said. "If you've replaced him."

"Hmm. Steve's supposed to be working on that," Amy said. "Hope he's got it under control."

"Knowing Steve, he's got a plan." Jackson grew silent for a moment. "Anyway, I just wanted to let you know that things are going better on this end. I'll see you in time for the dress rehearsal. Oh, and Amy…"

"Yes?"

"In case I haven't said it before, I think you're pretty amazing.

You've kept everything in balance, and that's not easy to do. You make a great director."

"Th–thanks."

"Oops, gotta go. Gramps just pushed the wrong button and called for the nurse. See you in a while."

"Yes. See you…" She never got to finish. The call ended. Not that she really knew what to say in response to Jackson's flattery anyway. One thing was for sure, though. The guy certainly knew how to make a girl feel good. Yes, he certainly did.

* * * * *

Steve glanced out the window of his office, troubled by storm clouds overhead. He ushered up a quick prayer that the weather would cooperate. If they ever needed clear skies—symbolically or otherwise—it was today.

A rap on the door caught his attention. He turned to find Mickey standing there.

"Glad you could come," Steve said. "Take a seat."

"Am I in some sort of trouble?" Mickey asked as he sat. "Still mad at me after that last article? Did those pictures of Amy and Jackson bother you?"

"No, I'm over that." Steve walked around his desk and took a seat facing Mickey. "I feel like we've had the time to get to know each other over the past several weeks, and that's a good thing. And it's because we're friendly that I feel comfortable asking for a favor."

"A favor?" Mickey shifted his position in the chair. "What sort of favor?"

"You were there when Sarge had his stroke," Steve said.

"Of course. How is he?"

"He's going to recover, but it's going to take time. From what I hear, he's already talking, telling the nurses his war stories."

"Glad to hear it."

"I met with Woody last night to talk about how to handle Sarge's absence. We weren't sure at first how to go about replacing him in the jousting scene. But then Woody mentioned something you'd said to him about horseback riding. You grew up on a ranch?"

A look of terror settled into Mickey's eyes. "Wait. What are you asking?"

"We need someone to take Sarge's place in the jousting scene. Someone who's experienced with horses. Or mules." Steve chuckled. "Shoot, you could be experienced on a carousel pony and we'd take you."

"You want me to...what? Be in the show?" Mickey paled. "Take Sarge's place?"

"It's the only chance we've got of going on tomorrow," Steve said. "I need you, man. And don't tell me you don't know the part. You've been here for nearly every rehearsal. If anyone knows this show, you do."

"Well, sure, but that doesn't make me an actor. And if I take Sarge's part, I have to dance in that maypole scene." He shook his head. "Ain't happening."

"Sure it is." Steve slapped him on the back. "We need you. And you're part of the family now. You've grown on us."

"Like a fungus?"

Steve laughed. "I guess you could put it like that." He paused. "So, just one question. Can you really ride a horse? Or, I guess the better question would be, can you ride an old donkey?"

Mickey gave him a sheepish look. "I won barrel races in high school. And my father owns over forty horses at our family's ranch just west of Knoxville."

"You're kidding."

"No. You need horses?"

"Do we need horses? Does a skipper need a first mate?"

"I don't know." Mickey looked confused. "Does he?"

Steve laughed and patted the fellow on the back. "He does. And yes, we need the horses. The sooner, the better. Dress rehearsal starts in two and a half hours."

"Hmm. Might be doable." As Mickey paused, he gave Steve the funniest look. "Okay, so can I ask you a question? And please be honest with your answer."

"Sure."

A pained expression came over Mickey as he spoke. "Why are you so nice to me? You always have been, from the very beginning. But why? Everyone else around here treated me like I was some kind of enemy or something, but you were always kind."

"Well, I'll be honest—it's Charlie Hart's doing," he confessed. "He told me from the beginning that I needed to include outsiders at our round table. That we were all on the same team, working together. So I guess I've just never seen you as a real enemy, even when things were tense. You know?"

"I guess." Mickey ran his fingers through already-messy hair. "Until that day in the pest control van, I didn't really think about all of you as regular people."

"Excuse me?"

"Sorry if that sounds blunt," Mickey said. "But when I'm writing an article, the folks I'm writing about are just a means to an end. A way to get a paycheck. I've never really stopped to think about—or care about—them. Ya know?"

Steve shrugged. He didn't know. Couldn't even imagine what it would be like to live like that. "We're definitely real people with real problems," he said.

"I guess that's why I felt comfortable hanging around," Mickey said. "I've always considered myself such a screwup. Felt good to land in a town where everyone else was just as messed up as me."

"I'm not sure if I should be flattered or offended."

"Flattered," Mickey said. "Knowing you are all flawed gave *me* permission to be. And hearing all the guys talk about women the other day…" He shook his head. "Strange, but it did something to me. Got me thinking about falling in love again. Don't know if it's possible, but maybe."

A thousand thoughts rolled through Steve's head at once. He wanted to tell Mickey that in order to find real love, he needed a relationship with the One who created the idea in the first place. Before he could open his mouth to say anything, though, Eula Mae rushed into the room.

"Boss, I don't know why you're sitting here. It's a madhouse out there. Ellie Parker nearly caught the diner's kitchen on fire trying to cook those turkey legs, and there's a water leak out at the RV park. Darrell's run into some sort of problem with a sewer line backup at the theater, and Amy's in meltdown mode."

"Amy's in meltdown mode? Why?" He rose and took a few steps toward Eula Mae.

"Couldn't make sense of her last phone call. I think she's worried about Sarge. I tried to ease her mind. She also wants to know what we're going to do about that jousting scene." Mickey raised his hand. "Let her know that I'll be taking Sarge's place."

"You—you are?" Eula's Mae's face paled. "Seriously?"

He nodded.

She rushed over to him and gave him a kiss on the forehead. "God bless you. And here all this time I thought you worked for the enemy, just like that Fred Platt fellow."

"Worked for the enemy?" Mickey laughed. "The only enemy I face each morning is myself. So, no, I don't work for the enemy. And right now I'm going to be working for—or with—you guys. But I'd better track down some horses first." He looked at Steve. "Go ahead and call Amy if you like. Tell her not to worry."

Steve nodded. "I'm headed down to the theater, so I'll let her know everything's under control."

Mickey gave them a nod as he headed out the door and down the hallway.

"Let me ride with you," Eula Mae said, turning her attention to Steve. "That way we can iron out some of these other problems on the way."

"I live to iron out problems with you, Eula Mae," he said, sweeping her into his arms and kissing her on the top of the head.

"Don't let Woody catch you kissing me," she said. "He's liable to come after you with a shotgun."

"Let him." Steve kissed her white curls again and laughed.

"You're kissing the wrong woman, Steve Garrison," she said, a scolding look in her eyes. "In case you've forgotten, there's a beautiful young woman out there who's crazy about you."

"Hmm." He paused, not sure how to respond. "Well, I'll make you a deal, Eula Mae. You leave my love life to me and I'll leave yours to you."

"Like *that* would ever happen." She laughed. "C'mon, Mr. Mayor. We've got some big fish to fry today. Better get out of here."

"I always loved a good fish fry," he said, giving her a wink.

Still, as he followed her down the hallway, the only fish on Steve's mind was the one he hoped to hook later this afternoon when he finally —heaven help him—opened up and shared his heart with Amy.

And maybe, just maybe, he'd even sing her a song in the process.

Chapter Twenty-Two

....

The art of acting consists in keeping people from coughing.

BENJAMIN FRANKLIN

Steve arrived at the theater an hour before the scheduled dress rehearsal, anxious to find Amy. Already, the melody rang in his heart for that goofy song he and the other men had written. It offered a strange sense of courage. With the song leading the way, he could speak his mind—finally.

Not that he really had time for a heart-to-heart today. Not with the tech people, musicians, actors, and stagehands rushing about and shouting orders to each other. Still, he would give it the old college try.

Caroline grabbed him by the arm. "I know it's early, but you need to get into costume right away. Amy's orders."

He saluted, offered a quick, "Yes, ma'am," then headed inside to change.

It didn't take long to get into his costume for the first scene. Thankfully, Caroline had adjusted the stretchy pants, letting the seams out a bit. Much better. And she'd adjusted the shoulders too. Once dressed, he checked his appearance in the bathroom mirror then headed back outside.

"Steve, glad you're here." Woody drew near with a panicked look on his face. "After the problems we had with your lav microphone during our last rehearsal, I decided to locate a new one. Took some doing, but here it is." He held up the tiny black pin-on microphone. "Do you mind doing a sound check?"

"Of course not."

"Take center stage, if you will," Woody said. "Just recite your lines from your soliloquy. That should give our sound guy enough time to set your levels."

"Okay." Steve walked up the steps to the stage, completely blown away by the set. The whole area had been transformed into a Camelot-like forest. Eerie medieval-looking trees hung suspended from wires overhead, and Chuck had hand-painted the backdrop to create the illusion of a deep forest. Perfect for the opening scene.

Steve turned to face the sound booth at the back of the auditorium. As he spoke his lines, his heart swelled with excitement. He looked around the new theater, encouraged by the ever-growing crowd of workers and the amazing work Darrell and the others had done on the facility. He got so carried away thinking about the transformation that he apparently forgot to continue talking.

"Keep going, Steve," the sound tech called out. "Sounds good, but we need to make sure we've got the volume set right. Won't be much longer."

"Okay." Off he went again, speaking his line from that infamous scene, the one where he released Guinevere and Lancelot from their sins. He closed his eyes, the emotion of the words wrenching his heart. *Lord, is this how You feel when we betray You?* The depth of meaning nearly swept him away to another place.

Until a spotlight hit him in the face. Steve opened his eyes and squinted against the glare.

"Sorry," someone called out from the back of the auditorium. "Just checking the angle of the lights."

"Okay." After a few seconds the light went out, but tiny flashes still danced before his eyes. Steve stood still for a couple of minutes, hoping the sensation would pass. He happened to look out to the center aisle as one of the musicians walked toward the orchestra pit—or, rather, the area in front of the stage that would serve as a makeshift orchestra pit. The unfamiliar female with long dark hair carried a cello. Or tried to, anyway. She tripped over a wire and nearly went sprawling.

Darrell happened along beside her at just that moment, a smile wider than the Atlantic on his face. He stretched out his arms, steadying her, and then took the instrument and walked beside her up the aisle. Coincidence? Steve doubted it.

His gaze shifted again, this time settling on Natalie, who greeted her brother, Mark, as he took his place at the keyboard. The two began a lively conversation, one that kept him plenty distracted.

"Keep talking, Steve," the sound tech called out. "Just a few more lines and we'll be set."

He began to speak, the words to his soliloquy front and center in his mind once more.

Well, until Grady entered the stage dressed in an odd getup. "I think something must be wrong with Natalie today," he muttered. "Look at this here getup she's makin' me wear fer the rehearsal." He pointed down to his shorts and then up to his medieval-looking shirt.

"Why?" Steve asked.

"Split my pants."

"What?" Steve couldn't help but chuckle at this news. "You split your pants?"

Several of the musicians started laughing—Steve's first cue that he'd just delivered that line through the sound system for all to hear.

At this point, Amy entered the stage dressed as Guinevere.

Her beauty stunned him. He could hardly breathe as he took in the medieval gown. It matched her eyes perfectly.

"Wow." Just one word, but it was all he could manage.

"You like?" She twirled to show off the skirt.

"Very much."

"Thanks." She gave him a shy smile—his first glimmer of hope in some time. "We need to get started. You guys ready?"

"I was just checking my mic," Steve said, his heart nearly thumping out of his chest. "But since you're here…" He paused, realizing everyone could hear him. "Do you have a minute?"

She gave him a curious look. "Sure."

"We need to talk." He put his hand over the microphone and whispered, "Privately." Her eyes widened and she nodded. Steve looked back at the sound guy. "Are we done?"

"All done," the guy said. "Thanks."

Steve took Amy by the hand and led her to the edge of the stage, past Prissy and the twins and beyond Grady and Blossom, who were giggling over his odd attire.

Finally, he could share his heart. Let her know what he'd been thinking. Feeling.

Unfortunately, at the very moment Steve opened his mouth, Chuck approached, dressed in knightly attire but looking a little green around the gills. In fact, as the fellow grabbed his midsection, he looked as if he might be ill.

"You okay?" Steve asked, rushing his way.

Chuck shook his head. "N-no."

"What's wrong?" Amy asked, stepping up beside him. "Are you sick?"

"Maybe. Do I have a fever?" Chuck gripped his belly.

Amy put her palm on his forehead. "Nope. Cool as a cucumber."

"I feel horrible. Don't think I can go on."

"What?" She looked terrified. "But you have to. The show must go on. That's our motto." She paused and gave him a curious look. "What's really going on here, Chuck? Something you want to talk about?"

Chuck shook his head, his gaze shifting to the ground. "I'm just scared."

"Scared? Of what?" Steve asked.

"Th-this." Chuck pointed out to the stage and the auditorium. "I've—I've never done this before. And I'm not sure I can do it now. I'm not cut out for this. Thought I could do it, but I can't."

"Chuck, none of us have done this before," Steve said. "You're in good company. Trust me. We're all terrified."

"You are?" The tight lines around his mouth softened a bit.

"We are." Amy and Steve spoke in unison.

Steve looked at her, wondering what scared her more—directing the show or playing the part of Guinevere. He'd just started to ask when a frantic male voice called from offstage.

"Look out below!"

One of the Styrofoam trees began to swing wildly overhead, nearly hitting Chuck in the head. Steve grabbed him by the arm and pulled him to safety just as the huge tree broke free from the wire that had held it bound to the bar above. It hit the stage with a *thud*, a horrible scraping sound reverberated in the monitors.

Amy let out a shriek, which brought several of the men running from backstage.

"Everyone okay out here?" Darrell asked. "Anyone get hurt?"

"That stupid tree almost knocked me in the head," Chuck said. He turned to Steve. "You should've let it hit me. Then I could've slept through this whole thing. Pretended like it never happened."

"No more pretending," Steve said. His thoughts and his gaze shifted to Amy. "From now on, we only move forward, no matter how difficult." He reached to take Amy by the hand, once more ready to spill his heart.

Unfortunately, he'd only gotten three or four words into his rehearsed speech when the sound of an explosion ripped through the building. Seconds later, the power went out...and everything faded to black.

* * * * *

"No way." Amy groaned and slapped herself in the head. "Don't tell me." She turned her attention from Steve, who'd started some sort of cryptic conversation, to find out what had happened to the lights.

"Don't worry, Amy," a voice shouted from the booth at the back. "We did that on purpose. Had to repower the soundboard. Everything should be back up in a minute and we'll be ready to roll."

"Ah." She turned back to Steve, who gripped her hand. "Do you think we could talk after the show?"

"Sure." The pained sound in his voice threw her a little. Strange that he wanted to talk now, with so much going on. Was he upset with her about something?

The lights came back on, offering her hope that things could move forward.

Amy walked to the center of the stage, which amplified her voice. "Okay, everyone. Let's get together and pray; then we're going to dive in. Act One, Scene One."

Actors and tech people came from out of the woodwork for the prayer, which Steve led with great passion. His prayers never ceased to amaze her. Why was it he could share his deepest feelings with the Almighty but not with her?

Probably not an appropriate question.

The dress rehearsal got off to a healthy start. Woody took his seat in the front row, his script on a music stand in front of him. The orchestra warmed up then began to play the overture. Her heart went crazy as she listened. *This is really it. We're here…doing the very thing we only dreamed of doing.* Oh, it felt so good. So right.

She watched as Steve entered the stage as Arthur for the first time. Something about his demeanor, his words, pricked her heart. She forced her attentions to the stage, awaiting her cue.

Off in the distance, a male voice interrupted: "Who stole my pants?" She turned to find Grady running across the backstage area dressed in his shirt and a pair of shorts.

"Don't ask." Jackson stepped into the spot next to her, his nearness giving her a bit of a jolt. "Just stay focused on the show."

"I've been kind of freaked out all day," she whispered. "I heard that Pete and some of the other guys have a rubber chicken they're planning to insert into one of the scenes, so I'm on my guard. And I'm terrified Lucy's going to sneak Fiona in here somehow."

"Heard all about the rubber chicken," Jackson said. "But they haven't told me yet which scene they're planning to use him in. And as for Lucy sneaking Fiona in, well, I'd say that's a given."

"I'd rather they get their pranks over with tonight, when no one's here," she said. "Because tomorrow night, that auditorium will be filled…." She stopped talking, caught up in the beauty of Steve's speech. "Wow."

Jackson leaned in close, his breath tickling her ear. "He's doing a great job, isn't he?"

"Yes, he is." Amy smiled. "He was born for this."

"I think you're right." Jackson's tender gaze seemed to reach all the way down to her soul. "And so were you." A long pause followed, and he whispered, "Which is just one of many things that makes the two of you so perfect for each other, I suppose."

"W–what?" She turned to face him, but he'd slipped away into the shadows of darkness backstage. Still, he'd given her a lot to think about. Not that she had time to think right now. Right now she needed to stay focused on Arthur's lines. What was her cue again?

Ah yes. There it was.

She made her way onstage as Guinevere and finished the opening scene with her heart in her throat.

Well, almost finished the scene. About three lines from the end, her lavalier mic went out. One of the techs came running onto the stage holding a package of batteries.

"Sorry," he muttered. "Meant to swap these out before we started."

He shot off the stage and she wrapped up the scene, then raced backstage for the scene change.

Caroline met her, a tiny flashlight in hand. "Time to get dressed for your wedding, honey."

Amy smiled, her heart now racing. Almost felt like the real deal, especially with Caroline leading the way.

"I thought Natalie was going to help me with costume changes," Amy said.

"I made her sit down. She's not feeling well."

"Oh no."

"It's going to be okay," Caroline said. "I'm working on finding someone to take her place backstage."

"Good idea."

The orchestra began to play the music for the wedding scene.

From across the stage, Amy caught a glimpse of Steve in his wedding costume. "Wow." She could hardly believe her eyes. With the crown sitting perched atop his head, he looked very much like a real king.

King of my heart.

She smiled as a rush of emotions washed over her. And as she stepped out onto the stage in her wedding gown, the whole experience felt surreal. She looked up, mesmerized by the twinkling stars overhead. Well, fake stars, but twinkling ones nonetheless. They made a beautiful backdrop for the wedding scene. So did the battery-operated candles, which flickered all over the stage.

As the music swelled, she stepped onto the stage and took a few steps toward Steve. Her eyes never left his. When they met in the center of the stage, he reached for her hand. She took it willingly and turned to walk with him toward Pastor Crane, who had donned a priest's robe for this particular scene. As the wedding scene moved forward, Amy found her throat tight on more than one occasion, especially as Steve spoke his vows. He squeezed her hand so tightly that she flinched...until she realized what he was trying to say. The words—albeit scripted—were straight from his heart. He left no doubt in her mind. Oh, how she wanted to skip all of this nonsense and just throw herself into his arms—forget about all of the chaos from the past few weeks and just go back to where they started, that day in his office when he'd kissed her for the first time.

The orchestra continued to play, the music taking a slow turn. Ah, the end of the wedding ceremony. Time for the big moment. The one she'd waited for all evening.

Amy and Steve had just leaned in for the kiss when something distracted her. "W–what's that?" She pointed to the stage, sure she saw a large rat scurrying from one side to the other. "R–rat!"

"That's no rat!" Steve said, taking off after it. "That's Fiona!"

Off he went, running until he caught the little rascal. Lucy entered the stage with a sheepish look on her face. "I hadn't planned to send her out until the next scene," she said. "I promise."

Woody entered the stage and lit into Lucy, who looked as if she might cry...until a noise from backstage stopped them all where they stood.

"Wait." Amy put a finger to her lips, trying to get everyone to stay quiet so she could hear. "What is that? You guys hear it, don't you? It's coming through the sound system."

Confusion registered in Steve's eyes.

"That sound. It's amplified. Coming from backstage," she whispered. "Sounds really...odd." She grew silent once more and tried to make sense of it. Off in the distance, a girlish giggle resonated through the sound system, followed by—what was that? Smacking? Was someone chewing gum with a lav mic on? If so, they had to be stopped immediately.

Then the words, "You silly man!" came through, clear as a bell. In the pit, the orchestra members stopped playing and began to laugh. Off in the wings, cast members doubled over with laughter too.

The voices spoke again, sounding more and more familiar. At once, Amy realized who—and what—she was hearing.

"No way." She looked at Steve, wondering if he'd figured it out.

Not that she planned to stick around long enough to find out. Amy raced backstage, beyond stagehands and the props director. She sailed past Grady—still dressed in his shorts and doublet—and into the very darkest corner, behind the props table. She grabbed a penlight from the table and turned it on, pointing the tiny ray of light on two people who happened to be wrapped in each other's arms...kissing.

"Dad?" Amy whispered.

No response.

"Dad!" She flashed the light in his direction and he turned her way, looking like a kid who'd been caught with his hand in the cookie jar. He took a giant step back and paled.

So did Caroline, whose nervous stammers morphed into sense-less giggles.

"Oh, uh…" Amy's father raked his fingers through his hair. "We were just…"

"You were rehearsing a love scene in front of approximately forty-five people," Amy explained. She pointed to her father's mic, and his eyes widened.

"Don't tell me…" A look of sheer terror passed over his face.

"Okay, I won't tell you," Amy said, still reeling. "But I will ask you to reach down and flip the switch on that microphone so that your love scene isn't broadcast to everyone in the theater. The guys in the sound booth have enjoyed your performance so far, and so have the people in the orchestra."

From out front, a round of applause sounded, confirming her words.

"Oops." Caroline's giggles started up again, and she threw her-self into Amy's father's arms, clearly unable to get control of herself.

By now, at least half the cast had gathered around, many of them chuckling. Steve pushed through the crowd, sounding a little out of breath. "I lost you back there in the dark, Amy," he said. "Didn't know where you went."

"I just followed the trail until I found the culprits."

"Caroline?" Steve said after a moment's pause. "Something you want to tell us?"

She turned to him with a smile. "Mm-hmm." Caroline put her

left hand out for all to see, a diamond ring shimmering under the glow of the penlight.

Amy let out a squeal. "You two are engaged?" She ran toward them, wrapping them in an embrace and nearly dropping the light in the process. "I don't believe it."

"No, not engaged," Amy's father said, his voice a little shaky. "We, um…"

"We're married!" Caroline released the words with a triumphant look. "Have been, for three weeks."

"W–what?" Amy leaned against the props table, overcome. "You're…married? And you didn't tell us?"

"Yep. And nope." Her father took her hand. "Are you mad at me?"

"Not mad." She shook her head. "Just confused. Steve and I thought that Caroline was…" She paused. "We thought you were sick."

"Sick?" Caroline laughed. "What in the world made you think that? I've never felt better in my life."

"Well, you were acting so secretive," Steve said. "And you were gone so much. I thought maybe you were in Knoxville at the doctor's office or something. I don't know."

"Well, we were in Knoxville." Amy's father drew near and slipped his arm around her waist. "Saw the justice of the peace three weeks ago."

"And spent the night at the prettiest little bed-and-breakfast," Caroline threw in. "I'll have to tell you all about it."

A couple of the older men whooped and hollered their response to that news. Still, Amy couldn't quite process all of this. How had her father managed such a thing…behind her back?

"Dad, you mean to tell me you weren't fishing that night like you said?" she asked.

"Oh, I was fishing, all right." He grinned and gave Caroline a kiss on the cheek. "Caught the most beautiful fish in the pond too."

"Oh, this is the most romantic thing ever!" Blossom clasped her hands together. "It's the stuff movies are made of!"

"No, it's the stuff *stage plays* are made of," Woody said. "Which reminds me, we still have a show to rehearse."

Amy knew they should get back to business, but nothing about this made sense. Her father...and Caroline? Really?

Suddenly all the emotion she'd held pent up over the last few stressful weeks came bubbling out. Amy began to laugh—quietly at first, and then louder. Before long, Steve joined her, their voices blending together in giddy harmony. Finally she managed to get control of herself. Amy dried the tears of laughter from her eyes and drew in a deep breath, knowing she could no longer put off the rehearsal.

As she turned to her father to give him a celebratory hug, Amy had just one lingering question. "Dad? Can I ask you something else?"

"Sure, honey."

She pointed to the rubber chicken he'd been holding in his left hand the whole time. "Want to tell me what you were planning to do with that?"

"Oh." He glanced down and chuckled. "Almost forgot about this poor little guy. We were planning to use him in the lusty-month-of-May scene. But now you've gone and foiled our plan."

"Looks like I've foiled your plan, all right," Amy said. "But I don't think it has anything to do with rubber chickens."

She reached up and gave her father a kiss on the cheek, hardly able to contain herself, before heading back onstage to continue her wedding scene.

* * * * *

Steve somehow made his way through the rest of the dress rehearsal. Still, every time he thought about Caroline kissing Amy's father, he couldn't help but laugh. Something about their hidden relationship struck him as funny. Here he was, struggling to share his heart with Amy, and her father had up and married his mom's best friend without telling anyone. Just seemed... ironic.

The rehearsal continued for the next three hours, presenting the cast and crew with multiple bumps and bumbles. By the time they reached the curtain call, Steve was exhausted but psychologically prepared to speak his mind. He looked around, hoping to find Amy. He searched the backstage area...and couldn't locate her.

As he passed by Annabelle and Blossom, Steve paused. "Hey, have you ladies seen Amy? I need to talk to her."

Blossom pursed her lips and shook her head. "Where does she always go when she has a lot on her mind?" A chuckle followed. "She's in the restroom, Steve. Probably contemplating all the wacky things that have taken place tonight."

"Not again. Can one of you ladies go in after her? It's really important. Tell her to meet me at center stage in five minutes."

The two women looked back and forth at each other and shrugged.

"Oh, and by the way," Steve said, "gather all the ladies too. Tell them to sit in the front row and wait for the show to begin."

Annabelle looked confused. "What do you mean? We just finished the show."

"Trust me." He smiled. "You might find out that knights

in shining armor do exist after all. So take your seats, front and center."

Blossom's eyes grew wide and she nodded before the two women disappeared in the direction of the ladies' room.

Steve had a few words with the guys in the sound and light booth and then headed for center stage, praying all the way. *Lord, give me the words. Not a script, necessarily. Just words.*

Moments later Amy walked onto the stage, dressed in her jeans and T-shirt. Though she was still at a distance, her face lit up when she saw him. "Hey, you're still in costume."

"Yep. Thought it would help me stay in character."

She gave him a curious look. Steve stood his ground at center stage until she met him there. Then he slipped an arm around her waist and a spotlight hit them.

"Thanks, fellas," he called back to the tech booth. "I needed that."

She gave him a suspicious look. "What are you up to?"

"Oh, a couple of things. First, there's something I want to say to you. Been trying to say it all night, in fact, but…well…a couple of things have gotten in the way."

He'd no sooner spoken the words than one of the Styrofoam trees swung his way, coming loose from the bar above. It whacked him on the shoulder, sending him plunging headlong into Amy's arms.

"Well, that's one way to do it." He staggered to an upright position, unable to keep from laughing. "Not quite what I had planned, though. That was a little more dramatic."

"Sometimes God's plans are better than our own," she said and grinned.

"Yep. Usually."

"So, you were saying...?"

Steve squared his shoulders and looked her in the eyes. "Amy, we've talked a lot about what the real Camelot was like. I wasn't sure if I believed the legend or not. I'm still not sure. But there's one thing I do believe in, and that's you and me."

"Really?" She smiled.

"Yes, and I'm sorry it's taken me so long to say this." He swallowed hard and gazed into her eyes, garnering all the courage he needed. "I'm crazy about you. Head-over-heels, can't-walk-straight, have-trouble-sleeping crazy." He paused, knowing he had to take it a step further. "I love you, Amy. I've loved you since the seventh grade."

At this point, a cheer went up from the front row and he heard the words, "You go, Steve!" Eula Mae, of course.

Steve looked out to see that the women of Camelot had arrived, just as he'd instructed. Perfect. But they would have to wait a moment for their performance. Right now he had to finish this one-on-one scene with Amy.

"With the fog, sometimes it's hard to see what's right in front of you," he whispered, grateful that the microphones had been turned off. "We get caught up in our imaginings and begin to wonder if a far-off place is better. Sometimes what's right here is what we've dreamed of all along."

"I'm not fictional." Tears rose and covered Amy's bottom lashes. "I'm real."

"Very," he whispered, kissing her hair.

"And I'm not going anywhere," she said, her voice now shaking. "Emotionally or otherwise. No dreams of far-off lands or knights in shining-armor. This is my home. *You* are my home."

He stared into her eyes for a moment then leaned in to give her a kiss she wouldn't soon forget. As their lips met, every bit of emotion he'd left bottled up inside over the past few weeks rushed out. And as the kiss intensified, so did the roar of approval from the front row. After a few moments, he couldn't take their cheering anymore and released his hold on Amy, before taking a sweeping bow.

"So glad to see our scene meets with the approval of the audience. But if you like that, hang on for the ride. More is coming." He turned to Amy. "If you don't mind, m'lady, go join the other women in the front row. We've got a little encore presentation."

"We?"

He nodded and she left the stage, a puzzled look on her face.

"Okay, fellas," Steve called out to the men waiting in the wings. "Just like we practiced it."

Grady, Pete, Woody, Darrell, Mickey, Fred, and Chuck entered the stage, dressed in knightly attire. Well, all but Grady, who still wore his shorts instead of pants. The men took their places, looking a little weak-kneed, and Steve led the way, singing the first few notes of the song they'd written that memorable day in the pest control van.

Okay, it was a little cheesy. Really cheesy, in fact. But from the cheers coming from the front row, he could tell that the audience members didn't seem to mind. In fact, if the way the ladies of Camelot rushed the stage afterward was any indication...Steve would have to conclude they rather liked it.

Chapter Twenty-Three

....

Well, I think one of the main things that you have to think about when acting in the movies is to try not to make the acting show.

JAMES STEWART

On the afternoon of the first performance, Steve whittled down his to-do list. One by one the final details of the show were ironed out. By three thirty in the afternoon, he found himself free to take a drive through town. Rumor had it—Eula Mae, of course—that the whole place was packed out with tourists. He could hardly wait to see for himself.

First stop, the diner. He inched his way past the parking lot, mesmerized by the number of cars with out-of-state tags. Unfamiliar people lined the sidewalk, waiting to get inside. In all his years living in Camelot, he'd never seen anything like it.

Next Steve drove by the parking lot at Lance's, equally as stunned by the amount of people he found there. He parked and got out of the car, then walked from booth to booth. The sights and sounds nearly overwhelmed him. Several of the locals handed out hot dogs, popcorn, kettle corn, sodas, and more to people Steve had never seen before. Other Camelot residents sold jewelry, paintings, and various trinkets with a Smoky Mountain feel. And the Camelot-themed art seemed to be a big hit, as was evidenced by the line forming outside of one tent.

After getting back in his car, Steve headed out to the new RV park. He drove up and down, counting all the RVs, Fifth Wheels, and campers. Forty-two. Who would have dreamed such a thing would be possible?

Oh yes. Amy. She'd envisioned this from the start. Well, envisioned putting on a show that would draw a crowd such as this.

After pulling away from the RV park, Steve picked up his cell phone and called her, just wanting to hear her voice one last time before curtain call. When her breathless voice came on the line, he realized he'd caught her in the middle of something.

"Don't want to keep you," he said. "Just needed to tell you something in case you didn't figure it out last night."

"What's that?"

"I love you."

A brief pause from the other end of the line caught him off guard for a moment...until he heard her giggle. "I love you, too, Steve. Who else would put up with me and these crazy ideas of mine?"

"Is that a rhetorical question?"

"Yes." She chuckled. "Please don't answer it."

"Okay." He glanced at the clock as he rounded the bend heading back into town. "By the way, where are you?"

"At the theater. Touching up some of the set pieces that fell last night and helping the ladies iron costumes. Natalie's looking pretty worn out."

"I'm headed there now."

"Awesome. I think Darrell and a couple of the guys could use your help rehanging a couple of the trees from that center bar. You up for that?"

"Of course. Hanging trees is what I do."

"Making me happy is what you do," she said. "So come on over and see me, okay?"

"I'm on my way."

Of course, the deed was easier said than done. Getting past the mob at the four-way stop in the center of town took some doing. And inching his way along the main road to the Civic Center was problematic. Folks kept stopping to take pictures of the hills and the amazing view near the bluff. Not that he blamed them. Oh no. There was plenty of beauty to draw people to Camelot.

Steve entered the theater at five fifteen. As he made his way up the center aisle, he glanced at the stage and watched with amazement for a moment as Annabelle practiced her dance moves. Crazy, how much she'd changed. Then again, they'd all changed, hadn't they? Some—like the bubbly Sack 'n Save clerk—on the outside. Others on the inside. In a thousand ways, the town had been transformed.

As he made his way up the stairs onto the stage, Steve passed Jackson and Gwen.

"Hey, you two." He stopped to smile.

"Hey yourself." Jackson extended his hand, a broad grin on his face.

"How's Sarge doing?"

"Coming home tomorrow. He's ready to spit nails that he couldn't come tonight, though. He's wanting to make it back in time for next week's performance."

"Hope there *is* a next week's performance," Gwen said. "Guess we'll have to see how tonight goes."

"It's going to be great." Steve reached over and squeezed her hand. "I've never prayed harder about anything in my life. And it will be great if Sarge can come see the show as soon as he's able."

"We were just ironing out the details of his care," Jackson said. "Gwen's putting together a team of women from the church to bring meals to the house once he gets back home. She's been such a big help through all of this." He turned to give her a comfortable smile.

"Nice." Steve nodded. "Glad things are progressing."

"Oh, by the way, Amy's looking for you," Jackson said. "She's backstage with Natalie and Caroline."

"I'm on my way." Steve headed back behind the curtains in search of Amy. He found her bent over an ironing board, pressing wrinkles out of her bridal gown.

She looked up with a look of contentment on her face. "Hey, you."

"Hey, you." He drew near and wrapped her in his arms—grateful she'd put the iron down. "Ready for tonight?"

"As ready as I'll ever be."

"It's going to be great."

"I'm going to photograph it in my mind," she said. "So I won't forget a thing."

"Well, photograph this too." He gave her a kiss. Then another. And another. He found himself swept away...until Eula Mae's voice rang out.

"You two kiss entirely too much. Don't you realize that kissing spreads germs?"

Steve step back and chuckled. "That would explain why you and Woody both had a sore throat this morning."

Eula Mae rolled her eyes. "Very funny. Just wanted to tell you that tonight's performance is officially sold out."

"No way." He and Amy spoke in unison.

"Yes. Heard from Pastor Crane. Every seat is taken. And tomorrow's matinee is nearly sold out too."

"If you build it, they will come." Steve gave Amy a wink. "You had it right all along."

"No one is more surprised than me," she said.

He gave her another quick kiss on the nose then headed off to find Darrell. The next hour or so whizzed by at breakneck speed.

With so much to do and so little time to do it, Steve felt a little overwhelmed. Only when he reached the men's dressing area and slipped into his first costume did he pause to take a deep breath and whisper up a prayer that tonight's show would go well. Then he walked back out to the wings and peeked around the edge to spy the incoming crowd.

The patrons were now arriving in steady succession, filling first the center section. Then the sides. Then the back. Whoa.

Eula Mae drew near and whistled. "You look mighty handsome, King Arthur."

"Thank you very much." He bowed.

"Wish you'd shave those whiskers off your face, though." She gave him a scrutinizing look.

"I've been trying to grow them out so I'll look more kingly."

She snorted. "Whatever. Guess your mama didn't raise you right. Good boys don't wear hair on their face."

"Take that up with the Lord," he said. "He's the one who put it there."

"Hey, speaking of your mama, she called the office earlier today. Wants you to call her cell phone a half hour before showtime."

"That's right now."

"Yep." Eula Mae nodded. "Better get to it, then. Don't want to keep your mama waiting."

Steve reached into his pocket for his cell phone and punched in his mother's number. She answered right away with an excited, "Hello," but with all the noise in the background, he could barely make out her voice to understand the rest of her conversation.

"Mom, we're about to go on."

"I know." She laughed. "Can't wait."

"Can't wait?"

"Well, sure, son. We're sitting in the third row. Center section. Stick your head out and give us a wave."

"No way." Steve peeked around the edge of the stage and searched the audience until he saw his mother and Bob sitting in the third row. "Hang on, Mom, I'm coming." He ended the call then sprinted across the stage, costume and all, eventually bounding down the steps.

She met him at the edge of her row, face alight with joy. "Well, hello there."

"I can't believe you came."

"We drove all day. Bob didn't mind. He knows it's for my boys." Her mother gave him a warm hug and a kiss on the cheek, and Bob offered up a wave from his seat.

"Well, you've made my day," Steve said.

"I'm so glad about that. But I came for another reason too. The minute I got the news that Caroline had up and married Charlie, I had no choice. I still can't believe she went behind my back and did that. What's a best friend for, if not to tell your secrets to?"

"We were all shocked," Steve said. "But I'm glad you're here now. She needs you." He gestured to the stage. "We need you. Does Darrell know you're here?"

"I just sent him a text. He should be…" Her voice drifted away and she pointed to the stage. "Right there."

Steve turned to find his brother standing stage right, a broad smile on his face. Moments later, he joined them. They entered into a lively conversation…until a loud gong went off, letting patrons know that the show would be starting soon.

Steve gave his mother another quick hug. "Sorry, Mom. Gotta run. The show must go on."

"So they say." She blew him a kiss.

As he headed back to the stage, Steve caught a glimpse of Fred Platt seated in the first row with his wife and children. Steve gave them a wave before heading backstage to join the others for what he knew would be one of the greatest nights of his life.

* * * * *

Amy scurried around backstage, making sure everything was in place. "Five minutes, everyone," she said.

She glanced over at Woody, who sat in a chair while Lucy applied stage makeup to his face.

"I have the best makeup crew in the world," Woody said. "Same folks who restored the Statue of Liberty."

Lucy slapped him in the arm. The good arm. "Stop that, Woody. If you keep talking, how will I ever get enough makeup on you?"

"Oh, the eternal question." He chuckled.

Annabelle approached, dressed in her lady-in-waiting attire. Amy couldn't help but gasp when she saw her with the cinched waist and flared skirt. She had a true hourglass figure, one that apparently made Chuck's eyes pop. He stood off in the distance with his eyes riveted on her.

"Annabelle, look at you." Amy found herself almost speechless.

Annabelle turned in a circle, showing off her dress. "Don't you love this shade of blue?"

"Yes, but even more than that, I love the way the dress is made. Really shows off your new figure. Just look at that waistline. And your new hair looks great."

"Oh, that's Blossom's doing." Annabelle giggled. "Can't believe I let her talk me into it. I've never had my hair in an updo like this before."

"It's beautiful, and so are you."

"Thanks, Amy." Annabelle's cheeks turned pink. "I do feel transformed. Guess that's the right word."

"Transformed is right," Amy said. "You're breathtaking." She leaned in and whispered, "And a certain handsome knight has taken notice, hasn't he?"

"You mean Chuck?" Annabelle grinned. "Definitely. He offered to drive me home last night after the fellas sang that awesome song."

"On a white steed?"

"No." Annabelle giggled. "And not on a stubborn mare, either. He drove me home in his car. We had the best talk ever. He's such a great man, Amy. I really think..." She paused. "I really think he was worth the wait."

"Perfect."

The opening music to the Camelot theme resounded from the orchestra pit. Amy's heart raced—in part because she realized that tonight's performance was the fulfillment of a dream for her. This event could very well change the town of Camelot forever.

Lord, what if I hadn't stepped out and followed my heart?

A joyous feeling rose up inside of her as the words "followed my heart" flitted through her mind. They reminded her of Steve.

Steve! Where are you?

She glanced across the stage, seeing him in the wings on the other side—exactly where he was supposed to be. Yes, that was her Steve. Always where he was supposed to be. Doing the thing he was called to do. Caring for the people he'd been called to care for.

The music swelled, and she watched as King Arthur took the stage, the forest scene magnificently framing his entrance. His first words filled the auditorium with his presence. Then again, a real king could always command an audience, couldn't he?

Amy closed her eyes and breathed a prayer. Then, when the

moment came, she entered the stage, taking on the role of Guinevere—the love of Arthur's life. Could anything be sweeter?

The next hour was a blur. After all of the weeks of rehearsing, after all of the hours of agonizing, the first act of the play soared by at lightning speed. With the exception of a couple of dropped lines and one costume faux pas—Chuck entered the stage wearing his cowboy boots with his tights—the whole thing came off without a hitch. Amy could hardly believe it.

Only when the musical crescendo announced the beginning of the intermission did she feel the weight of the world lift from her shoulders. Well, for a minute, anyway.

Exiting the stage on the left, she was approached by Annabelle, whose eyes were wide. "Um, Amy?"

"Yes?" Amy pulled off her headpiece and ran her fingers through her hair.

"I thought you'd want to know that Natalie's in labor."

"What?" The headpiece slipped out of her hand and landed on the floor.

"Well, at least she thinks she is. Could be those...what do you call them? Bragging Higgs contractions?"

Amy rose and shook her head. "I don't have a clue what they're called. But if they're contractions, shouldn't someone be driving her to the hospital?"

"Well, that's the problem. Pastor Crane has gone back to the sound booth to fix some sort of computer problem. Jackson has gone to get him."

"Okay." Amy sprinted toward the stage then turned back to Annabelle. "Where is she?"

"In the ladies' dressing room."

"Gotcha."

She rushed to the dressing room, where she found Gwen kneeling next to Natalie, who sat in a chair with a look of pain on her face. The poor woman made a few puffing sounds then closed her eyes, wincing.

"That was a strong one," she whispered a few seconds later.

"How far apart are the pains, Natalie?" Gwen asked, glancing at the clock on the wall.

"About every three minutes," Natalie responded. "From everything I've read, that means I'm getting close."

"Why didn't you tell us?" Amy asked.

"The contractions started in the second scene," Natalie said. "Didn't feel like much at first. But by the time we got to the wedding scene, I knew I was in trouble. There was no turning back."

"Definitely no turning back from this point on," Amy said. "But we'd better get you to the hospital before you have this baby in the dressing room."

"I can think of worse scenarios," Natalie said. "Honestly, Amy, this production is the best thing that's ever happened to our little town. Since I moved here, I mean. I'm so proud of you." She put her hand on her belly and then winced again. "Oh, there's another one." Once it had passed, the pained expression on her face shifted to one of relief. "That was a big one."

Pastor Crane and Jackson arrived in short order and gently helped Natalie to her feet.

"You okay, honey?" her husband asked.

"I—I—" Natalie paused and took a few deep breaths. "I will be. But promise me one thing, Brent."

"Anything."

"Under no circumstances will I give birth in that hearse. Understand?"

"Of course." He chuckled. "Though the stories we could one day tell our kids would be pretty unique, don't you think?"

She shook her head. "No, thank you. I can think of a thousand other stories I'd rather tell them, trust me."

"Okay." He grinned. "But that means we have to hit the road."

"Someone needs to tell my brother," Natalie said.

"I'll tell him," Jackson said. "The musicians are on a break right now but should be heading back to their places soon. The second act starts in six minutes."

"Yikes." Amy glanced at the clock. She'd never seen time pass so quickly. And from the looks of things, things were only going to get crazier from here on out.

* * * * *

"Steve, we have five minutes to find someone to take Pastor Crane's place."

"What?" Steve turned as he heard Amy's voice. "What happened?"

"He just left with Natalie. She's in labor."

Steve felt his heart lurch. "No way."

When Amy nodded, he tried to compose himself, tried to think. Who could fill in for Pastor Crane? There were just a couple of brief scenes, primarily the one where Guinevere was burned at the stake. *Hmm.*

A couple of ideas rolled around in Steve's head, and one took root. "I know the perfect person. He's certainly been around enough."

Seconds later, he bounded down the steps into the seating area, his gaze fixed on one man: Fred Platt.

"Sorry to take you away from your family," Steve said, "but I need to ask a favor."

"Sure." Fred shrugged and rose from his seat. "What is it?"

Off in the distance the orchestra members settled into their seats.

"We just lost Pastor Crane," Steve said. "Need someone to take his place."

"W–what?" Fred paled. "Oh, but I couldn't…" He shook his head.

"You can do it, Daddy!" his son called out.

"You might as well, Fred," his wife said. "You may never get another chance to be a knight in shining armor."

Ouch.

"You're one of us now," Steve said, giving Fred a slap on the back. "Might as well join the family. We won't bite."

The fellow looked terrified but followed along behind Steve as the orchestra began to play the opening number for Act Two. As for what would happen next…well, that was up to the Lord. For now, Steve was content, knowing that Camelot was safe in His hands.

Chapter Twenty-Four

·····················

Good night! Good night! Parting is such sweet sorrow
That I shall say goodnight 'til it be morrow.

WILLIAM SHAKESPEARE

The second act rolled by at lightning speed. Steve rushed from place to place, scene to scene, grateful to be surrounded by such a great throng of people. He was a bit mesmerized by how well everything seemed to be going. Even the jousting scene was a hit with the audience. Mickey soared through it as if he'd been born for the task. And Fred—though nervous—had pulled off Pastor Crane's role with no problem.

The moment the show ended, the cast and crew went crazy. Steve had never heard so much whooping and hollering in his whole life. Not that he could blame them. The whole thing had been surreal, in a wonderful sort of way. If the standing ovation was an indicator, the audience had loved it too. Didn't look like they would be asking for their money back. That alone was worth celebrating.

After the final curtain call, the cast met backstage for a quick we-did-it! moment. Woody gathered them in a circle and offered his congratulations; then everyone scattered to the winds. Well, all but Amy, Steve, and Jackson, who remained fixed to Woody's side, chattering nonstop.

"How can we ever thank you for all you've done, Woody?" Amy asked, her eyes brimming with tears. "We owe you so much."

"This has been the best experience of my life," he said, giving her a hug. "So no thanks are needed."

"Oh, happy day!" Eula Mae's voice rang out. She slipped into the spot next to Woody and put her arm around his waist. "I love a man who loves the theater."

"I love a woman who loves a man who loves the theater," Woody said and then kissed her on the cheek. "And you have to admit, there's a strange sense of euphoria after the first show. I think it's triggered by relief."

"Relief that the show wasn't as bad as the dress rehearsal?" Steve asked.

Woody chuckled. "Maybe. Probably. But I was going to say it's because the tension of doing the show for the first time has lifted. Every subsequent show gets easier, and the actors and actresses grow more and more sure of themselves."

"I hope you're right about that," Amy said. "Because tonight was nerve-racking. I thought I was going to lose my lunch a couple of times. And did you see that part where I dropped my lines in the scene with Lancelot?" She groaned and gave Jackson a sheepish look.

"I did," Woody said. "But it didn't matter. Jackson covered beautifully for you."

"Yes, he did." She gave Jackson a smile. "He's a consummate pro, isn't he?"

"Thanks." Jackson shrugged. "But to be honest, I just feel like one of the family here. There's no pro or non-pro. Ya know?" He laughed. "I think I just made a rhyme."

Steve watched as Gwen approached and gave Jackson a little wave. He smiled then headed off to her.

"Jackson is a brilliant actor," Woody said. "One of the best I've seen. We were blessed to find him."

Steve cleared his throat. "What am I? Chopped liver?"

Woody slapped him on the back with his good arm. "No, my boy, you're not chopped liver. You're ham and cheese on wheat with a pickle on the side."

"I beg your pardon?" Steve shook his head. "What does that mean?"

"It means you delivered—in the same way a great sandwich offers multiple layers of goodness. Your acting was great, the singing was out of this world, and your on-screen chemistry with Guinevere—er, Amy—was completely believable." Woody grinned. "I almost believed you two were a couple in real life. Oh wait...you are."

"Ah." A sense of contentment settled over Steve as he contemplated Woody's words. "Yes, we are."

"I'm not the only one who thought you were great, by the way," Woody added. "I happen to know that Mickey is giving the show a great review. He told me so himself."

"Awesome," Amy said.

"Gotta love those good reviews," Woody said. "It's like a stay of execution. It means the show will live to see another day."

"How many days, do you think?" Amy asked, slipping her arm through Steve's. "How long can we keep the show going?"

"Don't suppose it matters." He gazed at her, his heart full. "We'll leave that in the Lord's hands. He knows how long we'll need to keep this thing going to bring in adequate revenue. And He knows what we can stand, physically and psychologically. We'll just follow His lead."

Several of the ladies drew near, distracting Amy. After a lengthy giggle-fest, she disappeared with them, heading to the dressing room. Steve watched as she disappeared behind the curtain and then returned for a moment to blow him a kiss.

He caught it, not even trying to hide the smile. With his heart so full, how could he help but smile?

Woody gave him a curious look. "Anything you want to tell me about Fair Guinevere there?"

"Yes, spill the beans, mister," Eula Mae added.

"Only one thing is really important in this story," Steve said. "She ends up with the right man and they live happily ever after."

"I see. So Lancelot doesn't steal her away?" Eula Mae's gaze narrowed.

"Not a chance."

"Is the king going to take the lady as his bride?" Woody asked, giving him a pat on the back.

"If she'll have me."

"Oh, I feel pretty sure she'll have you," Eula Mae said, giving him a hug. "If you'll just shave those ridiculous whiskers off your face." She reached up and gave him a kiss on the cheek.

"That's why we keep you on the payroll, Eula Mae," Steve said. "To keep us walking the straight and narrow."

"My boy has always walked the straight and narrow." His mother's voice rang out. Steve turned to face her, and she threw her arms around his neck. "Son, that show was amazing. *You* were amazing." She released her hold on him and took a step back to stand beside Bob. "You look so…kingly."

"Thanks." He gave her an exaggerated bow. When he straightened, Darrell stood in front of him.

"Thanks, bro," Darrell said, "but it's not necessary to bow every time I come around." He chuckled and slapped Steve on the back.

"Right. No bowing necessary," Steve said. "But the Bible says I should give honor where honor is due, and you did an awesome job— both with the build-out of the theater and with your performance.

You amaze me, big bro." He threw his arms around him and gave him a tight squeeze. When he stepped back, Steve noticed his mother's eyes brimming with tears. "You okay, Mom?"

"Yes, this is just such a special moment. My heart is so full." She slipped her hand into Bob's and released a breath. "This is the perfect opportunity to share our news."

"You're having a baby?" Darrell tried.

She smacked him in the arm. "No. Bob and I are thinking of moving."

"Again?" Steve said. "But you just moved to Memphis a few years ago. Are you sure you're up to another move so soon?"

"I think so." Bob grinned and pulled her close. "She's been after me for months to bring her back home."

"Home?" Joy consumed Steve as the realization set in. "To Camelot?"

"Yes." Tears spilled down his mother's cheeks. "I've been aching to be with my boys. And with Caroline too." She paused. "There is one little problem, though."

"What's that?" Darrell asked.

"Well…" She stared at them both. "When I left, I handed the house over to you boys. If I come back, we'll have to figure out the housing situation."

"I could build you a house," Darrell said. "Or…" His eyes lit up. "I could build myself a house and you could move back to your place."

"But what about Steve?"

Steve looked her way, an idea surfacing. "Might be just the right timing," he said. "Could be I'll need a new house soon too." He gave his mother a knowing look. "By the time you two arrive in town, you'll have your old place to come home to. And I…" He paused, his heart fuller than ever. "I'll be ready to make a move of my own."

* * * * *

Amy joined the other ladies in the dressing room. She laughed as Annabelle stared at her reflection in the mirror. "I'm going to need power tools to get all of this makeup off. Lucy was pretty heavy-handed." Giggles followed.

"What else is new?" Caroline said. "The woman has skill. What can I say?"

"We've all got skill," Blossom added. "I'm floored by the talent in our little town. Completely floored."

"So am I," Amy said, giving her a hug. "You were all great."

"Could you believe those guys in the jousting scene?" Annabelle's eyes widened. "They blew me away. Those horses were spectacular. Who did you say they belong to again?"

"Mickey. The reporter. The horses are his dad's."

"They *made* the show," Caroline said. "I loved them."

Amy listened in as the ladies carried on, sharing their favorite memories of the night. Off in the distance, Gwen sat staring at her reflection in the mirror, slowing removing her makeup.

The crowd eventually cleared, leaving Amy alone with Gwen. Her heart twisted as she felt the Lord's nudge to say something to her. "Are you coming to the after-party?" Amy asked, taking the seat next to Gwen.

"What would be the point?" Gwen looked her way for a second then turned her gaze back to her reflection. Amy couldn't help but notice the sadness in her eyes.

"What do you mean?"

"Name one person who would care if I didn't show up." Gwen dabbed at her eyes, removing the heavy eyeliner.

"Me."

"What?" Gwen turned and stared at her, eyes misting over. "Since when?"

"Since always, Gwen." Amy spoke the words from her heart, meaning them with every fiber of her being.

"I seriously doubt you or anyone else in this town really cares about me."

Amy gave her a curious look. "Of course we do. Everyone thinks you hung the moon. And you were pretty amazing the other day with Sarge. If you hadn't been there, there's no telling what might have happened." She smiled. "I know Jackson appreciated it."

"Jackson." Gwen blew out a breath. "I have to wonder if he even realizes I'm alive. Just like Steve never knew I was alive when you were around. You're so…" She quickly turned, as if embarrassed to be caught wearing her emotions on her sleeve.

"Gwen, what happened to us?" Amy reached out to touch her arm. "You were my best friend. We did everything together. And now it seems like we're on opposite teams or something. It's weird. I don't like it."

"Me either." Gwen's words were whispered but genuine.

Amy pulled her chair a little closer, looking at Gwen intently. "It's been great working with you on the show. I love that whole Knights of the Round Table thing. I've enjoyed watching everyone work together…no one being more than—or less than—anyone else."

"That's just it." Gwen faced her, eyes filled with tears. "I could never compare myself to you because you always won out."

"W–what?"

"Yes. You were every teacher's pet. You were so friendly, and everyone loved you. Then when Steve came along…" She shook her head. "Anyway, it's not always easy being friends with someone who's so perfect. That's why I ended up stepping away, if you want the truth. I couldn't stand the comparison."

Amy shook her head, completely dumbfounded. Gwen's words stunned her. "You've been comparing yourself to me? Don't you realize what a screwup I am? I'm the last person you want to compare yourself to."

"You're the one who always gets the guy at the end of the story," Gwen said. "And from the time Steve became your best friend, there wasn't room for me anymore."

"But..." Amy couldn't find the words. Nothing made sense. She finally worked up the courage to speak. "I'm sorry if I pushed you away, Gwen. I never meant to do it. Maybe I just wasn't paying attention."

"Who knows." Gwen faced her reflection once again. "Maybe I was just too caught up in the fairy tale. Thought I'd capture the guy and ride off into the sunset. But that's not going to happen now, so I need to just get over it."

Amy shook her head. "Don't be so sure. I know that God has someone special for you, Gwen, because you're so special."

An awkward silence rose up between them, followed by a little sniffle from Gwen. "I'm clueless about all of that." Her words sounded strained. "Sometimes I think it's easier just to go on pretending. The real world isn't much fun."

"Well, I hear ya on that one," Amy said. "Trust me when I say that I'd just as soon put on rose-colored glasses and pretend everything's perfect when it's not. But that's not an honest way to live. Facing reality is really the only way to accomplish anything. It's a hard lesson, but it's one I've definitely learned in the past few weeks, thanks to *Camelot*."

"Camelot was a fictional place." Gwen returned to her makeup removal, working the cotton ball until every last bit of eyeliner had disappeared.

"I used to think that," Amy said. "I'm not so sure anymore."

"What do you mean?"

Amy paused to collect her thoughts. She wanted her response to be just right. "The more I think about it, the more I realize that Camelot symbolizes something far greater than any earthly kingdom."

"What's that?" Gwen tossed the cotton ball into the trash can and looked at Amy.

"We need to live in the real world, for sure," Amy said. "But we've also got to have faith that God is leading us toward an ideal home—a true Camelot, as it were. A place where the weather really is perfect year-round and a King—*the* King—rules in wisdom and power."

Gwen shrugged.

"We can trust Him, Gwen." Amy rose and stood beside her friend's chair, gazing at their reflections in the mirror. "He loves us. You know?"

Gwen's eyes filled with tears, and she reached for another cotton ball. "Look what you've done, Amy. Ruined a perfectly good makeup removal." Her words were followed by a hint of a smile.

Not exactly outstretched arms, but a step in the right direction. Not that Amy expected the relationship to be mended in a day. After all, good things came to those who were willing to wait. If this production hadn't proven that, nothing would.

* * * * *

Steve took a few steps toward the Civic Center, looking through the sea of people for the woman who'd stolen his heart. Unfortunately, he couldn't seem to find her.

"Looking for someone?" Pete asked, coming up beside him.

"Yes. Haven't seen Amy for a few minutes." His gaze darted to the right and then the left. Where was she?

"You know how women are. She's probably gabbing with the other ladies or fixing herself up to look beautiful for you."

"She definitely doesn't need to fix herself up to look beautiful," Steve said. "She's never been the kind to wear a lot of makeup, and I'm fine with that."

Pete laughed. "My daddy used to say, 'Powder and paint make a girl what she ain't.' " His paused, a reflective look on his face. "Not sure what that says about Lucy Cramden, but I have learned to admire her artwork."

Steve laughed. "You are a man who appreciates fine art, to be sure."

"And willing to work hard to get it," Pete added. "Which reminds me...I have something to tell you."

"Oh?" Steve looked Pete's way. "What's that? Did you decide to pop the question?"

"No. I bought a ferret."

"You what?" Steve stared at him, confused. "On purpose?"

"Yes." He nodded. "I've named him Fabian."

Steve shook his head, not quite believing this. "And you did this because...?"

"I decided Fiona must be lonely. That's why she's always in trouble. And I thought it might be a surefire way to win Lucy's heart. If she knows how much I care about her pet, she'll realize how much I care about her. Right?"

Steve chewed on that idea. "Makes sense. So when are you going to tell her?"

Pete glanced across the stage and drew in a deep breath. "Right now. Pray for me."

"Will do."

Steve watched as Pete sprinted into the Civic Center, his head held high.

"Lord," Steve whispered, "I'm not sure why You've planted me in this crazy town, but I do find it all pretty entertaining."

"Entertaining?" Eula Mae's voice rang out. "You find us entertaining?"

"Very." He pulled her into his arms and kissed her soft white curls.

"Ah. Well, then, you'll like this," she said, wriggling out of his arms. "I've just been told there's going to be a funeral. That ought to be good for a laugh."

"A funeral?" Steve looked up, fear gripping his heart. "Who died?"

Eula Mae rolled her eyes. "Bugsy."

"Well, yes, but…a funeral?"

"Yep." She nodded. "According to Jackson, Sarge feels awful about what he's done. He didn't mean to shoot Bugsy. The whole thing happened accidentally while he was out taking a few practice shots. Apparently Sarge called Pastor Crane this afternoon and asked him if he'd perform the service. He wants to go all out for poor Bugsy."

"Isn't Pastor Crane a little busy right now?"

"Yes." Eula Mae chuckled. "Just got a call from him, by the way. Natalie's due to deliver anytime now, so the funeral will have to wait a few days. Just wanted you to know, since you're the mayor and all."

"Thanks." He paused to rake his fingers through his hair. "I think."

Eula Mae narrowed her gaze. "You might want to shave between now and then. Wouldn't be right to go to a funeral looking like that. This is going to be a pretty big shindig. They're going to bury Bugsy proper-like. Sarge is buying a coffin and everything. Not an expensive one, mind you. One from the back room of the mortuary. The kind they use for county burials." She paused. "By the way, I signed you up to bring a casserole."

"A casserole?"

"Well, sure. Folks always bring casseroles to funerals, don't they? For the family and friends to eat afterward. We'll have a big party in the fellowship hall after we drop Busgy into the ground. I think I'll drive through the Cluck 'n Stuff out on the parkway and pick up some chicken. They've got a special on dark meat."

Steve closed his eyes, completely sure he must be imagining all this. When he opened them, Woody was standing beside Eula Mae, giving him the strangest look.

"You okay, Steve?" Woody asked.

"Just another day in Camelot." Laughter rose up, and he didn't even try to force it down.

Off in the distance, Amy called out his name. He waved in response. Her smile broadened and she waved back.

As he watched the woman he loved sprint down the center aisle toward him, Steve was struck by the most amazing thought. Maybe…just maybe…it wouldn't be the last time he would see her coming down the aisle. Maybe next time he'd meet her at the altar, ready to carry her off on a white steed toward their real happily-ever-after.

Epilogue

....

I love acting, but it's much more fun taking the kids to the zoo.

Nicole Kidman

Amy cleared the table, carrying the last of the dishes back into the kitchen. She didn't care much for loading the dishwasher but would never think of complaining. Not with all the other joyous things going on in her life right now. She kicked off her shoes and stretched her aching feet. *Ah. Much better.*

"What did you think?" Steve asked, slipping up behind her. "Did you have fun tonight?"

"I always love it when Gwen and Jackson come over," she said. "And you know I love a good game of Yahtzee."

Her husband pulled her close and gazed into her eyes. "No, I mean, what did you think of the conversation we had?"

"About you running for Senate?" Her heart swelled with pride. She placed the last plate into the bottom rack and dried her hands then turned to face him. "Is that what you mean?"

"Yes. So…?"

Amy smiled, her heart overflowing. "I think it's a fabulous idea. You're such an amazing leader, Steve, and people really respect you. And I know your heart better than anyone else."

"You do." He kissed her on the brow and offered a smile.

"You want to make a difference in the world."

Steve nodded, his eyes glistening.

"I can't wait to see what the Lord does," she whispered. "It's going to be exciting."

"Mom!" Seven-year-old Timmy's voice rang out, interrupting their private moment. "Why did Uncle Jackson have to leave? We were going to play army."

Amy turned to her son with a smile. "He and Aunt Gwen have to be up early in the morning. She has a doctor's appointment."

"Is she sick?"

"No, honey. They're going to find out if their new baby is a girl or a boy."

Timmy's nose wrinkled. "Hope it's a boy. Girls are so dumb."

"I used to think that too, son," Steve said, tousling his son's hair. "But I was wrong." He looked at Amy with such tenderness that it melted her heart. "On every conceivable level I was wrong." Looking back at his son, he added, "Your mommy was my lady-in-waiting."

"Lady-in-waiting?" Timmy shrugged. "What does that mean?

"It means she was worth waiting for. One day you'll understand, trust me."

Timmy didn't look convinced.

"And your daddy is my knight in shining armor," Amy said, her heart rising to her throat. "Always has been."

"What about me?" Timmy asked. "Can I be a knight too?"

"I don't know. What do you think, Steve?" Amy looked her husband's way with a grin. "Is Timmy old enough to accept the challenge?"

"I am! I am!" the youngster cried out.

"Are you ready to give your allegiance to the King?" Steve asked.

Timmy's eyes widened as he nodded. "Yes, sir."

"And are you ready to join with the other knights in service for the betterment of the kingdom?"

Timmy's emphatic nod let them know he was. "I want to be in the play too."

"Someday, son," Amy said. "We'll talk about that later."

"And now, the most important question of all…" Steve leaned in close and whispered, "Are you willing to listen to Lady Guinevere when she tells you it's time to turn out the lights and go to bed?"

"I guess." Timmy groaned.

"Well, then…" Steve knelt beside him. "The time has come at last." He put his hands on his son's shoulders and spoke in a kingly voice. "I hereby knight you Sir Timothy Charles Garrison. From this point forth, you will carry out your Father's orders, only going into battle as He leads. Understood?"

"Yes, sir." Timmy's eyes grew wide.

"You will grow up and make a difference in your world."

"Just like your father," Amy threw in.

"And you will share the story of Camelot wherever you go."

"The story of a King who led others with a kind and compassionate heart," Amy added. "And who loved unconditionally."

Steve looked her way, his eyes reflecting his joy.

"I'm a knight!" Timmy jumped up and down. "Finally!" He did a funny little dance around the room then stopped and put his hands on his hips. "Tell me the story of Camelot again," the youngster begged. "I need to memorize it, so I can tell it like Grandpa does. He's the best!"

"First, let's get you into bed, young man," Amy said. "*Then* you can have your story."

"If I hafta…"

Amy followed behind him as he headed into the bathroom to

brush his teeth. Then he settled into his twin bed, the sheet twisted around his ankles. She knelt beside him.

"Now, Mom," he implored, "tell the story."

Amy nodded and drew a deep breath. "Once upon a time, in a land far, far away..."

"How far?"

"Not as far as you might think," Amy said as she pulled up the covers and tucked her son in for the night. "It was in a land of knights and castles, kings and queens."

"The land of Camelot!" Timmy sat up in his bed, a childish giggle erupting.

"Yes, Camelot," Steve said, entering the room. "A land where would-be kings shared a round table with ordinary men. Where knights in shining armor would give their lives for a noble cause."

"Why don't you take over from here?" Amy said. She rubbed her expanded belly. "This little girl is tossing and turning, making it hard for me to stay down here on my knees."

"Of course." Her husband drew near their son's bed and helped her stand. Amy settled into a spot near the door, watching as Steve eased his way down to sit on the side of the bed. He smiled in Timmy's direction. "Are you sure you want to hear that same story, son? Don't you ever get tired of it?"

"No way!" A smile lit the youngster's face. "It's the best story ever."

"Okay, then." Steve started at the very beginning. "Once there was a king named Arthur. He lived in a kingdom shrouded with mystery, one that even the best of storytellers could not do justice. He lived in the kingdom of Camelot."

"Camelot," Timmy whispered. "Like our town."

"Yes, Camelot." Steve wove the tale from beginning to end, his voice carrying just the right amount of magical wonder to keep

Timmy's eyes wide. When he reached the end of the story—changing it slightly so that Arthur and Guinevere lived happily ever after—Timmy yawned.

"I like your version better than Grandpa's."

"Me too," Amy said, drawing close. She joined her husband on the edge of the bed, taking his hand. "I've always been a sucker for a happily-ever-after story."

"Me too," Steve said then kissed her on the cheek.

"Does the story *have* to have kissing in it?" Timmy yanked the covers up over his head and groaned.

Amy pulled the covers off and kissed her son on the forehead. "Yes, it has to have kissing. Wouldn't be much of a story without it."

"I guess." He yawned once more.

Amy rose and walked over to the light switch. She flipped it, and the room fell into shadowy darkness. The tiny night-light at the foot of Timmy's bed illuminated her husband's face. Steve's voice rose out of the mist, strong and secure as always, pulling her in as it had done all those years ago when he'd first stepped onto the stage as King Arthur.

"Don't let it be forgot…"

"That once there was a spot…" Timmy chimed in.

"For one brief shining moment…"

Steve rose and took Amy by the hand. Together they whispered the words to end the beautiful tale….

"That was known as Camelot."

About the Author

....

Award-winning author JANICE HANNA, who also writes under the name Janice Thompson, has published more than sixty books for the Christian market, crossing genre lines to write cozy mysteries, historicals, romances, non-fiction books, devotionals, children's books, and more. Her passion? Romantic comedies! Janice currently serves as vice president of the Christian Authors Network (christianauthorsnetwork.com) and was named the 2008 Mentor of the Year by the American Christian Fiction Writers organization. She is passionate about her faith and does all she can to share the joy of the Lord with others, which is why she particularly enjoys writing.

An avid theater buff, Janice taught drama classes at a Christian school of the arts for many years while also directing a missions-oriented drama team. She continues to write and direct musical comedies for the stage at a Houston-area Christian theater.

Janice lives in Spring, Texas, where she leads a rich life with her family, a host of writing friends, and two mischievous dachshunds. She does her best to keep the Lord at the center of it all. You can find out more about Janice at www.janicehannathompson.com or www.freelancewritingcourses.com.

POST CARD
CARTE POSTALE
Love Finds You

**Want a peek into local American life—past and present?
The *Love Finds You*™ series published by Summerside Press
features real towns and combines travel, romance,
and faith in one irresistible package!**

The novels in the series—uniquely titled after American towns with romantic
or intriguing names—inspire romance and fun. Each fictional story draws on
the compelling history or the unique character of a real place. Stories center on
romances kindled in small towns, old loves lost and found again on the high plains,
and new loves discovered at exciting vacation getaways. Summerside Press plans to
publish at least one novel set in each of the fifty states. Be sure to catch them all!

Now Available

Love Finds You in Miracle, Kentucky
by Andrea Boeshaar
ISBN: 978-1-934770-37-5

Love Finds You in Snowball, Arkansas
by Sandra D. Bricker
ISBN: 978-1-934770-45-0

Love Finds You in Romeo, Colorado
by Gwen Ford Faulkenberry
ISBN: 978-1-934770-46-7

Love Finds You in Valentine, Nebraska
by Irene Brand
ISBN: 978-1-934770-38-2

Love Finds You in Humble, Texas
by Anita Higman
ISBN: 978-1-934770-61-0

*Love Finds You in Last Chance,
California*
by Miralee Ferrell
ISBN: 978-1-934770-39-9

*Love Finds You in
Maiden, North Carolina*
by Tamela Hancock Murray
ISBN: 978-1-934770-65-8

*Love Finds You in
Paradise, Pennsylvania*
by Loree Lough
ISBN: 978-1-934770-66-5

*Love Finds You in
Treasure Island, Florida*
by Debby Mayne
ISBN: 978-1-934770-80-1

Love Finds You in Liberty, Indiana
by Melanie Dobson
ISBN: 978-1-934770-74-0

Love Finds You in Revenge, Ohio
by Lisa Harris
ISBN: 978-1-934770-81-8

Love Finds You in Poetry, Texas
by Janice Hanna
ISBN: 978-1-935416-16-6

Love Finds You in Sisters, Oregon
by Melody Carlson
ISBN: 978-1-935416-18-0

Love Finds You in Charm, Ohio
by Annalisa Daughety
ISBN: 978-1-935416-17-3

Love Finds You in
Bethlehem, New Hampshire
by Lauralee Bliss
ISBN: 978-1-935416-20-3

Love Finds You in North Pole, Alaska
by Loree Lough
ISBN: 978-1-935416-19-7

Love Finds You in Holiday, Florida
by Sandra D. Bricker
ISBN: 978-1-935416-25-8

Love Finds You in
Lonesome Prairie, Montana
by Tricia Goyer and Ocieanna Fleiss
ISBN: 978-1-935416-29-6

Love Finds You in Bridal Veil, Oregon
by Miralee Ferrell
ISBN: 978-1-935416-63-0

Love Finds You in Hershey,
Pennsylvania
by Cerella D. Sechrist
ISBN: 978-1-935416-64-7

Love Finds You in Homestead, Iowa
by Melanie Dobson
ISBN: 978-1-935416-66-1

Love Finds You in Pendleton, Oregon
by Melody Carlson
ISBN: 978-1-935416-84-5

Love Finds You in Golden, New
Mexico
by Lena Nelson Dooley
ISBN: 978-1-935416-74-6

Love Finds You in Lahaina, Hawaii
by Bodie Thoene
ISBN: 978-1-935416-78-4

Love Finds You in
Victory Heights, Washington
by Tricia Goyer and Ocieanna Fleiss
ISBN: 978-1-60936-000-9

Love Finds You in Calico, California
by Elizabeth Ludwig
ISBN: 978-1-60936-001-6

Love Finds You in Sugarcreek, Ohio
by Serena B. Miller
ISBN: 978-1-60936-002-3

Love Finds You in
Deadwood, South Dakota
by Tracey Cross
ISBN: 978-1-60936-003-0

Love Finds You in Silver City, Idaho
by Janelle Mowery
ISBN: 978-1-60936-005-4

Love Finds You in
Carmel-by-the-Sea, California
by Sandra D. Bricker
ISBN: 978-1-60936-027-6

Love Finds You Under the Mistletoe
by Irene Brand and Anita Higman
ISBN: 978-1-60936-004-7

Love Finds You in Hope, Kansas
by Pamela Griffin
ISBN: 978-1-60936-007-8

Love Finds You in Sun Valley, Idaho
by Angela Ruth
ISBN: 978-1-60936-008-5

Love Finds You in
Tombstone, Arizona
by Miralee Ferrell
ISBN: 978-1-60936-104-4

COMING SOON

Love Finds You in
Martha's Vineyard, Massachusetts
by Melody Carlson
ISBN: 978-1-60936-110-5

Love Finds You in
Prince Edward Island, Canada
by Susan Page Davis
ISBN: 978-1-60936-109-9

Love Finds You in Groom, Texas
by Janice Hanna
ISBN: 978-1-60936-006-1

Love Finds You in Amana, Iowa
by Melanie Dobson
ISBN: 978-1-60936-135-8

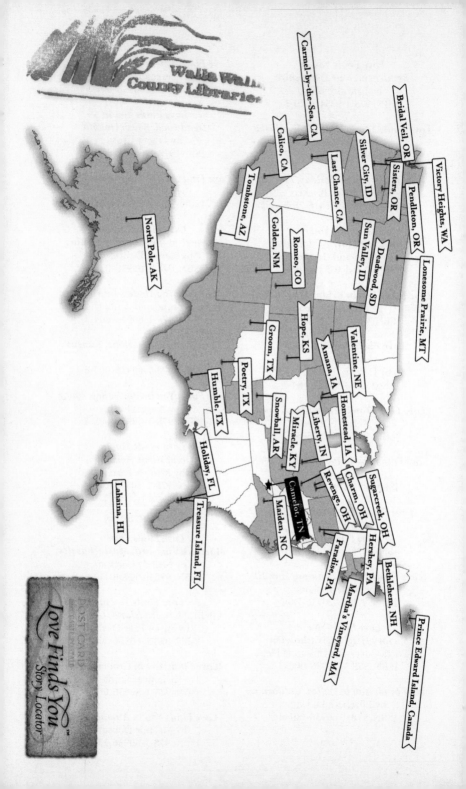